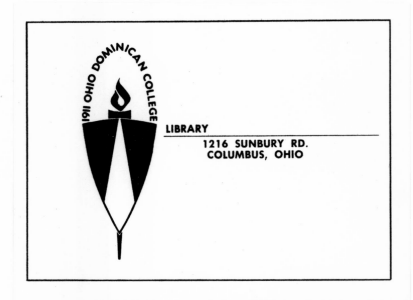

THE
LION'S
PAW

THE LION'S PAW

by D. R. Sherman

Doubleday & Company, Inc.
GARDEN CITY, NEW YORK

/1975

Library of Congress Cataloging in Publication Data

Sherman, D. R.
  The lion's paw.

  I. Title.
PZ4.S5529Li3   PR6069.H459   823'.9'14
ISBN 0-385-07545-6
Library of Congress Catalog Card Number 74–25122

First published in Great Britain by
Cassell & Company, Ltd., 1974

*For Mike Thomas and Carl Brandt
and also for Peter Spaedes . . .*

*I just have to tell you about Pete. He was a guard on the
Rhodesia Railways, working between Bulawayo in Rhodesia
and Mahalapye in Bechuanaland. We used to hunt and drink and
beat our gums together, and in those affluent days I owned a tape
recorder. On the next page I offer you a couple of his drunken gems,
in the same open and hesitant spirit in which he offered them to me.
If he ever gets to read this book, I think he might like the love
story I have written.*

The ability to exercise compassion must be constantly renewed: to renew it, I must either inflict pain, or by default permit other agents to do so, on the subject which is to be the object of my compassionate exercise.

SPAEDES

All lepers are as dependent on saints for their care just as much as those who aspire to sainthood are dependent on outcasts to achieve their ambitions. Who then are the lepers?

SPAEDES

THE
LION'S
PAW

PART ONE

I

HE WAS a few months under six years of age, and he weighed five hundred and sixty-two pounds. His huge black mane swept back across his shoulders and reached half way down his front legs, and his big paws left prints in the sand that were nine inches across.

His fur was a tawny gold, and the colour merged smoothly into the creamy white hair of his belly. His face and flanks were scarred in places. He had been cut by thorn and cut by hoof and claw, but he had no memory of the encounters which had marked him.

The territory over which he ranged covered almost a hundred square miles. Some quirk, some defect in his nature had made him different to other lions. He did not run with a pride. He had mated three times in his life, with all the savage fury of his kind, but when it was over he returned to his solitary life.

He had slept through the heat of the afternoon and into the late evening in a thicket of black thorn. He had risen at dusk and moved out. It was three days since he had eaten, and he was hungry and thirsty.

He prowled through the bush and scrub of the Kalahari, his loose belly swinging to the rhythm of his stride. His head was held high, and he moved it from side to side, his sensitive nose testing the air, reading the messages that each little puff of breeze brought to him. He moved with a sure confidence, secure in the knowledge that there was nothing to challenge his supremacy.

He was wary of elephants and crocodiles, but there were neither in the land he now owned. He feared nothing, and all creatures of the desert were afraid of him. He was a king, and he accepted it in the same way as the fact that he had to kill and eat.

The night darkened, cold and still. He grunted softly to himself, and then suddenly halted. The massive head lifted. The broad fleshy nostrils contracted and quivered as he sipped at the air. The black tufted tail lashed once from side to side and then became still.

It had come to him, the scent of carrion, but so very faint that there was no certainty to it. After a few seconds the building tension in him began to dissipate itself.

He snarled once, a low purring rumble that came from deep in his

belly, and as the black-edged lips peeled back they revealed the two
and a half inch daggers of his canines.

The king moved on, threading his way through thorn and scrub.
He felt the familiar give of the coarse sand beneath his pugs. He
moved confidently through the night, with nothing but the pale
water light of the stars to guide him.

On the perimeter of his territory he came across his own scent. He
freshened it, squirting two small jets of urine against the camel
thorn.

He swung left and continued his prowl. The thorn and scrub
thickened. He had gone about a quarter of a mile when a swirl of
air feathered against his face. He froze, his nose pointing, and the
scent he had picked up before came in strong and heady. Carrion,
and there was no mistaking that smell, rich and ripe with the be-
ginnings of decay.

He held still a moment longer, fixing its direction, and then he
went after it. His stride lengthened till he was moving at a fast trot,
and now the scent was in his nose all the time and the belly hunger in
him grew. The sand spurted from under each of his big feet as they
left the earth: there were others who might also have picked up the
scent.

Twenty minutes later he was bearing down on the source. He
slowed and came to a halt, his nose sampling everything else that
was in the night around him. Satisfied that he was alone he padded
forward.

He was a few yards from the bait when he halted again. There
was a strange taint to the air. It was so faint and subtle beneath the
overpowering aroma of the decaying meat that he could not isolate it
entirely. It was a strange scent too, and in all of his life he had
never known it before.

It made him uneasy, and for a while he was reluctant to go forward, but in the end his hunger drove him. He moved up to the
thicket of thorn. It was a solid barrier, and there was no way in.

He began to move round it, the smell of the meat strong and
overpowering in his nose. He came to the gap in the circle of thorn.
His mouth was full of saliva now, and the hunger to feed cramped
the muscles in his jaws.

Then he picked it up again, a little stronger now, that faint and
alien scent. He stiffened, and the big head swung from side to side,
but he could not locate the direction from which it came. It was all
around him, that taint in the air.

He backed off, his tufted tail stiff and standing almost straight up in the air, the big muscles in his body tightened up and ready to explode.

Nothing happened. The stiffness ran out of his body after a while, but he was still uneasy. He eyed the gap in the thorn, and then padded closer. He halted again, listening to the night, smelling it and feeling it with every nerve and fibre of his being.

His tail dropped, and it lashed from side to side. He prowled past the inviting gap in the thorn, still uneasy. He went right round the thicket, but it was all solid and there was no way in.

He came back to the gap. He hesitated, that strange scent strong in his nose, and then he padded round the thicket again.

The smell of the meat was overpowering, and the pain of emptiness grew in his belly. He circled the thicket twice more, but there was only the one way in. Once more he came back to it.

He stood a moment, three yards from the opened arms of the waiting thorn. The massive head lifted and he growled, rumbling it up softly from deep down in his empty belly.

He moved forward warily, one step, his right front paw coming down lightly, delicately, no weight on it, the pad just touching the sand, testing it, and then his body coming forward, the earth yielding a little and then becoming hard and firm, supporting him, taking the weight of his huge forequarters.

He took another step, his confidence growing. The saliva streamed from his mouth, a slimy string of it on either side, catching on the white hairs of his chin.

The right front paw went forward again. There was sand beneath the rough pad, the touch of it familiar and reassuring. Thorn caught in the mane which covered and protected his big shoulders.

The sand began to give beneath the weight of his body, the grains spreading and separating. The pads under his big foot touched lightly against the steel pan of the trap. The pan pressed down on the dried desert grass, and the grass in its turn bore down on the brittle twigs over the hole in the ground.

The twigs snapped, and in that instant, with his weight suddenly falling forward, the lion reacted, knowing instinctively that something was wrong.

He jerked his foot back. The reflex movement was fast, but the trap was even faster.

He felt the first faint caress of the jaws on either side of his leg and then the shocking hammer-hard blow as they closed, with the steel teeth driving through the meat and on into the bone.

White hot pain exploded inside his leg. He leapt into the air, all four feet off the ground, and he roared with shock and rage and surprise. The night split and shivered with the thunder of his voice.

He felt the tug of the trap round his leg. It shot the pain right up through his shoulder and into the back of his skull. When he hit the ground again he began to feel the pressure of the jaws, continuous and unrelenting.

He sprang forward, smashing straight through the thorn he had avoided in the beginning when he had circled the thicket. He blasted his way right through, pulling the drag on the trap after him.

In his rage and madness he did not feel the pain, but he became aware of the thing that was biting into his leg.

His head flashed down, jaws open. His jaws closed over his leg. One of his front canines drove into his own flesh, the other splintered slightly and broke off at the tip as it met with steel. Fortunately for him, the nerve remained unexposed.

He roared and roared, his voice filling the night and shaking it. He savaged his foot and bit at the chain, and he slashed at the drag with his claws and his teeth.

When he found that he couldn't get free of the thing that had wrapped itself round his leg, when he found that it could not be destroyed, he felt the first insidious touch of fear, he who had never been afraid in all of his adult life.

His fear drove him again into a self-destructive paroxysm of fury. For a while there was no pain in him, only rage, but when his rage diminished he felt the pain again. And with the pain, his fear mounted.

He ran off into the night, silent now, heaving the chain and the drag along behind him. Lightning flashes exploded in his brain each time he moved his right leg.

In the beginning he ran at a crippled trot. He ran blindly, without any sense of direction. The pain in his leg slowed him quickly to a walk, and then his instincts took over.

He changed direction, heading for the safety of a distant thicket he knew, wanting to get as far as possible from the place where he had been hurt and chained.

There were others in the night who had heard the king when he roared out in his anger and his pain. One of them was a Bushman youth called Pxui.

He was a little over sixteen, but he had not counted the years of his life, and he had no idea how old he was. The desert was timeless, and he was a part of it, and it did not concern him that he did not know.

2

IT WAS after eight at night when the Land Rover pulled into camp. For a while they had been lost in the vast darkness. The fire which looked so huge and bright now had been nothing more than a pin-prick of red when they first saw it in the night and homed in on it thankfully.

Jannie had only just killed the engine and flicked off the lights when Joseph and his assistant hurried up to him. Joseph was the camp cook. He was a grey-haired, snaggle-toothed drunkard, but he could bake bread in an empty biscuit tin that tasted better than anything produced in a bakery.

"Morena!" he exclaimed breathlessly. *"Tau!"*

"What's that?"

The word itself had an electric sound. Together with its meaning and the images and memories it evoked it was enough to make the heart of any man who had known them beat faster.

"Lion, morena, in the trap, you must have heard it," Joseph blurted out. "He roared and roared, so loud that the earth shook and the sky trembled."

Jannie heard the slight tremor in his voice, and he smiled to himself in the dark, not at him, but at his own thoughts. There was something about the king, just the mention of his name, or the sound of his distant voice in the night, that made people afraid and drew them closer together. He was no exception.

"Where?" Jannie demanded. "We were far out and heard nothing."

Joseph waved vaguely in a southerly direction. Jannie nodded, knowing which of the four traps had taken it.

"You hear that, Spartala?" he asked, speaking to the African on the seat beside him.

Spartala wasn't his real name. It was the Setswana corruption of hospital. Jannie had christened him with it long ago, because everyone he brawled with invariably finished up in hospital. Now most people had come to call him by that name, but he was indifferent to the accolade it implied.

"I heard."

"So," Jannie breathed softly, and he began to think of the coming morning, when he would follow him and kill him. "The bastard walked into my trap."

"Let us hope it took him good and hard," Tsexhau murmured. "And not just by the toes."

He was seated on the other side of Spartala. He was a half-breed Masarwa, or Bushman, and he was the best tracker Jannie had ever had.

"Amen," whispered Jannie, lapsing into English for the first time.

He remained seated a few moments longer. He had been driving all day and he was tired, but thinking about the lion his weariness began to fall away. He opened the door of the Land Rover abruptly and climbed out, stamping his feet and flexing his legs from the knee to shake off the stiffness.

"Help them get the meat out and cut it up," he told Joseph. "And then bring the skoff."

He had shot a gemsbok late in the evening. They had skinned and butchered it out in the desert, but the meat still had to be cut up and salted and hung.

He walked over to the Chev. pick-up. He siphoned a basin full of water from one of the 44-gallon drums in the back.

He placed the basin on the ground and stripped off his shirt. He squatted in front of it and then washed himself down, his face and his arms and his chest. He used the soap sparingly, conscious of the dogs which were already gathering behind him and waiting patiently for him to finish.

He stood up and dried himself, refreshed by the sluice. The dogs immediately grouped round the basin of scummy water. They lapped it up with relish, their tongues slurping and slapping as they jostled for position.

They weren't his animals. The dogs belonged to Spartala and Tsexhau. They weren't hunting dogs in the strict sense of the word, and at times they were a damn nuisance, trying to follow the Land Rover out in the mornings. He knew that the only reason their owners brought them along was to fatten them up. In a few days they gobbled down more meat than they saw in a whole year. But there was always plenty of meat, and he didn't mind. He buttoned his shirt and left them licking at the basin.

He dug out a bottle of Viceroy from his stores box. He turned it upside down and checked the level of the dark gold spirit.

"Joseph!" he called out.

"Morena?"

The African straightened up at the back of the Land Rover, a shoulder of meat in his hands. He saw the bottle, and he immediately assumed an expression of righteous indignation.

"You've been at my brandy again."

"Morena is mistaken."

"Don't tell me I'm mistaken, you black-enamelled bastard," Jannie said, but there was no anger in his voice. "From now on I think I'll lock it up."

He had threatened it many times before, but somehow he could never bring himself to do it. That would have been an open declaration that he knew Joseph was stealing. Sometimes he was certain that Joseph knew this and banked on it too.

"Perhaps that would be best, morena."

Jannie waved the bottle in a gesture of dismissal. He didn't really mind about the brandy, but he had to remind him now and again that he knew what was going on otherwise the old thief would think he was going soft in the head.

"Get on with it," he said, simulating a vast disgust.

Joseph grinned victoriously and lurched off under the load of meat. He dumped it on the wet hide of the gemsbok that had been spread on the ground and went back to the vehicle for more.

Jannie poured himself a half-glass of brandy. He topped it up from one of the hanging water bags and then sat down on his sleeping bag which was rolled out on the tarpaulin near the fire.

He sipped at his drink, quick short sips that emptied half the glass in a matter of seconds. He put it down and lit a cigarette. He sat back, his left arm draped loosely over the knee of his bent left leg, his right leg stretched out straight and the weight of his upper body on his braced right arm.

He began to feel the effects of the brandy a few minutes later. The good warm feeling came up from his belly and spread through his body, stealing softly into his mind.

He glanced idly round the camp. It was in its usual state of chaos, with empty and half-empty cartons lying scattered all over the place.

There was something reassuring about the disorder. His gaze fell on the rows of drying meat, and he studied them with satisfaction.

They were hanging from ropes stretched between the branches of trees. Each blackened strip of meat was suspended from the rope by its own wire hook. He had spent a whole afternoon preparing them, and it was a good feeling to know that they were being used, that they were fulfilling the purpose for which they had been made.

He had been out in the desert five days now, and he had another two to go. He loved these periodic sojourns in the Kalahari, for the hunting, as well as for the isolation. They refreshed him, putting new life into his spirit, and he always returned to the cares and worries of the farm feeling like a man reborn.

He began to wish that he could stay another week. But he knew it was impossible. He had brought only enough water for an anticipated stay of seven days. That in itself was not the decisive factor, because he knew the desert and he knew the ways men could live without water. What was important were his cattle, and the railing quota he expected to receive when he got back.

He finished his brandy and mixed himself another drink. He sat down again. For a while he watched his boys, busy cutting up the meat, and then abruptly he began to think of the lion.

A good skin, with a decent sized mane, would fetch him somewhere around sixty rand. It would pay for the fuel and cartridges he had burned. He wished the night had gone and that it was morning already, because then he would be out after him. He felt a fine flutter of excitement and anticipation. He wanted to see him, this lion that had walked into one of his traps. To see him and kill him.

He pictured him in his mind, limping through the night. The pain would be appalling, especially when he had to move the trapped leg, with the weight of the chain and the drag adding to his agony. He had made the traps himself, and he knew just how hard they bit.

He felt a momentary surprise that he should be thinking about the pain, because he had never given it a thought before. He shook his head, as if trying to deny the knowledge that had surfaced from somewhere deep down within him. He pushed the thought of the lion's pain from his mind.

He finished his drink and got to his feet. He collected his rifles from their brackets at the back of the driving cab of the Land Rover and returned with them to the fire.

He began to clean them, first the .375 Holland & Holland Magnum, and then the Winchester which was a .264. He did the barrels with a wire brush on the end of a ramrod, and he finished them off with a piece of flannel to get rid of the excess oil. He cleaned and tested the actions, wiping off the dust and rubbing them over with a rag that left behind just the faintest smear of oil.

He worked methodically and without haste, and he handled his rifles with a loving care. They were more than just weapons to him: they were old friends, tried and tested, and there were many hours of his life and so many of his good memories bound up with them.

Sometimes when he held them in his hands he got the impression that they were living things, with an intelligence and life of their own. He knew it was nonsense, but it was difficult not to be beguiled by their sleek beauty and functional deadliness.

He finished wiping them down. He reloaded both rifles and returned them to their brackets, and then he put away his cleaning equipment.

He fixed himself another drink and sat down by the fire. He glanced across to where the Africans were working. They had cut out the fillets and stripped the haunches and shoulders of meat. The bare bones gleamed yellow in the dusky light of the fire, and he knew it wouldn't be long before they were finished.

He stared into the fire, nursing the glass in his hands. He could feel the growing cold of the desert night on his back. A shiver ran through his body and he hunched his shoulders and moved closer to the fire.

He began to think about the lion again. He wondered if the trap would hold, if it was still tight round his leg, or whether even now he had thrown it and was driving himself as fast as he could deep into the desert.

He felt it then, mounting within him, the consuming desire to find out, not in the morning when it was light again, but now. He wanted to see the king, to close with him, to see all that great strength and beauty and freeze it forever in his mind in that moment just before he took its life.

Perhaps the hyenas were already on his trail. He would be too fresh and strong for them at the moment, but the thought of it was nauseating. The king deserved better than that.

His reverie was interrupted by Joseph who brought him his food. It was in a tin soup-plate, hartebeest stew in a thick brown gravy, boiled potatoes, rice and canned peas. Jannie set the over-loaded plate down between his legs. He picked up the spoon and began to eat.

Moments later the Africans drifted over with their own heaped plates, huge mounds of mealie porridge, swimming in gravy and buried beneath chunks of meat. They squatted round the fire and began to eat. They ate with their hands, licking their fingers fastidiously after each mouthful.

"That lion," Joseph commented. "He had a very big voice."

"Tau!" breathed Spartala, and there was a hushed reverence and excitement in his voice.

"Ghum!" Tsexhau echoed, and there was the same muted awe in his.

The meaning that they put into that one word, the inflection they gave it, electrified Jannie. He stopped chewing abruptly. His gaze moved between the pair of them, from one to the other and back again. He swallowed the food in his mouth.

"Now!" he exclaimed abruptly. "Let's go and get him now."

He knew he was mad even to think about it, let alone suggest it, but he couldn't help himself.

Spartala started. He stared at Jannie. The look of disbelief in his eyes was replaced by a flicker of excitement.

"In the night?"

"We can use the spot!"

"The big light?"

"Yes, the big light."

Spartala was silent for a few moments. The excitement in him mounted as he thought about it. He swung suddenly to face Tsexhau.

"What do you think?"

The tracker swallowed the half-chewed lump of meat in his mouth. Its passage down his gullet was plainly discernible. The magic of the lion had reached out through the night to touch him too, and he felt his heart flutter with fear and anticipation. Killing a lion was different to killing any other animal. To kill a lion was to kill a king, and the man who killed a king . . .

"I think we are mad," he said.

"Why?" Jannie demanded.

He knew he could order them to accompany him. They would have obeyed, but it was better to get their agreement, because their minds would not be clouded with the anger and resentment of having been forced to do something against their better judgement.

"It's dark, and he is hurt."

A lion was unpredictable at the best of times, a wounded one even more so, and it was not unusual for the hunter to become the hunted. Sometimes the situation became evident a little too late.

"I know, but we can be careful," Jannie said. "Extra careful."

He knew he wasn't thinking rationally then. He was always careful, and there was no real way he could be extra careful. He had hunted lions all his life, and he had trapped them before, but he had never been so foolish as to go out after a trapped lion at night.

"We are mad," Tsexhau went on. "Even to think about it."

"Then you don't want to come?"

"I did not say that."

"For God's sake!" Jannie exclaimed, his voice rising in exasperation. "What are you saying then?"

"I am saying," Tsexhau said slowly, "that I am as mad as you."

Jannie stared into the inscrutable black eyes. He felt a flicker of unease, but it was drowned in the sudden liquid excitement that spurted through him. In his mind he saw the lion again, and the vision of it drew him like iron to a magnet.

"Eat up," he snapped, "and let's get going."

He shovelled the rest of his food down, hardly bothering to chew it. He put his plate aside and stood up.

"Come on, Spartala, give me a hand."

He pulled on a sweater and then strode over to the Land Rover. He checked the radiator water, and then with Spartala helping him he siphoned gasoline from a 44-gallon drum into a jerry can and filled the petrol tank of the vehicle.

After that he dug the spotlight out of his equipment box, checking on the spare bulb. He unwound the flex and plugged it into the dashboard points and switched it on.

The powerful beam speared into the night. He swung it from side to side, ripping the darkness apart, and then he switched off the light, satisfied with it.

For a moment he was blind, seeing nothing, but then his vision returned slowly. He shut the door of the Land Rover, leading the flex out through the open window. He laid the spotlight down carefully in the back of the vehicle.

"Okay, Tsexhau," he said briskly. "In the back, and mind the light with your big feet."

He lifted down the .375 Magnum. He had checked it recently, but he did it again. He inched the bolt open, just enough to see the gleam of brass in the breech, and then he held the trigger down and closed the bolt. As an afterthought he took three spare rounds from the box on the dash tray and slipped them into his shirt pocket.

There were four rounds in the magazine of the rifle, and one in the breech. It was more than enough for what he had to do, but the extra rounds in his pocket gave him a feeling of added security.

"Now, Spartala," Jannie said, and he was strangely disconcerted to find that his voice had dropped to a whisper. "If I want you to stop, I'll tap twice, just like always. When I want you to go on, I'll tap once. Have you got it?"

"Yes, morena."

"You know which trap it is?"

"I know the one Joseph pointed out."

"You can find your way to it?"

"Oh yes."

"Okay, get in and drive."

Spartala climbed behind the wheel. He shut the door, and as a further precaution he slid the window closed. Two years ago Jannie had taught him how to drive. He didn't have a licence, but he could handle the vehicle as well as anyone who did. He started the engine and drove out into the night.

The headlights cut a passage into the darkness, and beyond the range of their beams the single finger of the spot probed, sweeping from side to side.

From the back of the Land Rover, his legs spread wide and his body pressed against the back of the driving cab for support, Tsexhau operated the spotlight.

Jannie stood beside him, the rifle cradled in his arms and resting on top of the cab, his right hand curled tightly round the bolt handle, ready to flick it up and shut and cock the rifle instantly.

He followed the sweeping beam of light, oblivious to everything else. The tension in him mounted as they penetrated deeper into the bush, and his straining eyes felt as if they were slowly being sucked from their sockets.

He doubted that the lion would have come this way, towards the camp and their fire, but neither could there be any certainty that he hadn't.

He saw two jewel-bright flashes of luminous blue a little way above the ground. They looked like fallen stars. His heart lurched, even though he knew it was only a buck.

The probing beam backed up. It held on the frozen duiker for a moment and then swept on, giving it back to the sanctuary of the darkness.

The Land Rover wove its way in and out through the thorn. A few minutes later it slowed, picked up speed again, and then slowed once more and came to a faltering halt.

"Have you seen something?" Jannie cried.

It just wasn't possible, that from his position of vantage he had missed something that Spartala had seen. The beam of the spotlight swung instantly, and he had no more time to think about it.

It made one quick furious sweep right round them, and then it went over the same ground again, going backwards and forwards over each quadrant before moving on to the next one. He saw nothing, and he became conscious of the ache in the wrist of his right hand. He relaxed his grip on the bolt handle of the rifle.

"What is it, Spartala?" he cried urgently, leaning down to rap on the closed window.

It slithered open. "I've lost the way."

"Jesus!"

The word came out as a sibilant explosion. There was a relief in it, and also disappointment.

"To the left," Tsexhau called. "Much more to the left."

Jannie heard the window sliding shut and then they were rolling again. Approximately fifteen minutes later Tsexhau steadied the beam of light on a thicket of distant thorn and jabbed him excitedly in the ribs.

Everything looked strange and different at night, but after a moment of incomprehension he recognized the thicket in which he had set his trap. He rapped twice on the roof of the cab and the vehicle lurched to an abrupt halt.

The beam of light swung rapidly from side to side and then steadied on the thicket again. It tore into the shadows, revealing the untouched bait, and then it flickered away and took up its endless questing.

Jannie tapped once on the roof of the cab and Spartala drove forward, right up to the pocket of thorn. Jannie saw the place where the trap had been, the earth torn and disturbed, and as they circled the thicket he saw the hole in the thorn where the lion had blasted his way out. He tapped twice, urgently, and the Land Rover jerked to a halt.

The beam of the spotlight flickered over the thorn and then steadied. Tsexhau drew a short sharp breath. Jannie wondered what had startled him, and then he saw it himself a moment later, a knotted tuft of mane hair hanging from a branch. It was black and dark gold, and he wouldn't have seen it except for the gold in it which threw the light back.

On a sudden impulse he climbed down. He plucked the twist of hair from the bush and got back into the Land Rover.

He rubbed the tuft of hair between his fingers. It was coarse and soft and warm feeling to his touch. At that moment he felt very close to the lion. It was a mental proximity, not a physical one, and in his mind he could once again see it very clearly as it limped through the night while he held in his hand the hair that had been a part of it only a little time ago.

"Ghum!" whispered Tsexhau, and there was fear and an ancient awe in his voice.

Jannie stuffed the piece of fur into his pocket. He bent down and spoke quietly to Spartala through the open window.

"Can you follow the spoor?"

Spartala studied the twisting furrows which the branches of the drag had cut in the sand. "Easily."

"Let's go then."

The Land Rover went forward, winding in and out through the thickening scrub. The spotlight beam resumed its searching sweeps.

In places they had to make wide detours round the thorn, and they lost the drag marks time and again. These were moments of fear and tension, because no one knew just where the lion was. He might have been lying low in a thicket so dense that the probe of light would never reach to him, waiting for them to pass and leave him in peace. Or he might have been waiting to attack.

Jannie had never underestimated them, and that was one of the reasons he was still alive. They were quite unpredictable, and no two of them ever behaved in quite the same way. Even with a trap round its leg, dragging all that weight, he knew it could hit them from some unexpected quarter and be in amongst them before they knew what had happened.

The sweeping beam froze. Thorn and scrub sprang into sharp focus. Jannie saw the flash of reflected light. His heart leaped, and he was about to beat an urgent tattoo on the roof of the cab when he realized it was only the reflection from a dried leaf which was red and orange like the colour of a lion's eyes at night. The beam flicked away, and the tension in him faded.

The bush thickened, the scrub becoming taller and denser. The long white thorns on the bushes picked up the light and threw it back in dazzling splinters that blinded him. It was useless to go on, and he knew it. He rapped twice and the Land Rover skidded to a halt.

When the expected rifle shot did not come, Spartala cautiously slid the window open and eased his head out, a questioning expression on his face.

"Turn around and go back," Jannie ordered.

"But the spoor is still clear, morena," he protested. "A blind man could follow it."

The spotlight finished its protective sweep, and then began its slow methodical probing.

"The bush is too thick," Jannie explained. "And I can't see for the thorn."

"A little further," Spartala pleaded.

For a moment Jannie was tempted, but he knew it would be madness to go on. "I can't see, you silly bastard," he said patiently. "I can't shoot unless I can see."

"But morena——"

Jannie cut him off. "Maybe you want another one inside the truck again?"

Spartala stared at Jannie for a moment, and then he quickly withdrew his head and slid the window shut. He revved the engine and took off with the back wheels spinning. He swung the Land Rover in a tight circle and settled down to follow his own spoor back.

They had been following a wounded lion that day when it disappeared into thick bush. They had climbed into the back of the truck, from where their field of vision was greater. They had been studying the thicket into which the lion had vanished when it came at them from the opposite side.

It smashed into the side of the Land Rover with such force that it bent the iron of the chassis. It was half way into the truck before Jannie recovered enough to stick the barrel of the rifle into its wide open mouth and blow its head off.

The coach work of the Land Rover still carried the marks of its claws, and every time he happened to glance at them he could hear again the blood-curdling sound of its claws raking deep into the aluminium as it scrabbled for purchase against the slippery metal.

3

THE LION had been just over a mile from them when Spartala turned back. The animal had heard the vehicle, and he had begun to run again, on three legs, with his injured paw held up and clear of the ground, but now with the sound of it receding he slowed to a walk once more.

Since the trap had closed round his leg, he had been in pain all the time. There were different intensities to his pain, and he had come to know them all. Sometimes it wasn't too bad—such as when he lay down to rest briefly. Then it was just a steady pounding throb that pulsed with metronomic regularity, like a series of hammer blows.

But he had to move, to get away, and it was then that he really suffered. Each time he dragged his right foot forward white-hot shafts of pain lanced through his leg and flashes of light danced before his eyes. He had come to dread his brief moments of rest, because the temporary respite made it more difficult to go on. He was learning about his pain, and the pattern that it had.

He was limping along when the drag snagged and caught just as he was moving his right foot forward. This was the thing he had come to fear the most, and all of his other pain was as nothing compared to it.

He felt the first tentative tug of the chain. He froze in mid-stride, but his reactions weren't quite fast enough. The explosion began in his metatarsals, and the shock waves that it generated numbed his brain.

Carefully he lowered his right foot to the ground, no weight on it, the pugs just touching the earth. He inched it forward experimentally, but the pain made him check the movement instantly.

He was fast again. He knew what he had to do now if he was to keep going, and this was the terrible part of it. He would have to jerk his foot forward, using the great strength of his leg to free the drag. He had freed himself like that before, and he had come to know that this was the ultimate in agony.

He was about to jerk his foot forward when he thought he heard the sound of movement coming from behind him. He paused to glance back over his shoulder and then he pivoted and backed a little to the left. He stared into the night, his nose taking the air, but he saw nothing and he caught no scent. He was beginning to turn back when his glance fell on the branch of the drag.

It had scuffed along behind him, following him as if it were a thing alive. How it followed him was beyond his comprehension, but he had come to hate it.

He snarled suddenly, a vicious rumbling growl. He sprang on the drag. The links of the chain clinked softly as he moved. He took the drag in his mouth. He lifted it up and began to shake it. Silently and furiously he shook it from side to side, heedless of the fiery stabs of pain that spurted through his leg with each movement of the chain.

When his rage diminished he tossed it aside savagely, almost contemptuously, and then he turned to go on. In his brain was the knowledge that he was still held fast, and an awareness of the price he would have to pay in pain to set himself free.

He moved forward cautiously till the chain tightened. He inched forward a little more, testing its resistance, expecting that sharp warning tug to come at any moment.

It never came. He was puzzled for a while. He moved forward hesitantly, and then with more confidence, and when he found that he was no longer held fast he kept going, concentrating on doing the things he had to do to minimize his pain.

The next time the drag snagged he was on the point of ripping it loose when two recently acquired pieces of information fused in his brain. He savaged the branch that moved endlessly behind him, and when he had finished mauling it he found to his gratification that it no longer held him prisoner.

The inference was instant and instinctive: attacking the drag somehow freed him, and that in its turn prevented the great pain he had come to associate with the snagging of the drag.

The next time it happened he turned back and shook the branch as he had done before. He tossed it aside and moved forward warily, and once again he found that he was free. The process of learning continued, till in the end he found he did not have to shake the drag. He merely lifted it high in his mouth and tossed it aside.

Sometimes it snagged on something else, so he tossed it again, and if necessary again and again till he could move on without having to tear it loose.

A mile further on he lay down to rest. He began to lick at his swollen paw, and then he licked at the jaws of the trap which were tight round his leg, tasting the acidity of the steel on his tongue through the taste of his own blood. He licked tenderly at the trap, as if it were a part of his own flesh, seeking to heal himself in the way he had always done.

His chipped tooth hurt him too, but it was a small pain and it did not cause him much discomfort because of the greater pain in his leg which captured all his attention.

He was busy with his leg when the hyenas came upon him. They had not come together, because they were by nature solitary scavengers. They had arrived from different sectors of the night, drawn by the scent of blood and the unerring instinct which guided them to the sick and the crippled.

They closed in on him warily, with that strange gait of theirs, the front and back legs on one side of their bodies moving forward together at the same time and then alternating with the legs on the other side.

They approached to within ten feet of him and then halted, one on either side. Their fur was sparse and greyish, and they were spotted with dark brown blotches.

The lion remained motionless, his head down and watching. He knew what they were. They were the ones who waited and fed on what remained after he had killed and eaten. They sometimes killed for themselves, but only the weak and the lame. He did not know that they were as necessary to the scheme of things as he himself was, and even if he had known he would not have cared. His prime concern was his own survival.

He felt a moment of fear as they came to a halt. But there were only two of them, and it passed quickly. He was hurt, and his movements were greatly restricted, but the huge strength of his body was still there.

He lay and watched them, waiting for them to move. He knew that if he got up and went on they would follow him. And with the patience of their kind they would wait, and when he was truly weak and enough of them had gathered, they would attack him and satisfy their hunger. It was the way of all life.

The hyena to the right of him circled his flank and took up a position behind him. The lion turned his head to keep it within his vision. His tailed lashed from one side to the other and then stiffened. He studied the hyena behind him for a moment longer and then swung to face the one in front. He realized instantly that it was a little bit closer than it had been before.

He sensed movement behind him. He turned his head quickly. The moment he did the hyena froze. As he stared at it he heard the one in front begin to inch its way closer to him. He let it come, paying it no heed, apparently intent only on the one to his rear.

But he was listening to it, and he heard its sly movements cease. He continued to ignore it, concentrating on the one behind. Long minutes passed, and the three of them remained perfectly still, watching each other in hunger and in fear.

The hyena to the front, emboldened by the lion's lack of aggression and its apparent disinterest, began to creep forward.

The king heard him, the soft whisper of his feet in the sand. He remained motionless, continuing to stare at the hyena behind him. The great muscles in his hind legs tensed. The smooth hide rippled as it accommodated their expansion, but neither of the scavengers observed it.

The hyena to his front was about five feet from him. It paused, uncertain and apprehensive. It started forward again, cautiously and almost reluctantly, ready to whirl and flee if it had to. Still the lion made no move.

The hyena was beginning to inch closer when the lion whipped round and catapulted itself forward. The left front paw drew back and struck. The blow caught the hyena high up on the side of its head, and the force of it lifted it into the air. It landed six feet away and rolled over once, its neck broken and the life already gone from it. The dust began to settle again.

The lion whirled, but the other hyena had retreated to safety. He growled softly and then limped off into the night.

The hyena followed him a little way, but then it turned and went back to the one that was lying motionless in the sand. It approached warily, slinking up to it.

When the king looked back over his shoulder it was already feeding. Within his own body there was no hunger now: there was only fear and the need to reach the security of the thicket he had been heading for.

He moved on through the night, the paw of his right leg twisted slightly outwards: he had found that the pain was less that way.

A night plover called, its weird echoing cry coming faintly from far off in the night. It sounded lost and mournful, like the plaintive wail of a ship's siren, the inarticulate protest of a dumb beast about to be driven out to the loneliness of the open sea.

4

TO THE EAST, the black curtain of night was beginning to lift. The stars began to dim, and the darkness gave way to a smudged greyness, barely perceptible at first and so indistinct that it might have been taken for a momentary illusion. Watching for it, Pxui, the Bushman youth, knew that it was not.

He rose silently from the skin on which he had been lying down. He moved to the small fire he had fed periodically throughout the night. The morning cold of the desert set him shivering.

He placed a few twigs on the ash-filmed embers. He blew softly into them. They glowed, turning from dull red to orange. The ashes blew back in his face, and he squinted his eyes till they were almost shut, feeling the heat against his lids. He continued to blow, and then suddenly the twigs burst into flame.

Tsonomon woke and raised himself instantly. He studied the boy, the fire, his waking wife, and then he turned and looked eastwards. The sky was opening up, and the low stars were already beginning to fade and go to their rest.

He began to think of the food that remained to them, and his eyes strayed to the thorn branch on which were hanging four pieces of blackened half-dried meat. It wasn't much, and if they were to go on eating, he would have to kill again soon. A week ago he had led them from their camp by permanent water, pushing deeper into the desert, driven by the ancient need to be on the move again. But the game had not been plentiful, and it was time once more to retrace their steps.

When the fire was going to his satisfaction, Pxui walked off a little way into the bush. He urinated, and then adjusting his loin cloth of steenbuck skin, he came back.

He drank water from one of the ostrich egg shells. He drank sparingly, because it was precious, and he plugged it up again carefully and returned it to its bed in the sand.

There were nine shells in all, with a single hole bored into the top of each. Two of them were empty, and the one he had drunk from was now only half full. It was all the water they would have for the next three days, until they returned to their winter camp and their secret underground water.

He took one of the pieces of meat and threw it onto the coals of the fire. After a while it began to spit, and the smell of the meat coming into his nose made his jaws tighten and ache. He took the meat from the fire, and he cut it into three equal pieces.

He handed a portion each to his mother and father, and then he began to eat himself. He chewed each mouthful for a long time before swallowing. It required a certain amount of restraint on his part, because his belly was empty and he wanted to wolf the meat down and try and fill the gnawing pain in there.

When he had finished the meat he cut a piece from one of the tubers he had grubbed up the evening before. He bit into it, careful not to lose a drop of the juice. It was slightly bitter, but he had been eating them since he was an infant, and it was no kind of hardship.

The sun began to edge its way up over the horizon. It was blood red, and it coloured the sands of the desert with the same colour. He slung his quiver of arrows and picked up his bow and spear.

"Where will you go?" asked his father.

He had no fear for his son. He was a man already, a skilled desert hunter. His one fault was that he had not as yet learned to exercise an iron control over his excitement and impatience. If he had learned that, their bellies would now be full, and the little steenbuck they had been stalking yesterday would have given them the strength and nourishment of its body.

"A quick look, to read the sands," replied the boy.

"If you see anything, be patient," the man said. There was no rebuke in his voice, but it shamed the boy all over again. "Also, do not be long, because we must be moving."

"How long?"

The man glanced at the sun, a big red ball just clear of the horizon now, separated from the earth by a thin sliver of sky. He stared at it for a while, its presence permeating his whole being, not only seeing it, but hearing it as well. It had a strange sound, the sun, especially in the early morning. He heard the noise it made, not so much with his ears, but within his body, a silent tremor that plucked at the strings of life within him and set them vibrating in response.

"When the sun is as high as a tall camel thorn," he replied.

The woman regarded her son affectionately, the only one of her children that had lived, this one that she had given first to the stars.

"Go, hunter, I feel something waits for you," she said, tapping at her breast, her brown slanted eyes burning with the light of some inner vision.

Her words made his heart stumble, and then it began to beat

faster. Ever since he could remember she had been that way. It had baffled him until a few years ago, this ability of hers to see without seeing. And then one day he himself had had the same extraordinary kind of premonition, and he had begun to understand.

He had been out hunting with his father, searching the sand for fresh spoor. He had seen nothing and heard nothing, neither had the wind brought him any scent. Suddenly he had frozen and pointed to the crest of a dune a little way off, his whole being vibrant with a feeling so strong that it left no room in him for doubt or wonder.

When they reached the rise and looked down, they saw the herd of wildebeest. He had known that they would be there, with the same absolute certainty of seeing them, but how he had come to know it was beyond his understanding. It was enough that it had happened.

"What do you feel?" he asked.

"I feel a sleepiness. I think it waits for you, and sitting here I feel it. I feel that it waits for you even as I sit here and listen to its waiting."

He started and turned away, his heart beating harder. It was well known that sometimes an animal would make a hunter feel sleepy. It was a magic that they had, to protect themselves, and the bigger and stronger the animal, the greater the feeling of sleepiness it induced. He himself had never been subjected to this particular magic of theirs, and over the years he had begun to wonder if it was really true.

He set off at a slow trot, his small supple body moving with an easy grace. He had the loose, muscled limbs of a runner, and his ankles were shapely and slender. He travelled at a speed of about nine miles an hour, and if necessary he could keep it up for hours on end.

He angled off to the right, travelling on a mental arc which would eventually describe a circle and bring him back to where he had begun.

His keen eyes swept the sands, searching for fresh spoor, and at the same time he drew and recorded in his mind a comprehensive picture of the land over which he passed. He did it unconsciously, without having to think about it, a process that had developed over the years till it was now an inherent part of his nature and came to him as naturally as breathing.

He saw plenty of spoor, but all of it was old. Sometimes he would hold onto a particular set of tracks for a few yards, intrigued by some slight peculiarity about them. And even though the spoor was old, the images it evoked in his mind were so vivid that he could visualize the animal which had made it as if it were before him at that very moment, and reading the subtleties of the marks in the sand he knew almost everything it had done, and in his imagination he became the animal, doing the things it had done and feeling the things it had felt. So close was he to the desert earth and its life.

His wandering eye fell on the two small leaves of a desert tuber. They grew close to the ground, and they looked like a pair of little floppy ears. He marked the spot in his mind, fitting it into the growing picture of the land that he was mapping and carrying in his head.

He began to think about the tubers as he ran, and why all the various kinds had such small leaves. He wondered if it was a kind of protection, showing as little of itself as possible to make it more difficult for the men and the animals to find it and dig it up and eat the life out of it. He wondered if it was that, or whether they just didn't have the strength left to make big leaves after growing such a huge and succulent water-filled root deep down in the hidden earth.

He loped like that for four miles, reading the sands as he went. Nothing escaped his wonderful eyes, and he saw even the narrow runs worn in the sand by the minute feet of the striped and long-nosed mice as they went to and fro from their holes in the ground.

He made a wide detour round an extensive thicket of mongana thorn, mentally noting the extent of the deviation and automatically calculating the angles and distances involved so that he could make compensatory corrections later and resume travelling in the direction he wanted to take.

He felt a sudden and inexplicable prickling at the nape of his neck. He cleared the thicket of thorn, and he came to a sudden heart-stopping halt.

He had seen lions before, but never as close as this, and never before had he seen such a majestic and formidable looking beast.

The lion's mane was huge and black. It surrounded the massive head in a ruff, and it swept down over his shoulders like a cloak and reached half way down his legs.

The lion remained motionless, about thirty yards away. Pxui stared at him in disbelief and astonishment, and for a few moments his mind refused to accept the reality of his presence.

The lion growled, lifting his head slightly and to one side as he did so, and the shock of hearing his voice snapped Pxui from the numbed trance into which he had fallen.

He stepped backwards involuntarily, and the act of moving

snapped him awake and he felt such fear as he had never known in his life.

His first impulse was to turn and flee. He was on the point of turning and running blindly when he realized that no man alive could outrun a lion from that distance.

He glanced about frantically, searching for something to climb. It was all scrub and low thorn, and there was only one tree that offered the smallest chance of safety, but it was just too far away.

He became conscious of the pounding of his heart against his ribs, short punishing blows that struck with such force that the impact of them made him feel faint.

The lion growled again, the sound like thunder coming from very far away. He heard the warning in it, and the menace, and he felt the echoes of the voice reverberating inside his body.

The lion took a step forward. The boy was about to turn and run when something about the way the animal moved caught his attention. He studied him through freshly alerted eyes, and it was then that he noticed what he had been too blinded by fear to see before.

He saw the trap round his leg, and the chain which ran from the trap to the drag.

In a flash it altered the whole situation. He glanced at the distant tree again. He wasn't all that sure, but under the circumstances he did have a very real chance of reaching it and climbing to safety.

It was a thorn tree, but he would get up it just the same. He would be stabbed and scratched and torn, but it would be nothing compared to what would happen if the lion got his claws and teeth into him. And it was big enough for him to climb, but not strong enough for the beast of prey that was standing there and watching him with his unwinking yellow eyes.

He was about to turn and make a dash for the tree when he realized that he had not been thinking clearly in the few seconds that had elapsed since he first came face to face with the lion in shocked surprise.

The way it was, with the trap round his leg and hurt, the animal would probably leave him strictly alone if he simply backed off a bit and moved out of his path. It would be the safest and most sensible thing to do.

He was beginning to back away when he remembered the bow in his hands and the quiver full of poison arrows on his shoulder. His hunter's heart began to pound with a different kind of excitement.

He halted, and thinking about it he began to feel very afraid once again. If he shot at the lion, he would probably charge straight at him. He might just have sufficient time to reach the tree, and then again he might not. And if he didn't, he knew that would be the end of him. He had seen them kill, and he knew just how strong and quick they were.

He tried to put it from his mind, this madness of even toying with the idea of shooting at the lion. But it persisted, and the more he tried to drive it away the more firmly did it become rooted.

He felt a fresh burst of fear, and he began to wish that his father was with him. He wondered what he would do, and whether he'd take a chance and shoot the lion and follow it up later while the poison did its slow and deadly work.

He thought that perhaps he might, because there was a lot of meat on the lion, and their bellies were empty even now. He remembered abruptly that it was his fault that they were hungry, and then he recalled the sudden anger that had come alive on his father's face. It hadn't lasted long, but the weary resignation that replaced it was even harder to bear.

Thinking about it his resolution began to harden. And then suddenly he thought of the great honour that would be his if he killed this huge lion. It would make him famous and respected, and it would be a story to tell his children and his grandchildren. The vision had the glitter and allure of gold.

He lowered his spear, bringing it down very slowly, not wanting to startle the lion with any sudden movement. He pushed the point into the sand, and then put a little pressure on it and drove it deep enough to hold.

He had nine arrows in his quiver. Each one was made in three sections, the short shaft of the iron head fitting into a hollow section which in turn telescoped into the length of the main shaft.

When an arrow struck its target, the head usually detached itself on impact. If for some reason or the other it failed to do so, separation occurred when the animal tried to dislodge the arrow by rubbing it against tree trunks or scrub. This insured that the poisoned head would remain behind to do its deadly work even though the shaft dropped off.

Three of the arrows were slightly longer and heavier than the others. They were for the greatest game of all, animals like the mighty eland and the giraffe, and the poison on their heads was the strongest and most virulent.

Pxui reached over his shoulder with his right hand. His exploring fingers found one of the arrows he wanted. He drew it slowly from the quiver, taking care that the poison-smeared head did not come near his own body.

The arrow was deeply notched, and he fitted it to the bowstring which he had made himself by plaiting the long tough fibres of wild desert sisal. The notch held it, truly and firmly.

He studied the lion for a moment, wondering just where to put his arrow. He was good with the bow, and at that range he knew he could place it wherever he liked, but the lion was facing him squarely.

The head was no good, with all that solid bone, and the chest and neck was obscured behind the thick flowing mane. He knew he could shoot right into that mass of hair, but he always liked to select a precise spot to aim at. And besides, he had a sneaking suspicion that his arrow might not penetrate that tangled matt. He decided he would have to work his way round the animal, if that were possible, and take him from the flank.

He slid his left leg along the ground, moving it so slowly that it hardly seemed he had moved at all. He transferred the weight of his body to his left foot and then carefully drew the right one in towards it. He paused for a moment, watching the lion, and he could hear the pounding of his heart like a drum beat inside his head.

He began to move again, slowly creeping further and further to his left. He didn't know how long it took him, but it seemed like a lifetime before he was in a position to shoot. He lifted the bow, and he felt the trembling in his arms as he brought it up.

He steadied it, the arrow gripped between his thumb and index finger, and the other fingers of his right hand curled tightly round the string.

The hair on the lion's shoulders wasn't as thick or matted as it was on his chest. There was a golden streak running through the mane, just behind his right shoulder. The boy fixed his eyes on it.

He drew back on the string, and the bow began to bend. He felt the muscles in his arms begin to knot with the strain. He bent the bow a little more, till it was at full stretch. Looking down the shaft of the arrow he knew it was pinned right to the target.

He was on the point of releasing it when the lion moved. He growled softly and came towards the boy, a low gutteral moan breaking from his foam-flecked mouth each time he moved his injured leg.

The lion came to a halt again, about twenty yards from the man. He snarled softly, a warning and a challenge. He had seen them before, these small creatures that walked upright on two feet. They were of the desert, but they were different. Fire was their servant, and through his pain he remembered dimly that he had once been driven from his kill by a group of them brandishing branches that were alive with the hateful orange flowers of flame.

They had taken his meat, but they had not harmed him, and that too he remembered. Their scent too, was different from that of all other creatures, in a category of its own. He was afraid of them, but it was not a fear that went too deep.

He continued to stare at the man. He did not know it, but had he taken another step, the thing in the man's hand would have leapt in a sudden convulsion and a poisoned arrow would have driven through his matted mane hair and plunged into the centre of his chest.

Suddenly he caught the thick and pungent smell of fear that came from the man. It was so strong that he felt it scorching the inside of his throat. All aggression was preceded by fear of one kind or another. His ears flattened against his head and his tail lashed from side to side. He was getting ready to make a mock charge when the smell diminished abruptly. His ears returned slowly to their normal position.

He lowered his head and licked at his leg and the steel around it. He was in great pain, and he was more tired than he had been in all his life. It was daylight already, and the thicket he had been heading for was still far off. He knew instinctively that he had to get as far as possible from the place where he had been hurt, but he had come to dread all movement. He was in trouble, and during the long hours of the night it had dawned on him that there was nothing he could do about it. Fear had followed the realization.

He looked up, staring at the man, and then in that instant, with the taste of the steel on his tongue, he sensed, by some strange process of divination that he had never before experienced, that only the two-legged creature in front of him could come to his help.

For the second time Pxui held his shot. The heart-stopping fear that had leaped through him when the lion turned and started in his direction became a little less acute. He threw a quick glance at the tree he would have to climb, checking its position. He began to back away, edging to the left as he did so, and it was then that the lion looked up from licking the paw and Pxui found himself staring straight into his eyes.

They were huge and transparently yellow, and they seemed to be looking at him and through him, and there was a strange and compelling intensity in their amber depths.

The lion took two steps towards him. He whipped the bow up and bent it. Once again the lion halted. The animal started to lick at the paw, and then he looked up at him once more. The boy began to back away. The moment he moved, the lion came after him.

He would have shot his arrow into him then and there, but the lion took only the two steps and then came to a halt. As before, he licked at the leg and then lifted his head to stare straight at the boy.

The big yellow eyes with their darker cores filled his vision hypnotically. They seemed to be trying to say something, but he could not read the language for the pounding of his heart.

He wondered irrelevantly and fearfully if this was a part of their magic, to stare with their calm eyes that seemed to see right into the soul of a man, to put him to sleep and then kill him. The thing was he didn't feel at all sleepy, only afraid.

The lion moved again. The boy stared in spellbound fascination as he carefully drew the injured leg forward, and he saw him snarl soundlessly with the pain. As the black-laced lips drew back he noticed the broken canine.

The lion came to a halt once more. He licked at the paw and then looked up at Pxui again. The repetitive act struck a chord within the boy. He struggled with it for a second, and then in a sudden flash he thought he understood. But the idea was preposterous, and the thought of it frightened him even more and made him feel strangely resentful.

Pxui started to back again, glancing in the direction of the tree. He was much nearer to it than he had been before. So much the better. He would work his way closer to it, shoot his arrow and then run for the tree.

The moment he moved the lion came forward. Pxui froze in midstride. The lion dragged himself painfully towards the boy, who watched in petrified astonishment. The animal halted a little way from him, and then once again went through the routine of licking the leg and then fixing him with his wonderful eyes.

The seed that had been planted in the boy's mind began to germinate. It was quite impossible, and yet there it was. He stared in disbelief, the bow in his hands forgotten.

The lion limped closer. It took all Pxui's willpower not to turn and flee. The huge animal came to within ten feet of him and then stopped. He heard the rasp of the tongue against flesh, and he saw the ticks on the flank. The hot raw smell of the lion struck at his nostrils, rank and overpowering.

The lion squatted suddenly, right there in front of him. The boy saw then, with a certainty he had not known before, that he had not been wrong in thinking what he had.

But it was still almost too incredible for belief. He himself was a hunter, no different from the lion, and yet this great beast had overcome its instinctive fear sufficiently to be able to approach another killer and ask dumbly for help. He felt a sudden awe and reverence for the courage he knew it must have taken. And now he wanted to help.

He stared at the lion, afraid of him still, his heart pounding wildly in his small chest. He was only a little desert man, a boy in fact, and the lion was so huge.

A sudden and frightening thought occurred to him. What if the lion were deceiving him? Perhaps the animal had touched him with his magic, even though he didn't feel sleepy. The lion was hurt and lame, and could never hunt the way he was. The boy wondered if the animal was using magic to draw him close enough to be killed and eaten.

He felt a quick rush of fear, but then the calm eyes of the lion found his own, and the terror in him began to subside. He became certain that no living creature could look at another with an expression like that if it was on the point of killing.

He studied the trap round the animal's paw, noting the laceration and the swelling. He thought he might be able to get the trap off, but what would happen about the leg later was a different matter. It would heal in time perhaps, but he would be lamed, and with a handicap like that no animal would survive in this land with its harsh and unrelenting code. It would be better and more merciful to kill him.

And with that thought in his mind, he felt the resentment creep into his heart again. There would be no stories to tell, about this lion he had killed.

He was thinking about that when another thought struck him. If he freed the lion, he would become a living legend, and the memory of what he had done would live on for ever and ever, and he himself would be revered for the rest of his days.

The golden bubble burst abruptly. He knew no one would ever believe such a thing, as he himself would not.

That in its turn angered him, and it increased his determination to do it.

The lion growled softly, and the sound of it startled him. He found the big amber eyes. They observed him unwinkingly, calm and confident. The boy knew then, that even if he wanted to, he could never kill him now.

Carefully he returned his arrow to its quiver. He laid his bow on the ground. Once again he wondered if he was wrong in thinking that the lion wanted his help. A curious numbness blanked his mind.

"Oh Dxui," he said silently in his head, praying to his God. "If I am wrong, it is my fault for not seeing to the heart of this beast. If I am right, you have sent him to me as a brother, and as a brother, I will try and help him."

He took a cautious step forward. One, he told himself. He took another and another, and then he lost track of the steps he had taken and he found himself standing in front of the lion.

5

JANNIE RUBBED at his eyes. They felt full of grit. He had slept fitfully during the night, his sleep broken by vivid dreams of the lion, the animal's teeth sunk into his flesh and his claws raking him up and down.

The sun was up, and in the pale early morning light the desert looked clean and fresh. When the sun rose higher it would wilt, but for now it was young again, with the air still chill and crisp.

Standing up in the back of the Land Rover with Tsexhau, Jannie had no eyes for the beauty of the day. They were fixed on the twisting line of scratches and furrows which the drag had cut in the sand.

He cradled the rifle in his arms and rubbed at his hands. The cold had reddened the backs of them, and he flexed his fingers to get the stiffness out.

The half-breed beside him was equally tense and alert. His eyes moved ceaselessly, sweeping the land on either side of the drag marks. Occasionally he leaned out over the side of the truck to study the spoor itself when they were running parallel to it. He would grunt and nod, as if confirming something to himself, and then he would go back to searching the thorn and bush with swift darting glances that missed nothing.

Fifty yards ahead the drag marks plunged straight into a dense thicket and disappeared from sight. Jannie rapped urgently on the roof of the cab. The Land Rover jerked to a halt.

"Keep your distance, Spartala," he whispered. "Circle round it and keep your distance."

Spartala nodded and drove forward, making a wide sweep round the thorn. Jannie slid his thumb to the safety-catch on the rifle, and he felt something tighten up inside his chest.

He became conscious of the fact that he was holding his breath. He breathed out noisily and then began to breathe again. His concentration on the thicket was absolute: nothing else existed for him. There was a black glitter in his eyes, of fear and anticipation.

They had gone three-quarters of the way round the thorn patch when Tsexhau spotted the emerging spoor. "There!" he gasped softly. "He has left the thorn."

There was disappointment in his voice, also relief. Jannie nodded, and he felt the high tension drain out of him. His thumb slid away from the safety-catch of the rifle.

They had gone another quarter mile when they came upon the remains of the hyena. Spartala brought the vehicle to a halt a few feet from it. The spoor of the drag was clearly visible beyond the half-eaten carcass.

"Get going!" Jannie called urgently. "Why have you halted when I didn't tell you to stop?"

"Let me take a look, morena," pleaded Tsexhau.

"What for? We're just wasting time."

"It's better," Tsexhau insisted. "Let me see how he's walking, how much strength he still has in him. Let me look at the marks of his feet and see what is happening to him."

"It's just a waste of time," Jannie snapped. "Let's get after him."

"Maybe it is a waste of time, but it's safer."

Jannie had been about to yell at Spartala to get the truck moving. He paused, turning to look at his tracker. He stared into the black expressionless eyes. He felt a faint shiver of uneasiness, why he didn't know. Maybe it was those eyes, so black and opaque that they revealed nothing.

"All right," he agreed reluctantly. "We'll take a look."

They clambered from the back of the Land Rover. Spartala switched off the engine and joined them. He could read spoor, but nothing like the way Tsexhau did. He was an expert, but that wasn't surprising, because he was half Masarwa and that made him half an animal. It was a comforting vindication of his own inferiority in this particular field.

Tsexhau studied the different spoor marks for a few moments. The picture began to take shape in his mind. He circled round, his eyes missing nothing, and then after that he moved into the bush a little way, picking up the spoor of first one hyena and then the other.

He came back to where they were standing by the half-eaten remains. He lifted his hand and pointed to a patch of scuffed sand about ten feet to his right. He began to speak, and though he was looking at the spoor and reading it as he spoke, he saw in his mind not the marks in the sand but the animals themselves as they had acted out their little drama of death. In his voice there was the quiet confidence of a man who is sure of what he says, and knows it.

"He sat there," Tsexhau began. "It is the fourth time he has rested, and he sat there. While he rests he licks his foot. Then——"

"How do you know he licks his foot?" Spartala demanded, a note of belligerence underlying the challenge.

"It is their way. How else can he try to soften his pain and heal himself?" Tsexhau replied contemptuously, pausing a moment to let it sink in before going on triumphantly. "Then these two filthy beasts come along, one from there and the other from there, and"—he pointed to a set of prints—"this one works his way round to the back of the lion. But he is not foolish, this lion of ours, and if he were foolish he would not . . ."

Jannie sighed. This was what he had been afraid of, but he knew also that it would be futile to try and interrupt now. The story was unfolding itself, and the vision of what had happened was so starkly real and immediate in the mind of the teller that it would take nothing less than the charge of an angry lion to cut him off. And if he did protest, his lack of interest would be a humiliation which would hurt the little tracker in one of the few places where he kept the remnants of his pride.

It was the third time they had halted, and he listened with a barely contained impatience. At the same time he could not help marvelling at the vast amount of information which the tracker garnered from the confusion of spoor. He knew something of the art himself, quite a bit, but his knowledge was like a child's in comparison.

"So then he went off into the night again," Tsexhau continued. "The other hyena followed him a little way, and then it came back to eats its brother."

He turned and began to follow the spoor of the lion. He crouched by one of the pug marks. It had been made by the right front paw, the leg which carried the iron. He examined it, seeing how slight was the impression, noticing how the foot had been twisted outwards.

He pictured the animal in his mind, limping, putting very little weight on his injured leg. He followed the spoor further, observing how the print made by the right front paw gradually became more and more distinct, and from this he knew that the animal was slowly but surely tiring, having to put more and more weight on his injured leg. When he turned back he was as closely attuned to the mind and the body of the lion as he could hope to be for the time being.

"Well," Jannie demanded. "What do you say?"

"He gets tired."

"That's natural."

"I am not sure, but I think he has also found a way to travel so that his pain is less."

"Tell me."

Tsexhau bunched his right hand into a fist, so that it looked a little more like the paw of a lion than a human hand. He twisted it outwards, to illustrate what he meant.

"He walks like that with his bad foot," he explained. "That in itself makes its own difficulties for him. There must be a reason, and if it is as I think, he learns very quickly, this one. He is no longer running blind with fear and pain. You remember the drag, how he learned to free it?"

Jannie nodded thoughtfully, thinking over what his tracker had just told him. Together with what he had deduced earlier, the picture which began to emerge was that of an exceptionally intelligent animal.

His right hand rose, and the fingers pressed lightly against his forehead. He trailed them down over the right-hand side of his face, the tips brushing lightly over his skin and exploring the contours. It was a habit he had, when something made him uneasy.

"Let's go and get him," he said abruptly. "We've wasted enough time already."

He signalled impatiently to Spartala and swung up into the back of the Land Rover. Tsexhau followed him up and seconds later they were rolling through the bush again.

The tension in him kept mounting the further they went. Sometimes it reached a peak when the spoor vanished into a likely looking thicket, and then for a minute and sometimes more he was held frozen on a pinnacle of excitement so intense that each subsequent descent left him feeling weak and a little more shaky.

"Morena!" Tsexhau shouted suddenly.

"I don't see anything!" Jannie cried. "For God's sake, where?"

Tsexhau pointed. For a few moments Jannie saw nothing, and then he rapped urgently on the roof of the cab. He hadn't seen it right away, because he had been expecting the lion, his senses keyed to the image he had of it in his mind, alert for that first flash of movement which would break the pattern of the bush and give its position away.

6

THE SMELL of the lion was thick and frightening in Pxui's nose. He saw the forelegs vaguely, through a kind of mist. They were huge and heavy, thicker than his own thighs. He bent slowly, poised to spring away, but knowing at the same time that he was already too close, that a lightning fast flick of that left front paw could rip him open before he even saw it coming.

He reached for the trap, inching his hands towards it, his eyes riveted on the lion. He touched the leg, and he froze in terror as the lion snarled. He tensed, getting ready to hurl himself to one side, and that was when the great head swung over and to his astonishment he found the rough tongue rasping moistly over the back of his right hand.

He took the jaws of the trap in his hands. They were slippery with blood, and he couldn't get a really firm grip on them. He knew he was going to hurt the lion, and he was afraid of what the animal might do in retaliation. He steeled himself, comforted by the remembered feel of the tongue on his hand.

He began to prise the jaws apart. He felt them give, beginning to open, but to his horror he also felt his fingers beginning to slip.

He became conscious of the lion's breath, beating against his face in hot gusts. He began to ease the jaws shut again, his arms quivering under the tension. He had almost got them closed again when he felt the metal begin to slip irrevocably through his fingers.

It happened in an instant, but it registered in his mind in slow motion. The terrible thing was that he knew it was going to happen, and there was nothing he could do about it.

The jaws slipped from his fingers and the trap clicked shut. Fear gushed through him as he waited in frozen apprehension. The lion snarled softly, but there was no anger in his voice, only pain.

He saw the left front paw stiffen suddenly. The inch and a half long claws sprang from their sheaths. They remained bared in a momentary paroxysm, and then slowly the stiffness ran out of the paw and the hooked talons retracted and slid back out of sight.

He stared into the beautiful eyes of the lion. There was a glitter in them that had not been there a moment before. He was beginning to feel afraid all over again when the head which was the size of his chest swung towards him and he felt the coarse stiff whiskers brush his wrist and then the hot rough tongue began to lick at his hand.

He tried again, getting the best grip he could, but there was only the narrow rim of the slightly arched metal jaws upon which to take a hold, and even before he had got them to begin opening he knew he would never make it.

He sat there on his haunches, deliberating over the problem. He decided there was only one way, but he didn't like the idea at all. After a few moments he got up and cut two small lengths of wood, each about nine inches long and as thick as two of his fingers together. He sharpened both of them at one end, and then returned to the lion.

He was apprehensive again, but the animal made no move as he squatted in front of him, and then in that instant he realized with a deep and completely instinctive knowledge that the lion would not harm no matter how much pain he was caused.

He put one of the sticks in his own mouth, with the sharpened end outwards, and then he went down on his knees. He gripped the jaws tight and began to draw them apart. When there was sufficient space he ducked his head forward and slid the stick in his mouth between the leg and one of the jaws. He repeated the operation and inserted the other stick.

He straightened up, breathing hard. The eyes of the lion were on him, calm but watchful. He saw that the left front paw had dug deeply into the sand.

He took a deep breath and took hold of the sticks. It was easy now, with the grip that they gave him, and he pulled the jaws apart with an even steady pressure. He felt the teeth come loose in little jerks, as if they were reluctant to give up their grip, and then he had the jaws wide, his arms trembling with the strain. He drew the opened trap over the big paw of the lion and allowed it to snap shut.

He saw the stuff which welled from the tooth holes. It wasn't dark like blood, but a pale watery red, and he had seen it before in the arrow wounds of animals he had spoored and finally killed.

The lion grunted softly. He was still in pain, but that monstrous and terrible pressure was no longer with him. A great rumbling purr started up inside him, and he began to lick at his foot, his eyes half closed in the ecstasy of release. He had born his pain for a little over eleven hours.

He cleaned his wounds, licking at them till his fur was slick and wet. After a while, the amber eyes opened wide again. He looked at the man, and the rumbling in him grew louder.

The boy reached out unthinkingly, intending to stroke his hand across its fur. The lion snarled savagely at him. He jerked his hand back in fright. It served to remind him of what he had almost forgotten: he was dealing with a wild predator, a killer.

The lion went back to working on his leg. Pxui got to his feet, retrieving his bow and his spear. For a while he watched the lion, wondering what would happen to him. He studied the mangled leg, noticing the deep indentation that had been made by the steel bracelet.

He doubted if the king would be able to hunt. And if he couldn't hunt and kill, he would become weaker and weaker until something else came along and killed him to fill its own belly.

Thinking of the inevitable course of events, the boy felt an inexplicable sadness steal through him. After a few moments he shook it off. It was the way of the desert, and there was nothing he could do to change it.

"Tshjamm!" he called softly. "Good day to you, big hunter, it is now that I must leave you."

He threw a quick glance at the height of the sun. He was turning away when he heard the sound. It was like the droning of a distant bee, so faint that he wasn't certain that he had really heard it. He cocked his head, straining his ears, and then the faint whisper of it reached him once again, the noise rising and falling and sometimes fading out altogether.

It was a sound alien to the desert, but he knew instantly what it was. He had spied on them before from a distance, and there was no mistaking the strange noise made by the beasts in which the red men sometimes rode through the desert.

He had never met a red man close up, or a black man for that matter, but he feared them, because he had listened to the stories of the oldest grandfathers. They themselves had not seen it, and they spoke only of what their own grandfathers had told them, of the red men and the black men who had in the past hunted them with guns, killing the men and stealing the women and children and taking them as concubines and slaves, driving his people deeper and deeper into the remotest parts of the desert to seek a safety which itself imposed so many hardships that it was no real safety at all.

That was long ago, and they were no longer hunted, but the red men had made laws, and even now his people were caught and carried away for killing certain animals, and he had heard they were put into the small stone houses which the red men built, and more often than not they died there, deprived of their music and their stories and the magic sight of the sun rising in the desert.

And if they did not die, they were broken men when they came out, their spirit gone no one knew where, living on the settled fringes of the desert and working as herdsmen, despised by both the red man and the black man, unable to break away, suspended between an old way of life and a new one, their hearts breaking with a longing to return that they could not satisfy. These things his father had told him.

It was incomprehensible to him, that he should be punished for killing certain animals. The red men and the black men, they had their cattle and they killed them. The animals of the desert were his cattle, and he killed them when he had to eat. It was madness, but it was the law, and for those who broke it and were caught there were the little stone houses which shut out the sun and the stars and the beautiful sky.

The thought of it made him tremble. He was turning away when out of the corner of his slanted eye he caught sight of the trap. The sound of the truck reached him again. In a sudden intuitive flash he knew that there was a connection between them.

They were hunters or policemen, or perhaps they were both, and they had trapped the lion and were coming after it. He had set it free, and their wrath would be terrible. He was a hunter himself, and he knew and understood the great rage a man felt when he was baulked of his rightful prey. A shiver ran through his body as he tried to imagine what it would be like inside one of those stone houses.

In a panic he turned and began to run. The boy had taken only a few steps when he skidded to a halt and whirled back. The lion had risen, but now he settled back on his haunches again.

"Go!" he shouted at him. "They are coming for you, the hunters are coming."

The lion stared at him in curiosity for a few moments and then went back to licking the leg. The boy ran up to him, waving his spear in the air.

"Go!" he screamed. "Run for your life."

The yellow eyes met his briefly, but there was no understanding in them. He was tempted to strike at him with his spear, to try and drive him away, but he was afraid of doing such a thing.

Frustration and despair mounted in him. He had gone to a lot of trouble, fighting and conquering his own fear in order to free the lion, and now all of it was in vain, because shortly death would undo everything he had done.

He forgot about his own safety, and his mind raced furiously, discarding ideas almost as soon as they had taken shape. And then it came to him, the only possibility. It wouldn't fool anyone for long, especially a man who could read the sands, but it would give the lion a little time.

It was all he could give the big hunter, and it would also give him the satisfaction of tricking the people who locked his own kind into those terrible houses.

He stuck his spear into the ground and laid his precious bow beside it. He didn't like the idea of leaving them for even a minute, but he would need both hands for what he had to do.

He cut some hollow-stemmed feather grass. He tied a dozen or so of the stalks together to make a soft-headed broom, binding them with a length of stem which he split down the middle and then twisted over and over till it was as good as cord.

He picked up the drag which was attached to the trap. He wrapped the chain loosely round his arm, letting the trap hang free. It was unwieldy and almost too heavy for him to manage, but he set his teeth and struggled with it. The chain tightened round his arm, the links pinching his flesh painfully.

The lion rose to his feet. He snarled angrily, his eyes on the trap hanging from the boy's arm.

Pxui started along the spoor that the lion had made. He brushed out the big footprints and the furrows that the branches of the drag had cut in the sand, at the same time whisking away the marks made by his own small feet.

When he had gone about fifty yards he halted. He dropped the drag and unwound the chain from his arm. Holding the trap clear of the ground, he moved off at an angle of ninety degrees to the old spoor which he had brushed out, the branch dragging behind him and cutting a new set of furrows in the sand. As he went ahead, he brushed out his own footprints. He did it carefully, but he was working in a hurry, and there was a single print that he missed.

He laid the false trail for about eighty yards and then dropped the trap. He knew it wouldn't fool them for long, and perhaps it wouldn't even fool them for a moment, because although the marks of the drag were realistic enough, the prints of the lion's feet were missing. He was banking on the fact that initially they would follow the drag marks for a while before realizing their mistake, simply because it was the most prominent aspect of the spoor. When later they came to the empty trap they would back up along the spoor. They would discover the deception then, and the puzzle of it would probably delay them a little more.

He swung in an arc after that, brushing out his own footprints. It took him back to where he had left his bow and his spear. To his consternation and annoyance the lion was still there. He tossed his grass whisk into a thicket and picked up his spear and bow.

"Go!" he shouted at the lion.

A shift in the wind brought the sound of the vehicle to him. It was still distant, but much nearer than it had been before. He saw the lion stiffen, and its ears flattened against his head.

The sound of the engine rose, steadied for a while on a higher pitch and then abruptly died out altogether.

Pxui circled the lion. He brandished his spear and shouted, trying to drive him to his feet and get him moving. The animal merely continued to watch him curiously, and the purring in its belly increased in volume. His anger and frustration grew, and then he shrugged helplessly.

"Stay then!" he cried softly. "Stay here and die."

He turned away and set off at a quick lope. He had gone a little way when some sixth sense alerted him. He threw a hurried glance across his shoulder.

The lion was following him at a distance of about twenty yards, hopping along on three legs with the injured paw held out in front.

The boy spun to face the animal, his hand automatically tightening on his spear. His first thought was that the lion was closing in to attack him. He cast about frantically, but there were no trees near by. He took a fresh grip on his spear, but even as he did so he knew he had no chance against the beast.

The lion came to a halt about twenty feet from him. The animal sank to the ground immediately, and began to work on the leg. For a moment the boy was too astonished to think, but then relief poured through him. He shouted, prancing angrily and waving his arms in an attempt to drive the animal away. The lion stared back at him, calm and aloof, but made no other move.

The boy heard the sound of the engine starting up again, turned immediately and began to run. The lion got to his feet and hopped after him, the injured leg held like a banner in the air.

The boy glanced back across his shoulder. He saw that the lion was still following him, and another fear took hold of him. If the hunters found him, there was no knowing what they might do.

He lengthened his stride, and he began to choose his way, running over grass and rock and hard-baked ground where only the greatest of trackers would be able to follow his spoor.

The lion ran behind him. He did not follow out of any sense of gratitude or affection. He had decided instinctively that where the man went there would also be food. Now he was playing the role of the jackal or the hyena.

7

"HE'S THROWN IT!" Jannie gasped, and there was anger and anxiety in the explosive exclamation. "He's thrown the bloody trap!"

There was no lion, only the empty trap, about forty yards ahead of them. The abrupt termination of the drag marks was equally disconcerting. They had followed them for miles, over red earth and grey sand, with a single-minded concentration that had hypnotized them, and now there was nothing.

Jannie tapped urgently and the Land Rover came to a halt which slammed them forward against the back of the cab. Together with Tsexhau, he searched the bush, but there was no sign of the lion anywhere.

"Drive up to the trap, Spartala," he called down, easing his grip on the rifle. "Stay clear of the spoor and drive up to it."

Spartala drove forward and stopped beside the empty trap. Jannie stared down at it. Something he should have seen, but did not see, registered in his subconscious, but he couldn't pin it down. It continued to elude him, remaining tantalizingly just beyond the reach of his perception.

He studied the twisting furrows cut by the branches of the drag. He ran his gaze back along the trail it had left, but it told him nothing.

He stared thoughtfully at the drag. It was still wired to the chain. His eyes moved along the length of chain and finally came to rest on the trap itself.

He studied it for a few moments, and then his glance went ahead, and in that instant the knowledge he had been groping for seemed to leap right off the sand and explode in his face.

"The spoor, Tsexhau!" he shouted. "There's no spoor."

It had been so monstrously obvious that his mind had either not been able to grasp the fact or it had rebelled at the impossibility and refused temporarily to admit it. Beyond the empty trap the sands were unmarked, and there was no spoor that he could see anywhere to show which way the lion had gone. His mind boggled at the proposition. He spun to face Tsexhau, astonished and incredulous. What he saw in the black eyes sent a strange shiver of uneasiness through him.

"I know."

"Come on, let's look around."

"I do not like it."

"Now wait a minute," Jannie said quietly, and he thought he understood the other's expression for what it was. "You're not thinking of bloody ngakas and witchcraft and all that nonsense, are you?"

"What else could it be?"

"Don't be damn silly," Jannie snapped, and then his voice filled with stinging contempt. "What are you, a man or an old woman?"

With a last withering glance at his unhappy tracker he jumped off the back of the Land Rover. He was joined moments later by Tsexhau and Spartala.

"What is it, morena?" the big African asked.

"Switch the engine off," Jannie ordered brusquely. "We might be here a while."

Spartala leaned in through the doorway and turned off the ignition. The cylinders kept on firing erratically for a few moments and then the engine died with a final shudder that shook the whole body of the vehicle.

"What is it?" he asked again.

Jannie pointed. "Look."

"I don't see anything."

"You're right, but you should be seeing something."

Spartala stared in bewilderment, and then he shrugged and began to shake his head helplessly.

"The spoor," Tsexhau said ominously. "There is no spoor."

The grimace froze on Spartala's face, and then bit by bit it came apart till his expression had changed into one of fearful disbelief.

"It cannot be," he muttered, his eyes going over the ground once again. "Did he grow wings and fly away?"

"*That* is possible," Tsexhau murmured.

"You mean——?"

"It means you're both talking a load of old rubbish," Jannie cut in irritably. "Come on, let's start looking."

They cast about all around the trap, the three of them close together, neither Spartala nor Tsexhau wanting to get far from the protection of the rifle. They found no spoor.

They returned to the trap. Jannie squatted on his haunches and picked it up. He examined it, turning it over in his hands. There was dried blood on it, and bits of fur. He checked the spring tension, pulling at the jaws. It was in order, and he knew that if the lion had ripped its paw free it should have left a little more of itself behind.

He was trying to make sense of the paradox when an extraordinary idea flashed unbidden through his mind. But it was so utterly preposterous that he dismissed it immediately as imaginative fancy.

He pushed himself up off the ground, taking the rifle back from Tsexhau. They began to walk back along the spoor cut by the drag. They hadn't gone more than a few yards when he froze.

"There's no lion spoor," he said tightly. "There's none here either."

They glanced at each other, their eyes holding for a moment, and then they moved on in silence.

To a hunter, everything that moved across the face of the land wrote its signature on the ground. To a tracker, these marks were his alphabet, the building blocks from which he created his symphonies of deduction.

Tsexhau was a tracker, and within him was fused the legend and superstition of both the Bushman and the African. His imagination was already in flight when he saw the single well-defined footprint. It was fresh, the edges sharp and clean and without any crumbling.

The sight of it stopped him in his tracks and made his heart leap. His rational mind told him that it was the footprint of one of the little desert men, the people of his mother. His ingrained fear of witchcraft and superstition told him something else.

It was well known that some ngakas were able to change them-selves into animals. Others, whose medicine wasn't as potent, rode on the backs of animals with saddles made from human skin. He him-self knew of one witchdoctor who rode on the back of hyenas. He had never heard of any of them mounting the king. The thought made him shiver, and his imagination ran riot.

That single footprint had probably been made when the ngaka descended from the sky in the shape of a vulture and changed into a man before mounting the lion. Other possibilities took shape in his fertile mind, but this was, for the moment, the most satisfyingly frightening. He pointed at it with a trembling arm.

"Look!" he exclaimed fearfully.

Jannie stared at it. "Masarwa!"

"A Masarwa that walks on one leg?" Tsexhau asked ominously.

Jannie flashed him a glance of exasperation. "That spoor?" he said eventually. "It's not old, is it?"

"As fresh as the lines cut by the drag."

For a while Jannie was silent. He stared at the ground, but he did not see it. The idea which had flashed through his mind earlier re-turned to haunt him, but it was so far-fetched that he still couldn't bring himself to consider it for long.

"So—what do you think?" he asked, not really expecting a rational answer, speaking only for the sake of something to do while he tried to marshal his own chaotic thoughts.

"I think it is a powerful ngaka," Tsexhau muttered. "I think we should forget about this lion and go."

"There's a simple answer to this," Jannie said, forcing himself to speak calmly and confidently. "And we're going to find it."

"We will find nothing."

Spartala shifted uneasily, exchanging a charged and frightened glance with the tracker. Jannie ignored the remark.

"Let's disregard that footprint for a moment," he said. "If we do, what do we have? I'll tell you. We have a trap that has walked by itself, and that isn't possible." He stared from one to the other. "Well—is it?"

Spartala began to shake his head, almost unwillingly, as if he were afraid to concur with such a facile deduction.

"We'll follow the spoor and see what we find," Jannie said.

Without giving them a chance to protest he started off. He fol-lowed the drag marks till he reached the place where Pxui had begun to lay the false trail.

"Spoor!" Jannie exclaimed softly, studying the pug marks. "So, up till here he walked on his feet, just like any other lion."

They packed up along his trail for a few yards, studying the good solid impressions of his pugs, and then they returned to where he had apparently taken wings.

"And what do you think now?" Jannie asked.

"I think we should go away," Tsexhau replied promptly.

"And I'll tell you what I think," Jannie went on. "I think——" He broke off sharply, even now unable to commit himself entirely to the suspicion which was slowly hardening in his mind. It was just beyond belief. "Come on," he continued grimly. "Let's find out how this lion learned to fly."

He felt a sudden spurt of anger as he set out and began to circle. If his suspicions were correct, it meant that someone had deliberately . . . He cut the idea dead in his mind. There had to be some other logical explanation, and what he was contemplating just wasn't logical at all.

It took them a little over ten minutes before they came across the profusion of tracks in the sand. There were the pug marks of the lion, with the faint scuffed indentation where he had lain belly down in the sand while the trap was being peeled from his leg.

There was nothing unusual in the spoor of the lion, but what made their minds revolt and unwilling to accept the evidence of their eyes were the small human footprints, equally fresh, in such close proximity to the huge pug marks.

"It's not—it's not possible," Jannie breathed. "I don't believe it. No one can walk up to a trapped lion."

"Only an ngaka," whispered Tsexhau, his voice hushed with fear and awe.

Jannie glared at him mutinously. His head was still swimming with the discovery, and he was half inclined to believe his tracker again, because it was even less absurd than the other alternative.

"What ngaka!" he shouted angrily. "You've seen them before, those little footprints in the sand. They were made by a Masarwa, a Bushman. He's not an ngaka. He's a man, just the same as you, the same as me."

Tsexhau refused to meet Jannie's eyes, and his face set stubbornly. "We have hunted a long time together, morena, is that not so?"

"What about it?"

"We have trapped lions before, and we have killed them after."

"Get on with it."

"We have seen their fierceness, have we not, and also their cunning?"

"Yes," Jannie agreed, and he became wary, because he thought he knew the direction in which his tracker was leading him.

"And where in all the world will you find a man who can walk up to a trapped lion and take the steel from his leg?" he asked, lifting his head to meet Jannie's gaze, his eyes bright and questioning. "This is what I want to know, especially since you yourself have already said it is impossible."

"It was just a way of speaking," Jannie said impatiently. "I didn't mean it like that, to be taken as the truth." He flung up his arm, pointing swiftly to first one set of tracks and then the others. "It's written there, in the sand. You're a tracker, you can see it, can't you? He came from that way, not an ngaka, a Masarwa. I don't know why or how, but he"—he faltered and then pushed on valiantly, unable to believe what he himself was saying—"he took the trap from the lion's leg, and then—and then he brushed out the old spoor and set a false trail and ran off that way. You see the spoor of his feet, dammit."

"And this was done by a man, a Masarwa?" inquired Tsexhau, and there was a wry and scathing irony in his voice.

"Of course it was. Isn't it written there for anyone with eyes to see?"

"Only an ngaka could do such a thing," Tsexhau cried. "And what lion will follow a man, follow him like a dog? I tell you it is magic, terrible magic."

Jannie clenched his teeth in exasperation. He knew that he could never persuade either of them otherwise, and that to try would be a waste of time. He was having a bad enough time convincing himself.

"Let's get back to the truck," he snapped.

He spun on his heel and strode off. After a moment's hesitation they hurried after him.

"Let us leave this big beast," Tsexhau pleaded. "Let us leave him, morena, and go far away and hunt for our meat."

Jannie felt his anger rising again, but then he saw the look of fear on his tracker's face. "I can't, Tsexhau," he said quietly. "That's a wounded lion out there, and I've got to get him."

"We will never find him," Spartala said ponderously. "And if we find him he will not be wounded."

"He'll be wounded," Jannie countered emphatically. "And he'll be dangerous."

"Forget him," Tsexhau urged. "What harm can he do out there in the desert, even if he is wounded, which will not be the case, as Spartala says. There are no men, there are not cattle, why bother?"

"There are Masarwas."

"They can look after themselves."

"Perhaps, but I'm going to get that lion if it's the last thing I do. And if I catch the little bastard that took—that set him free, I'll— I don't know what I'll do to him."

"Forget him, morena, leave him to the hyenas."

"Shut up!" Jannie roared suddenly.

He was immediately ashamed of his outburst, but the thought of the king being pulled down and torn up by those slinking scavengers made him lose his temper. He knew that they fulfilled a definite purpose and performed a very necessary function, but he had also watched them at work.

They walked the rest of the way to the Land Rover in silence, and he was conscious of their resentment and sullenness.

"Get that drag off and load the trap," he said.

Spartala bent to the task. Tsexhau squatted beside him, pretending to help. He heard them whispering, and he waited, wondering what they were cooking up between them. Eventually Spartala stood up, the trap in his hands. He lifted it up over the tail-gate of the Land Rover and put it in carefully, and then he turned to Jannie.

"Tsexhau says he will not go any further if you hunt for the lion," he said. "He is sorry, but he will not go."

Jannie nodded amiably: he had been half expecting something like this. "And you?"

"I also, morena."

His discomfort was evident, and Jannie knew that it must have taken a lot of courage, or a lot of fear, to rebel openly like this. But in their present state of mind, to try and force the issue would make them even more adamant and intractable.

"So," he drawled, injecting scorn and contempt into his voice. "You're even more of an old woman than Tsexhau."

"You're a white man, morena," Spartala replied sullenly, stung by the great insult. "You don't know about these things like a black man."

Inwardly Jannie was furious, seething at the delay, but he maintained a calm and unruffled exterior. "Maybe I don't," he agreed, and then when he saw they were beginning to relax he struck, his voice flat and grim. "But there's one thing I do know, and that's if you don't get behind the wheel, Spartala, and start driving, and if you don't get up into the back of the Land Rover, Tsexhau, you'll never come hunting with me again."

It was an idle threat. They had hunted together a long time, the three of them, and they were pretty nigh indispensable to him, both as hunters and as companions, but he didn't think they would know this, because in spite of their closeness, it was still basically a master-servant relationship. He paid them well, better than most, and they knew it. These desert excursions were gravy on top of their bread.

Both Spartala and Tsexhau started. Their pained dismay lasted a few moments, but then their faces hardened and became stubborn again.

"We will grieve, morena," Tsexhau said. "Surely there is some other punishment you can give us?"

"That's what will happen."

"Don't you see, morena, it's bad, bad, bad," Spartala pleaded. "Even to see such an animal, one that is the accomplice of an ngaka, is a thing that will bring great disaster."

"Are you coming or not?"

Spartala glanced at Tsexhau, found his confirmation and bowed his head. "For the rest of our days we will be in sadness," he replied. "But no, we cannot come."

"Morena!" exclaimed Tsexhau, cutting in with his own fervent plea. "A beast like that can never be found. His spoor will vanish into the sky, as will the spoor of the ngaka. They will fly away in the body of a vulture, because they are one and the same. And who can read the tracks which feathers make as they flash through the air of the sky?"

"All right," Jannie said. He racked his rifle inside the Land Rover and then turned to face the disconsolate pair. "I will follow him myself. I've got no time to take you back, so you'll have to walk."

They nodded eagerly.

"And while you're walking," Jannie continued, his expression grave and sombre, "I hope you don't bump into the lion, wounded or not."

He studied their faces covertly, trying to assess the effect of his words. At the first indication they gave of indecision and uneasiness he attacked again.

"Maybe you didn't think about it, but that ngaka, he knows who set the trap and where our camp is hidden," he went on, in the same sonorous tones. "He knows, and he might be wanting his revenge."

Spartala gasped and his eyes grew wide. Tsexhau was equally nervous. It wasn't an idea that had occurred to either of them.

"Perhaps we should go with the master," Spartala suggested hesitantly, addressing himself to the tracker. "It will be hard for him to drive and spoor and shoot, and besides, it is our duty."

"You have spoken the truth," Tsexhau affirmed immediately. "He cannot do everything by himself."

"You've changed your minds?" Jannie asked innocently.

"We will come," Tsexhau said, speaking with all the dignity he could muster. "But only because it will be dangerous for you to be alone."

"Let's get moving then," Jannie said abruptly.

He had refrained from making a sarcastic and cutting comment. In some ways they were no more than little children, and in others they were the greatest of men. Everyone was vulnerable somewhere, and he had never found it necessary or pleasurable to exploit weakness. Had they remained adamant, he would have gone after the lion on his own. It was quite a while since he had killed the last one.

Spartala picked up the spoor where Pxui had freed the lion and then he settled down to steer on the tracks. In the beginning they were easy to follow, the three pug marks of the animal and the footprints of the ngaka. In places where the spoor of the lion was superimposed on the spoor of the man, the dread in him grew more intense.

8

FROM FAR in the distance, the drone of the Land Rover's engine reached Pxui. It rose and fell, like the humming of a swarm of bees in flight. He knew that it was gaining on him.

A fresh burst of fear poured through him. The lion was still following, hopping along on three legs. Even now he found him a frightening sight, with the huge black mane looking like a cape made from the darkness of the night itself.

He wanted to halt and try to drive him away, but he had tried that already and it hadn't worked, and with every second that passed the hunters were getting nearer. He began to wish that he had never set him free. If he hadn't, the animal would not be following now, drawing with him the men who had crossed the lines of his fate and were hungry for his life.

I should have shot him with my arrow, he told himself. With the trap he was wearing, and the poison of my arrow in his blood, he would not be following me now.

He lengthened his stride, and breaking the rhythm of his lope he began to run. He felt the sand and the earth spurting from under his small flying feet, and it rose in him then as it always did, the hot sweet pleasure that came from running, with the blood pounding softly behind his eyes and making him feel so drunk that it felt as if he could leap into the air whenever he chose and soar like a bird on its wings.

It was almost the same kind of feeling he had at those times of the Rain Dance, when he lay down on his belly and drew the smoke of wild hemp deep into his lungs from the clay pipes sunken in the earth.

Through the pounding in his ears he heard the throbbing of the engine. It seemed louder now than it had been before. He began to run harder, and then just as he had adjusted to the faster pace the noise of the engine dropped to a quiet murmur. It started up again after a while, a different note to it. Once more it fell to a whisper, and then abruptly it died out completely.

He wasn't certain, but from the direction of the sound he was inclined to think that the hunters had reached the place where he had set the false trail. He wondered how long it would keep them there.

He looked back quickly, without breaking the rhythm of his stride. The lion was still with him, and as far as he could judge, maintaining the same distance. He felt a bleak despair take possession of him.

In a moment of madness he had given the animal the chance of life, and now he seemed bent on destroying him. He wondered if he knew what he was doing, and whether he was following him on purpose. Perhaps there was a plan in that huge head, some way of escaping in the end while the hunters were busy with Pxui.

The animal followed him as if he had a right to do so, as if he were his shadow. The moment the idea entered the boy's head he had a terrifying thought. He was running east, into the sun, and he glanced back directly behind him.

He saw his own shadow, right there where it should have been, hard and ink black and reassuring. Relief poured through him.

In that first instant of dread he wondered if the lion had somehow stolen his shadow and taken its place. A man without his shadow had lost the spirit of himself, and without the one that walked beside him he was as good as dead.

He heard the sound of the engine start up again. He began to run harder, driving himself, and then to his astonishment the sound did not get louder as he had expected but became fainter and fainter till eventually he could hear it no more.

He slowed abruptly and halted. He turned slightly, his head cocked in the direction from which the sound had been coming. He thought he heard it once again, but he couldn't be sure, because his ears were filled with the whistle and rasp of his own laboured breathing.

9

STARING AT the big pug marks and the footprints running together, Jannie felt all his previous incredulity returning. They unreeled hypnotically before him, making a mockery of all he had ever learned and believed in. At one point he even began again to entertain the idea that there might just be some truth in the theory expounded by Tsexhau, but the moment he began to contemplate it, his mind revolted at the idea. He would have to be out of his head to start believing in all that sort of stuff, so alien was it to his own way of thinking.

After a while the spoor became more and more difficult to follow. At times they lost it altogether, and then Jannie and the tracker would leave the vehicle and cast about till they finally found it again.

They lost it for the fourth time, and the moment the Land Rover halted he piled out of the back, calling impatiently to his tracker. Tsexhau climbed out without any enthusiasm.

He began by locating on the mental picture he had drawn in his mind his own position at the moment in relation to the direction the spoor had been taking when he had seen the last fairly clear prints about a hundred yards back.

"Come on," Jannie urged him.

Tsexhau refused to be hurried. He turned back to stare thoughtfully at the thorn-dotted land they had just traversed. There was a dreamy look in his eyes, but he wasn't dreaming. He was slipping himself into the mind of the lion, and with his knowledge of their habits, he charted mentally the direction in which it would most likely have travelled from where he had last seen its spoor. With that as a beginning, he studied the land which lay ahead, trying to imagine the path which the lion would have taken.

It came to him instinctively without conscious thought or effort.

He started slightly, as if coming out of a trance, and then he went forward, angling off slightly to the left, his eyes scanning the ground.

He was frightened and reluctant to go forward, but the habits of a lifetime drove him mechanically through the motions. It was one thing to track an ordinary lion, but this devil he had been forced to try and spoor was a very different matter.

"Let us give this up, morena," he urged once again. "We will find only terrible trouble, if we continue to find anything at all."

"Keep looking."

"What man can follow the journey of a shadow over the face of the desert?"

"You've followed him so far," Jannie said bluntly.

"This is only the beginning," whispered Tsexhau, a deep uneasiness rising in him again.

He went on for another fifty or sixty yards. He paused momentarily, as if at a loss, and then he cut sharply to his right and started off again. He began to wonder if there wasn't some way he could bring this foolishness to an end.

"Have you seen something?" Jannie demanded eagerly.

His thumb tightened on the safety-catch of the rifle. He threw a quick glance at the ground, hoping and half expecting to see fresh spoor right there in front of him. But he saw nothing, and he tore his gaze away reluctantly and once again concentrated on searching the brush ahead. It was the tracker's work to find and follow the spoor: his task was to keep a constant surveillance in case the lion should suddenly spring from the concealment of a thicket.

"Nothing," Tsexhau replied.

"Keep looking."

It was winter now, and five months since the last rains had fallen. The land was already burned and dry, and in places it was baked hard where the earth had melted under the deluge of the summer rains and then been turned to iron in the blistering heat of the sun.

It was in places like that where tracking became difficult. Any fool could follow a spoor over yielding sand. Where there were no visible prints, or an impression so faint that it would be meaningless to any but a trained eye, a tracker relied on his intuition and instinctive knowledge, and he searched for other signs—a broken twig, a crushed blade of grass, anything which had in passing disturbed the natural pattern of the desert.

To detect such minute indications was an achievement in itself: to interpret them with any reliability required a special kind of genius, together with years of observation and application.

Jannie had watched him at work before, and he had never ceased to marvel. He knew a little about the art, and still it astonished him at times. To someone who knew nothing about its subtleties, he was inclined to think it would appear to be nothing less than magic.

"What do you see?" Jannie whispered. "Don't you see anything?"

Tsexhau did not answer. He was in a strange, almost trancelike state, and he heard nothing. He had reached that peak of concentration where his mind felt as if it had detached itself from the rest of his body and was floating high above him, like some powerful and all-seeing eye. The acuity of his perception was stretched almost to breaking point, and he knew that soon his head would begin to ache if he kept it up.

He was angling off to the left again when he halted suddenly. It was unfortunate that the first spoor he saw was the vague and almost imperceptible print of Pxui's right foot. Terror knifed through him.

"Have you seen something?" Jannie demanded.

Habit, the discipline of obedience to the verity of his craft, almost betrayed him initially, but it was swallowed up in the next instant by a fear that was even more ancient and deep seated. He decided right then to put into operation the plan which had been shaping in his mind.

"Yes," Tsexhau said, and he pointed to an indecipherable smudge on the ground and swung right again, in the opposite direction to which the spoor was going. "There, morena, there!" he exclaimed. "That is the way he has gone."

"Can you follow it?"

"Oh yes."

"From the Land Rover?"

"To start with."

Jannie pursed his mouth and whistled, waving frantically at Spartala. Tsexhau felt a sudden blistering guilt at the deception he was about to embark on. It was a betrayal of himself and his craft, and also a betrayal of the man who was his master.

"Nothing good will come of this, morena," he said, pleading once again. "Let us give it up."

"I want that lion," Jannie said grimly. "It's wounded in any case, and you know I just can't leave it."

More than his code as a hunter was driving him. That alone would have been more than sufficient to keep him on the spoor of a wounded animal till he had found and finished it off, but in this instance he was being driven by a compulsion even more powerful.

He still could not bring himself to believe whole-heartedly that any man alive could walk up to a trapped lion and free it. His right hand strayed to the side of his face, the fingers touching and exploring.

He would have to see it for himself, this lion and this man. He knew that if he didn't, the dark mystery of it would haunt him for the rest of his days.

The moment the Land Rover halted he swung up into the back. Tsexhau followed him in. He called his instructions to Spartala and the vehicle rolled forward.

10

PXUI WAITED a little while longer, listening intently, and when he became certain the vehicle was no longer following him, he leaped into the air and let out a little yell. It was a soft meaningless cry, guttural with relief and gratitude.

He couldn't imagine what had turned the hunters aside: it was enough that they no longer pursued him. He wondered if they had failed to find the real spoor, but he didn't think that possible. Perhaps they had gone after some more immediate game. He didn't know, and for the moment he didn't care.

He glanced at the lion. The animal had come to a halt almost as soon as the boy had. He was belly down on the sand again, licking at the paw, lifting his head once in a while to stare at Pxui with those yellow eyes which seemed to look right through him and focus at some point in the vast distances beyond.

The boy broke into a sudden dance, his feet drumming quick and striking clean and hard against the earth, and then he brandished his spear and struck a pose.

He studied his shadow, admiring it, going over it inch by inch, relishing its size. He was a small man, like all of his race, and like all men of small stature, he was sensitive about it.

He made a stabbing motion with his spear, and he was gratified to see his shadow repeat the action simultaneously. In the crystal-clear light of the clean winter sun its definition was hard and sharp.

A man's shadow, he thought, was truly a wondrous and beautiful thing. It walked with him and kept him company, and it did all the things that he himself did. He wished again that he was as tall and big as his own shadow. He waggled the spear once more and assumed a theatrical and aggressive stance. He chanted aloud, his voice rising like that of a singing bird.

"Who is he whose shadow is so mighty that it darkens the whole earth?

"Who is he, who has set the greatest of all hunters free?

"Who is he who fears nothing and can walk beside a great beast of prey?"

He paused for a moment, as if listening to something within himself, and then he cried out joyously: "Why, Pxui, you child of a Bushman, it is you!"

He took a few prancing steps and then lifted his gaze to study the angle of the sun. It was late already, but it didn't perturb him. His parents would wait, or come looking for him, and even if they didn't and moved on, he would pick up their spoor and find them.

He eyed the lion for a moment and then set off at a steady lope, wondering if he was going to keep on following him. He wondered what his mother would say, and his father. That they would be astonished and dumbfounded he had no doubt, but somehow he had the intuitive feeling that there would be more to their reactions than just that.

He looked back, and he was a little disappointed to see that the lion was still belly down on the sand. He began to think of Xhabbo, whom he had last seen a week ago at their camp of secret water. Her name meant "dream," and she was a little younger than himself, and she was as beautiful and shy as a steenbuck doe, but she also possessed on occasion a caustic tongue that he was very much afraid of. He dreamed about her often.

He wondered what she would say if he were to return with a lion that followed him like a ratel following a honey bird. He wanted to look back again, to see if the lion had begun to follow him, but he didn't do it straight away, because now he truly wanted the animal to follow him, and he thought it might bring him bad luck. When a man wanted something it was best not to appear too eager, otherwise he invariably did not get it.

He looked back after a while, not really wanting to, but unable to restrain his anxiety about the matter any longer.

He leapt into the air, soaring high, and his feet did an ecstatic little jig before he came back to earth and faultlessly picked up his stride. The lion was once again following him.

And it was right then, with the happiness bubbling inside him, that he recalled the story his father had told him long ago about the young hunter and the lion. He had not thought of it for a long time, but he knew why it had come back to him now.

I I

TSEXHAU LED them away from the spoor he had seen, going in precisely the opposite direction. To give authenticity to his deception, he pretended to lose the spoor now and again. He was a consummate actor and he did it without difficulty.

Jannie, who had absolute faith in his tracker, made it even easier for him. He did not question him, nor did he bother with more than a quick and superficial glance at the faint indications which Tsexhau alleged was the spoor he was following. The only thing he did was drive him.

They ate on the move, sandwiches of roasted gemsbok and raw sliced onions. The thick slices of meat were butter soft and delicious, spiced with garlic and coriander. Jannie wolfed his down without even tasting them.

It was about three in the afternoon when Tsexhau stopped Spartala again. He made a great show of looking for spoor, casting around, the pattern of his search forming a large rectangle which he bisected diagonally. When he had finished he turned to Jannie. There was a peculiar expression on his face, compounded of both fear and triumph. It hadn't been difficult to assume, because by now he was so thoroughly brain-washed by his own game of make-believe that the dividing line between fantasy and reality had become blurred.

"He has gone."

It stunned Jannie, and it was a moment before he recovered. "What do you mean—gone!"

"I can find no spoor," Tsexhau explained. "He has gone, like I said he would. Perhaps he has gone into the air. Who knows?"

"There's no spoor at all? Not the lion, not even the nga—— the man?"

"Nothing."

Jannie stared at his tracker, incredulous and disbelieving. "Dammit to hell!" he exploded abruptly. "They can't just have vanished into—into thin air."

"There is nothing."

"Look again," Jannie commanded.

The desert air had dried his nostrils and the dust had caked inside them, adding to his discomfort. Perspiration had collected in his armpits, and he felt it begin to trickle down his sides. The stock of the rifle was sweating oil, and the wood felt clammy and greasy in his hands.

"Come on," Jannie urged. "What are you waiting for?"

"Morena, I have looked already," Tsexhau replied patiently. "I cannot find something that isn't there."

Jannie glared at him, his mouth opening, but then he shut it with a snap. He realized that he wasn't thinking or acting altogether rationally.

"We'll go back to where you last saw the spoor," he declared. "From there we can follow it up."

They drove back, following their tyre tracks. When they came to the location where he had last halted to look for spoor, Tsexhau hopped out smartly and began his pretence of searching. He knew he was going to be in trouble unless he came up with something.

He walked briskly off to one side, and then quickly, unobserved, he pressed his toes down on a patch of soft sand, lifted them, and then bringing his heel forward made a second impression with it. The result was the imprint of a small foot.

He moved away quickly, and Jannie joined him. They cast about together, but found no spoor.

"Well?" Jannie demanded. "Where is it?"

"It's bad country and the spoor was very faint, morena," explained Tsexhau. "I was following it with my nose more than with my eyes."

Jannie nodded. He knew that Tsexhau was referring to that intuitive sixth sense with which a tracker often had to work.

Tsexhau circled back slowly to where he had faked the diminutive footprint. "Morena, look!"

"Ahh!" Jannie breathed, studying the spoor, his eyes gleaming. "And the lion? You haven't seen any of his pug marks?"

"Nothing that would mean anything to you. I told you, half the time I have been working him with my nose."

"But you did see it? You saw *some*thing?"

"Yes."

"Let's walk then." Jannie threw a quick glance at the sun. It was going down fast, with only about two hours of daylight left. "We haven't got much time, we'd better hurry it up."

He was about to turn away when he paused. "Spartala!"

"Morena?"

"How much left in the tank?"

"About half."

"Under or over?"

"Just under."

That was a little less than ten gallons. Jannie thought for a moment, his fingers stroking the side of his face. "Follow us," he called out eventually.

They walked, and when after an hour and a half they had found nothing which he himself considered conclusive, Jannie called a halt. The sweat had glued his shirt to his back, and where it had run down his face it had cut streaks through the coating of powdery dust.

He thought about camping out, but rejected the idea. There was just enough gasoline to get them back to camp, and God only knew how far they would have to go the next day. He began to wish that he had fitted the extra tank he had been intending to install since last year.

"We'll go back now, back to where he got out of the trap," he informed them. "I want to have a good look at that spoor. I want to remember it, because I'm going out after him tomorrow. I'm going to get this lion if it's the last bloody thing I do."

He racked his rifle and piled in beside Spartala. Tsexhau got in after him and slammed the door, and a moment later they were rolling again.

Jannie passed his cigarettes and then lit one for himself. He drew the smoke hungrily into his body, and then he began to think about the lion again.

12

PXUI FELT a prickling at the back of his neck as the story ran through his mind again.

It was about a young hunter who had climbed to the top of a dune while out looking for game. When he reached the crest, from where he could see into the distance all around him, to his great surprise and consternation he began to feel sleepy.

He realized instantly that it must be the magic of some very great animal, but though he fought mightily against the sudden desire to sleep it overwhelmed him in the end.

A little while later a lion padded softly to the top of the dune. He had been on his way to water, the first thing of life, but the moment he saw the sleeping hunter he walked over and took him.

He was dragging him towards a tree when the hunter woke up from his sleep. He was terrified of making any movement lest the lion kill him straight away, so he remained limp and quiet, pretending that he was dead.

When the lion reached a nearby storm tree he picked the hunter up in his mouth and carried him up high and wedged him between two forking branches.

After doing that, the lion found himself in a terrible quandary. He had been on his way to water, for he was thirsty, and now he couldn't decide whether to eat the man first and then go for his drink, or keep to his original intention.

In the end, after a great struggle within himself, he decided to drink first and then eat later, because it was what he had been intending to do in the first place.

Having come to this decision, the lion wedged his prize even more firmly into the fork of the tree and then climbed down. He started off towards the water, but then all his earlier doubts returned to torment him, and he kept looking back across his shoulder to make sure that the man hadn't moved.

The further he went down the dune, the more difficult it became for him to see the man in the tree. Eventually when he got right to the bottom, he could no longer see him.

He began to doubt again, wondering whether he had really wedged the man securely enough in the tree. When his uncertainty became to much to bear, he turned and hurried back to the tree, to make sure one last time.

The young man watched the lion approach through squinted eyes. He knew that he was in even greater danger now and had to keep absolutely still. He was in agony however, and he had been crying quietly already, and it took all his willpower to remain motionless, because the lion had wedged him so tightly into the fork and in such a position that a protruding piece of branch was pressing painfully into his side.

When he reached him the lion saw the man's tears. He climbed into the tree and tenderly licked them away. They were bound to each other now as they had not been before, by pain and by pity.

After that the lion went away to drink his water, and the instant he was out of sight the hunter scrambled down the tree and ran back to his people.

He ran over broken ground, trying to hide his spoor, because he knew that the lion would follow him. It had licked away his tears, and for that there was a price to be paid.

When he reached his people he told them there was a lion following him, and he begged them to wrap him up in the skin of a hartebeest, which would make him invisible to the lion.

He was a handsome young man, a great hunter and provider, loved by all the people, and because of this they took pity on him and hid him thus.

When the lion eventually arrived, they attacked him with spears and arrows, because he was a common enemy. But their spears and arrows had no effect on the animal.

He spoke to them, telling them that he had come for the young hunter whose tears he had dried, that he had to find him.

As a last resort they offered the lion young children, and even a beautiful girl, but the animal refused, telling them again that he had come for the young man, and that no substitute would do, and further, that no one would be permitted to leave until he had got what he came for.

The sun went down, and it began to get dark, but still the lion would not leave. His eyes glowed red in the light of the fires which began to spring up.

The people were thoroughly frightened by now. Some of them began to perceive, dimly at first, but with a steadily growing conviction, that this was a matter in which they had not had the right to interfere. The reckoning had to be between the lion and the hunter, and if they persisted in trying to postpone the inevitable, the whole community would be in danger, because they would not be able to go out and hunt.

So in the end they took his protective skin away, and gave him to the lion, weeping bitter tears as they handed him over.

The animal recognized the young man and killed him immediately, and then he spoke to the people one more time, telling them that since he had now found the young man he had been searching for, they could now kill him too.

But before they could do that, the lion lay down beside the young hunter whose tears he had tasted, and died of his own accord.

This Pxui's father had told him, and there were many truths hidden there if a man hunted hard enough, and the one which he understood most clearly was that a person had to stand and face alone the consequences of his own mistakes, that if he fell asleep on his journey through life he could not expect others to pay the price.

He glanced over his shoulder once more, checking up on the lion. The animal was still behind him, and as he ran on he searched his mind to see if there was any way he could equate the story with what he had done, if there was any kind of similarity at all.

He tried, but he couldn't tie them together. It was all the wrong way round, and if anything, it was he who had metaphorically licked the tears of the lion. The animal had no reason to kill him.

In any case, the incidents in the story had all happened a very long time ago, to a young hunter who had been one of the first people of his race.

He wondered though, why the lion had not made him feel sleepy. He was beginning to doubt the truth of such a possibility when he realized that the explanation was quite simple. If the lion had used his magic on him, he would have fallen asleep and not been able to help him.

The logical corollary to this deduction was that the lion had purposely not used his magic. There was a definite tie between them now, but the exact nature of it eluded him.

It was then that it occurred to him that the lion might have conceived an affection for him. The idea was startling and gratifying, but he dismissed it after a moment's thought, remembering how the animal had snarled when he reached out to try and touch him.

He began to wonder if the lion would follow him forever, like the one in the story, and then thinking about Xhabbo he wished that it would at least follow him until they returned to their camp, because then she would see the proof of what he had done. No hunter that he had heard told of had done a greater thing.

The lion, on three legs, ran behind the boy. He was still in great pain, but it was nothing compared to what he had suffered before. He wanted more than anything else to be able to lie up in some impenetrable thicket, deep and dark, and there to lick and tend his wound.

His flanks heaved, and his breath blew gasping from his broad nostrils. He was not made for this long-distance slogging, and it clashed with the innate indolence of his nature. He was muscled and built for short lethal sprints which hurled him towards his prey at a speed which sometimes exceeded fifty miles an hour.

These were his finest and most exciting moments, and the excitement he experienced then was comparable only to that strange and subtly different quickening which electrified him when the air carried to him that pungent taint of a ready female.

It began with hunger, that dull belly-ache which had to be satisfied. It was followed by the prowling search for prey, the exquisite and almost unbearable tension of the stalk, and then finally, the murderous charge that catapulted him onto the back of his victim, where he killed in a burst of savage pleasure, biting through flesh and bone to crush a vital spot or hooking the claws of a forepaw into a spongy snout and jerking it back to snap the neck.

Feeding was the culmination of the cycle, soothing and calming and satisfying, dissipating the last of his accumulated tension.

The awkwardness of his three-legged gait began to tire him. It produced an imbalance that strained muscles which had not been meant to function in that manner and which had not as yet grown accustomed to having to compensate.

He lowered his injured leg and tried to put a little of the weight of his body on it. Pain shot up through it the moment it touched the ground, and he moaned deeply.

When the shock of it has passed and the agony diminished and the level of his pain was back to where it was before, he began to feel the depth of his hunger.

He knew though, that half-crippled and handicapped by his leg the way it was, he could never hope to kill and satisfy his hunger in the ordinary way.

There was carrion to be found at times, but it was not a commodity in regular supply. And even when it satisfied his hunger, it left him feeling strangely disturbed and incomplete. He did not understand that the cycle to which his inheritance had programmed him was disrupted by feeding on carrion. He was a hunter, a killer by instinct and training, and short-circuiting an essential part of the continuity of that cycle left him vaguely uneasy and dissatisfied. That was the extent of his awareness.

He kept his eyes on the man running ahead of him. It never occurred to him to equate the small running form with food. He moved on two legs and in an upright position, quite unlike any of the other animals on which he preyed. The smell of him was different also, and because of these differences and the fact that his knowledge of him was almost non-existent, he feared him still. But not to the same extent as he had done before.

And now he ran after him blindly, driven by a compulsion and an instinct he was unable to understand or deny. The small yellow-brown creature had unlocked the steel from his leg. It had taken the great pain away and made it into something more manageable, and it had not tried to hurt him.

Only once had it moved towards him, but he had given his warning, and the creature had left him alone. It was conceivable he had nothing more to fear, and where the man fed, there would be food and sustenance for him as well, and he could lick at his wound and work on it till the pain went away and the flesh grew back together and there was no longer any need to soothe and cleanse it with his tongue.

He saw the man moving wide to cut round a patch of thorn, vanishing behind it. He altered direction himself, the execution awkward and ponderous, a harsh reminder of the fact that he was no longer the same agile and fearless creature he had been before the trap took him.

The moment the lion cleared the thicket he came to a sudden startled halt. The man he had been following was a little way ahead, walking now, and just beyond him were two more of the same creatures.

"Father, oh my father!" Pxui called. "It is——"

He broke off abruptly as he saw the look of relief and welcome on the man's face change to one of utter disbelief which in turn was replaced by naked terror. He himself had got used to the presence of the lion behind him, but he had carelessly forgotten what the effect would be on someone who saw it for the first time.

After a few moments of shocked immobility Tsonomon found his voice. He shouted a shrill warning and then darted forward, his hand flashing to the quiver on his back. He ran straight at Pxui, and in the confusion of that instant the boy thought that perhaps his father was going to strike him for having freed the lion and allowed the animal to follow him back.

But the man pushed him aside, covering him with his own body, an arrow already notched to his bow, and it was then that Pxui realized that the man had not had any intention of punishing him, because he did not of course know what had transpired.

"Father!" he screamed, grappling for the bow in his hands. "It is mine, do not shoot my lion."

The man stared at the beast. The lion had halted, and his ears were flat back, his tail swishing and his black lips peeled back to show the big, yellowed teeth. The man lowered the bow slowly, letting the tension come off the string, but he held it poised and ready.

"Your lion?" he asked, flashing a swift incredulous glance at his son before returning his attention to the huge animal. "Is the time of the hyena upon you that you speak like that?"

"Listen, father, I will speak that you may listen to me," the boy replied breathlessly. "And listening, you will know that the hyena is not with me."

The times of the hyena were those times when disaster overwhelmed the spirit of a man and shredded his soul, so that he no longer acted or spoke in a rational manner.

"I listen."

"You know I went to read the sands, so that in reading them I would learn what has passed that way," the boy began. "I had not gone very far when I saw him. It halted me as suddenly as if an arrow had pierced my heart. In all my life I have never been so frightened. He stood there and looked at me, and then he spoke in his voice. You know how they speak, as if the sound comes from the earth itself, striking like a burst of thunder in the belly of a man?"

"And then?" the man asked, his own breath coming faster as he saw it so clearly that it was as if he had been there himself.

And then the boy went on to tell him how his first thought had been to run, but he knew also that no man could outrun a lion from such a distance.

The animal had started to come towards him, and his nerve had almost broken, but something about the way the lion moved caught his attention, and he saw the trap round the leg which he had not noticed in the beginning because of his fear and astonishment.

He went on, stressing the fact that he had wanted to kill him at first, for the meat of his body and also because of the great honour he would reap. He explained how he had tried to get a shot at him, and then described the incredible behaviour of the lion, and the slow-dawning realization that he was asking him for help.

He had taken his courage in his hands, and with the help of the little sticks had done what he had to do, driven by the knowledge that it was a thing no hunter had ever done before; and also because it was a challenge in a way, to overcome his fear and to find out for certain whether he had in fact interpreted the actions of the great beast correctly.

He told him about the trap, and the false trail he had laid, and how the lion had followed him even when he tried to chase him away.

He came to the end of his recital, and his eyes found those of his father.

"You do not believe me?" he asked softly, accusingly, and then: "But it is so, and it does not change even though you do not believe. It is thus, and therefore it is."

"I believe you," Tsonomon said.

"I believe you," echoed his mother, who had joined them to listen to the story. "When you were no more than a child in my arms I gave you a star. You were only a child, but I heard the star speaking."

She was old now and wrinkled, and the life of the desert had marked her as it marked all its children. She had been young then, still glowing with the wonder of her own motherhood, and as she went back in her mind to that night it seemed as if it had only been yesterday and that all the other years in between had never passed.

It had been a time of hunger, with the grass all burned and gone, and the game gone too, and every living creature in the desert anxiously watching the lightning and waiting for the first of the life-giving rain.

Since time immemorial all her people had followed the lightning in the same way that the animals of the desert did. In seasons of drought and deprivation, it was more than just a simple trekking towards the coming rain. It was that, but accompanying it was an inner compulsion that drew them like a magnet, giving them hope and strength and purpose, renewing the low-burning flame of the spirit in their thirst- and hunger-shrunken bodies.

She heard again the voice of her young husband, the rising inflection in it as he spoke of how far, far, far it was to the next secret water.

She had pictured it in her mind, the endless vista of sand and scrub and thorn, all of it shimmering and dancing and distorted beneath the huge sun which burned malignantly and without mercy in the heat-shocked sky. She had followed the lightning herself, but never before with one who was dependent on her, and the thought of it made her afraid.

The stars were hunting hard that night, she remembered, and from far away in the velvet distances she heard the sounds of their heavenly chase, an electric murmur that rose and fell like a distant sea sound.

She looked up, and the dog star caught and held her eye. Sirius, pulsing with light, the brightest star in the constellation of Canis Major. She did not know the name of the cluster, but grandmother

Sirius was an old friend, and she had prayed to her and danced for her many times before.

All the stars, she knew, were hunters, and it was one of the greatest in the sky, perhaps second only to the Dawn's Heart, the fiercest of them all, who hunted in such distant places that he only returned in the time before the dawn. She was thinking, of course, of Venus, the morning star of the southern hemisphere.

The sight of it filled her with a sudden overwhelming compulsion. The child was still too young really, but she disregarded the fact. She picked him up, and with her husband beside her she walked away from the fire and a little way out into the night.

She lifted the boy high above her head, her arms outstretched, her body taut and straining upwards as if by her effort she could touch the stars themselves with the offering in her hands. She threw back her head, her face lifted to the night sky and her eyes huge with the enormity of the moment. She began to sing softly, and in her voice there was a trembling reverence.

> "Oh you in the sky,
> Please take his little heart,
> And give him some part,
> Of your own great heart
> And your hunter's eye."

And so she had given him to the keeping of a star. She stared at the lion and a shiver ran through her. It seemed a strange answer to that prayer of long ago, but the way of the stars were dark and mysterious, as were the ways of all great hunters.

"I believe you," Tsonomon said again, eyeing the lion warily. "But it's difficult to believe. I have never heard of such a thing, since the first of all our fathers."

"But what of the story?" the boy asked. "The story of the young hunter and the lion? There is much that is the same."

"That is different. He was of the first people, and they were strange and different in many ways. In any case, he killed the hunger, don't you remember?"

"I remember."

The man was silent for a while, still apprehensive, studying the lion who had sunk to his belly and was licking at the wound.

"You did not feel a sleepiness?" he asked abruptly, anxiety and curiosity in his voice.

"No—I wanted to ask you about that."

"That is strange," the man mused, and then after a few moments: "It is a good sign, even if it is strange."

"Yes, it is strange."

The man was thoughtful for a while. "You say he follows you, that he has followed you all the way from that place where you set him free?"

"Yes."

"Good, we will lead him to a tree, and we will climb it, where we will be safe in the height of the tree," the man said. "I will shoot him, and we will spoor him till he dies, and in dying he will give us the food of his great body so that we may grow strong and great as him."

He was a hunter, and there were two others he had to feed besides himself, and though the boy was a hunter too, he was still his responsibility in the end, and here was good strong flesh that they needed.

"Father!" Pxui exclaimed, shocked, and thinking of Xhabbo and what he had thought before the bright rainbow colours of his dream faded till there was no brightness left in them.

"Yes?" Tsonomon answered, edgily and impatiently.

The boy did not know where he got the courage, but he found it somewhere. "Forgive me, oh my father, but you cannot kill him."

"I cannot kill him?" the man exclaimed incredulously. "What is it you mean?"

"He is my lion."

"Your lion?"

"It is so."

The man was puzzled for a while, but then the anger left his face and it cleared as he understood. "So he is, and you shall kill him yourself, with your own arrow."

The hope that had begun to flicker in the boy died abruptly. It was a terrible thing, he knew, to question his father, to defy him in this thing, but he was unable to help himself.

"I cannot kill him, and neither must anyone else," he said doggedly. "He came to me and I gave him life, and I cannot take it now."

For a few moments Tsonomon was shocked speechless, and then the anger flooded from him in a torrent. "I am your father, and you who are my son, how can you stand there in my body, which is the body of myself, and tell me such a thing?"

"Forgive me, oh my father," the boy murmured, his head bowed in shame, but when he looked up, though the pain was still in his eyes, there was also a look of defiance in them.

"And if I kill him?" the man asked, his voice dangerously low.

"The time of the hyena will be upon me," the boy whispered.

The man gasped slightly, but then his eyes slitted, and he said grimly: "Then let it be upon you."

"And also will it be upon you, oh Tsonomon," the woman said starkly. "Because the son is also the father. They are one, and it is so."

He was fearful for a while, for himself and for his son, but then he began to speak, driven by the urgency of the images which came into his mind one after the other.

"He has followed you, this great beast, and now he will follow us. He is lame, he cannot hunt. One by one he will eat us, in the night when it is dark, taking us from the fire as we sleep."

"He would have eaten me already, if that was in his mind," the boy protested. "I think perhaps he is one of the old fathers who walks in disguise. Or maybe he—he is lonely for me, and in being alone his heart cries for me, because I helped him."

The man stared at the boy incredulously and then burst into laughter. It wasn't cruel or mocking, but an expression of the amazement he felt at such a ludicrous idea.

"Oh Pxui, oh my son, you are dreaming dreams. Perhaps he is one of the fathers, but I do not think so. He is a beast of prey, a ghum, and he is alone for no one but himself. He follows you now like a hyena will follow a lion, waiting for his food."

"Then let him follow me."

"And what will he eat?" the man asked drily. "Will the bone splinters that remain after we have cracked the bones and eaten the marrow be enough to fill his big belly?"

"I will give him some of my food."

"And when your own belly is empty, how will you hunt?" the man asked brutally, his scorn thrusting like a spear, but knowing that it had to be done.

The boy lowered his head, silent, and he didn't think of Xhabbo any more. There were other hunters on her spoor, better than he.

"My son, oh my son, it cannot be."

"If I permit his death, the hyena will be upon me," the boy said again. He spoke without heat, telling only of the sure knowledge within him.

The man nodded, thinking it over. "Let us drive him away," he said eventually. "So that he does not follow us and begin to lust for our own flesh."

"I have tried," the boy said woodenly. "He does not move."

"With fire?"

The boy drew a sharp hissing breath. For a moment his eyes were bright with pain, but then they dulled with resignation. In a way, his father was right. He himself was a desert hunter, and he knew the demands that the land could make.

"Now make a fire torch," the man ordered, and as the boy turned to obey he called him back and said: "Make two."

He went to the fire and poked amongst the ashes, but they were all burned out and dead. He opened the skin satchel in which he carried his poisons and his weaving horns and the other things he used and he took out his fire sticks.

He collected a handful of dried grass. He laid it on the ground and squatted beside it. He picked up the pointed stick of iron wood. He placed the point in one of the charred craters on the broad flat surface of the other stick, and then, holding it between the palms of his hands, he began to rotate it rapidly backwards and forwards.

It took quite a while, and then in the blackened hollow in which the pointed iron wood twirled there suddenly appeared a pin-point of dull red.

"The torches!" the man called, and he threw a quick glance at the lion which was still ignoring them.

The pin-point of red grew larger. A few sparks flew upwards, and a wisp of smoke followed. When the boy walked over with the readied torches, Tsonomon dropped the stick in his hands. He snatched up the bunch of dried grass and placed it on top of the crater filled with the glowing dust. He blew on it gently, his breath no more than a caress, and the grass began to smoulder and then it burst into flame. He lit the torches. He passed one to his son and picked up his spear.

The boy armed himself with his own, and together they stood there, side by side, waving their torches gently in the air to get them burning properly. The flames grew and the wood and grass crackled as it burned.

"Come behind us, Xhooxa," the man said, speaking to his wife. "Who knows which way this beast will run."

She nodded, and she picked up her own skin sack which contained the ostrich egg shells and her stamping block and slung it on her back. She took up her position close behind them, her grubbing stick in her right hand.

Tsonomon inspected the flaming torch in his left hand. In the bright sunlight the flames were hardly visible. But there was plenty of smoke, and the air above the brand rippled liquidly in the heat like water. It was reassuring.

He glanced at his son. His slanted eyes were bright, glittering like polished black stone. There was apprehension in them, also uncertainty and excitement.

"Ready?" he asked softly.

"Yes."

"Let us give him our fire," the man said, his voice quiet, but with a quivering deep inside it. "Let him take our fire and run. We will give it to him and make him afraid."

The lion studied them as they approached, watchful and alert. He saw and smelled the fire in their hands, and an ancient fear rose in him.

He came up off the ground in one swift motion. He stood there, his injured paw just touching the sand but without any weight on it. He recognized Pxui, the one who had taken the steel from his leg.

It was confusing, because the man had helped him before and not hurt him, and yet now he came with fire in his hand. His ears rang with their shrill shouts and cries, adding to his fear and uncertainty.

They were about fifty feet from him when he lifted his head and growled. It wasn't loud, but it was a terrifying sound just the same, as if it had come from the bowels of the earth.

The three of them froze in their tracks, awed by his size, fearful of what they were going to do. The brands burned on forgotten in their hands, the half-dry wood hissing and crackling and occasionally bursting with a soft explosion.

Pxui touched his father lightly on the arm. The man jerked as if he had been shocked, and then his eyes cleared slowly.

"He knows me," the boy said softly. "He is not afraid because he knows me."

"The fire," whispered Tsonomon. "He must be afraid of fire."

He started shouting again, brandishing the torch, and the sound of his voice restored a little of his confidence and courage. They moved forward again, the heat from the brands in their faces and the smoke stinging their eyes.

The lion let them come closer. The animal's first instinct was to turn and flee from the dreaded combination of man and fire, but within his highly intelligent brain was a newer and more recently acquired piece of knowledge.

That fact, together with the pain in his leg and his own natural courage, helped him to stand firm. He allowed the group to come to within thirty feet of him, and then his tail came up stiff and straight and horizontal with the ground.

He growled, and the noise was like broken thunder. He saw them pause, come on again, and then he exploded into action. He went forward in a mock charge, his movements blurred with speed. He sank to a crouch and roared, in anger and defiance, and his thick heavy tail swept up a storm of dust as it lashed from side to side.

For a good twenty seconds none of them were able to move. They were stunned and shocked, paralysed by the terrible explosion of sound. Tsonomon was the first to recover, but it was not a recovery in the true sense of the word. He was still in a state of shock, half-insane with fear, his bowels hot and liquid.

He feinted at the lion, shouting and screaming at him. The lion sprang forward again, snarling savagely, his eyes on the group but his attention focussed on Tsonomon. The animal was ready to attack, but the presence of the boy held him back.

The burning torch in the hand of the man lifted again. The lion felt the heat of the fire against his face, and deep in his nostrils the fearful smell of the smoke. The big hind legs bunched beneath his body.

He was about to launch himself, the death spring, when the boy abruptly leaped forward to stand in front of the man. The bunched muscles relaxed, and snarling savagely, switching his tail in frustration, he backed up a little and then stood his ground once more.

"Enough!" the boy cried shakily, half-blind with his own fear and yet dimly conscious that the lion had backed away from him. "He will kill you, oh my father. He is not afraid, and he will kill you, and then he will kill us also once he has begun."

"I will kill him!" the man shouted, still high on the crest of his fear and excitement.

But he began to back away, and when he had put enough distance between himself and the lion to feel comparatively safe once more, he felt slightly light-headed with relief.

Staring at the lion, his eyes wide, his small golden chest rising and falling with the rhythm of his harsh frightened breathing, he felt his anger replaced by a growing bewilderment.

"What manner of lion is this?" he demanded softly, asking the question of himself, the lines on his weather-wrinkled face deepening with perplexity. "He does not fear fire, and he does not fear man.

He sits there on the ground, licking his big leg. He licks it carefully, and he fears neither man nor fire." He shook his head, a man confronted with something so extraordinary as to be beyond words or belief. "Perhaps he is one of the fathers," he concluded, but there was an edge of doubt in his voice.

"It must be so," the woman confirmed.

"And what will happen to us?" the man went on. "I cannot kill him, because the hyena will be on my son. It will be on him, therefore will it also be on me. I cannot drive him away, and now he will follow us. Will he take us one by one from the sand where we sleep? Will he frighten the game so that our bellies shrivel and the fat on our backsides melts till there is nothing left but skin? I do not know, I truly do not know." He turned suddenly to face his son, and there was resentment in his eyes, and also apprehension, because he was looking into the days ahead and he didn't like any of the things which he saw. "You should have killed him," he went on flatly. "I taught you to be a hunter. Therefore it should have been in your heart, not to set him free to hunt us, but to kill him."

"Forgive me, oh my father."

"I have forgiven you already, but my pardon means nothing," the man said, and after a pause he lifted his arm and waved it in a vague sweeping gesture. "The sands do not anger, nor do they grieve. They do not accuse, they do not forgive. It is all the same to them, whether a man is wise or whether he is a fool. The sands do not care for man or beast, wise or foolish. They are a place to live, or a place to die."

"Perhaps he will help us to hunt," the boy said, but without much hope. "Like that lion we stayed with after he killed the eland."

He had been young then, a small boy, but even now it delighted and awed him to remember. They had driven the king from his kill after he had eaten some from it. They followed him for three weeks after that, and when he killed they also ate. And when the game became scarcer and more wary, they took to driving it towards him, and he killed surely and easily.

Towards the end, after he had eaten, he used to move away and leave them what he had left the moment he saw them approaching, and it wasn't necessary to use fire to drive him away. It was as if he knew and understood that they had helped him, and were entitled to a share.

The man glanced at the lion and shrugged. He did not think this one would ever hunt again with any great skill. He signalled to his son, and beat his own torch out on the ground and then threw it down and with his foot scooped sand over it till the smouldering head was buried.

He slung his satchel and then picked up his bow. He set off heading to the east, moving with the unerring instinct he had for direction. The boy walked behind his father, and the woman brought up the rear, her grubbing stick of iron wood in her hand.

The boy glanced back over his shoulder. He saw that the lion was following. He felt a surge of elation deep inside, but nothing showed on his impassive face.

The man checked up on the lion also. He frowned, and he opened his mouth to say something, but then he closed it and shrugged instead.

His slanted eyes glittered briefly, but then he began to cast about, and soon he was engrossed with the many different stories that were written on the sands.

13

IT WAS after mid-day when they rested in the shade of a thorn bush. They divided one of the small strips of dried meat between them and ate it, chewing it down with bites from the wild tubers they had found and dug up. They finished their meal with a wild melon, and it gave sufficient moisture for them not to have to touch their precious water.

The woman collected the flat black seeds and put them away in her sack. She would pound them later to make meal, which would either be mixed with water and drunk as a gruel, or which she would cook in one of her clay pots to make a thick sustaining sort of porridge.

It was hot, even in the shade of the thorn. The boy dug into the sand, going down as deep as his elbow, and then he brought it up a handful at a time, sprinkling and scattering the cool sand over his body. He did it mechanically, without thinking of his actions, his eyes on the lion which was about thirty yards off in the shade of a low msita bush.

"He must be thirsty," he commented, his eyes straying to the skin which contained their water shells.

The man grunted unintelligibly, his narrowed eyes squinting against the violent light as he searched the shimmering land.

"And hungry," the boy went on.

"That's his business," the man said sourly.

The boy was quiet for a while. He dug another handful of sand, squeezing it hard, feeling it compress and yield and then trickle from his fingers. He sprinkled it against his bare belly.

He began to wonder whether the lion would continue to follow them. They were still a long way from their camp, and he didn't think the animal would, unless he did something to encourage him. He was reluctant to speak, afraid of what his father would say, but the thought of Xhabbo drove him.

"Let me try," he said abruptly, "to give him some water."

"To give him the heart to follow us? Are you mad?"

"Please, oh my father."

"We have almost three days to walk. There are six shells left, and we must walk for three days."

"There are melons and tubers."

"Then let him find them and dig for them."

"Father, it——"

"I have spoken," the man said sharply, cutting him off.

He got to his feet and slung his satchel and his quiver. The woman and the boy rose also, slinging their equipment. The man stared balefully at the lion. The animal stared back at him, mouth partly open and the tip of his tongue protruding between the lower canines. The man could see the flanks heaving.

He studied it a moment longer and then left the shade of the thorn bush. The sun struck at him. He felt the weight of it on his back, and his eyes slitted even further against the searing white light.

They moved over the endless face of the desert, neither hurrying nor loitering, three small figures dwarfed by the immensity of the land across which they trekked.

Others might have been overawed by their surroundings, and so diminished as to feel completely helpless, but they were not troubled by any such feelings of inadequacy. They were at home wherever they were, their needs minimal and adjusted to the essentials of survival, their possessions no more than they could pick up at a moment's notice and carry with them.

Time was meaningless. The sun rose, and the sun set. The winter fathered the summer, and the rains came and gave life to all the desert. It bloomed, and then it died, and the cycle began all over again. This was their life.

They had been walking for a little over two and a half hours when

Pxui felt that strange and inexplicable tightening in his chest, and a moment later the man in front of him froze.

The boy saw them almost immediately, even before the man lifted his arm and pointed. They were about a half mile away, moving slowly and unconcernedly across an open plain of grass and scattered brush, pausing to browse now and again—two blue wildebeest, looking like dark black beetles against the sun-bright land.

"Gnu," the man whispered, and he felt an old excitement begin to stir in him, the sight of the animals pushing everything else from his mind.

He sank to a crouch, and the boy and the woman did the same without question or comment. He turned to his wife.

"Wait here," he said, and then out of the corner of his eye he saw the halted lion and he drew in a sharp hissing breath. "I should have killed him. Now you will have to come with us. I cannot leave you alone here, not knowing what he will do."

"I can stay," she replied, but she was watching the lion uneasily even as she spoke. "I do not think he will trouble me."

He was tempted for a moment, but then he shook his head. In every man there was also a woman, and she was the flesh of the spirit of the woman within him, and without her he would be nothing. It was then that another calamitous thought occurred to him. He glanced again at the lion, and then at his son, and there was a bitter bleakness in his eyes.

"He will follow us, the lame and clumsy beast. He will frighten the game away. The buck being frightened will run and our bellies will remain empty." He checked on the slowly moving animals, and then looked at the boy again. "I will kill him if it happens that way."

In wordless communication he touched his son lightly on the arm. They started forward, moving at a crouch, running bent over from one bit of cover to the next, travelling in a direction which the man hoped would bring them to within bow range at the point of interception he had already computed, provided the animals held their present course.

In places there wasn't sufficient cover to enable them to dart unseen from one bit to the next. Then they crawled forward, flat on the ground. As they worked their way closer, the boy felt his excitement mount, his heart beating hard and fast, the drum-beat of it pounding back into his chest like an echo from the hot naked earth against which he was tightly pressed.

He glanced back once, past his mother, and to his surprise he saw the lion flat down on its belly and creeping forward, using the same cover that they were using and working his way from one piece of scrub to the next.

Pxui came to rest beside his father, behind a patch of thorn. He was breathing hard, and his chest was scratched and bleeding in two or three places. In the excitement of the moment he was not aware that he had been cut.

The animals had halted. They were grazing, about one hundred and sixty yards to the front and quite a way over to their right. Between them lay open ground, without any kind of cover at all. To their left was scrub and thorn, sweeping up in a long curving arc to the point of interception the man had planned on originally.

To his right there was also cover, but it dropped back in the direction from which they had just come, widening the perimeter of the pocket in which the wildebeest were grazing, the open land providing them with safety against ambush.

For minutes on end the man studied them. They were moving in circles, not in any one particular direction. He saw the swishing of their horselike tails, and one of them paused in its grazing to scratch at its flank with a rear hoof.

He wondered why they were alone, and not with a herd, and he wished that he could have seen their spoor, to read it and find out a little more about them.

A moment later, to his dismay, they turned nonchalantly and began moving slowly in the direction from which they had just come. He glanced back quickly, thinking his thoughts, and when he saw nothing of the lion anywhere, a guttural sound of disgust broke from his mouth, and he wondered where the big beast had gone and whether his scent was responsible for making the gnu change their direction and go back the way they had come. He didn't really think so, because they hadn't shown any alarm, but he was ready to believe it and lay the blame on the lion.

Long before the men had first seen the wildebeest, the lion had scented them and spotted them. His mounting exhaustion had dulled the hunger pains in his belly, but the raw strong smell of the animals brought them back to life.

He flattened himself automatically, preparatory to making his stalk. Inadvertently he put some of the weight of his body on his injured leg. Pain shot through it, and in that instant he realized fully that he was in no position to do anything about the wildebeest.

It was then that he noticed the behaviour of the men. They were down too, moving from one piece of cover to the next, doubled up and bent over, sometimes flat down on their bellies and crawling the way he himself crawled when he wished to remain unseen.

Their tension and excitement communicated itself to him, like a blood taint in the air. He followed them, crawling on his belly, his pain still there, but exercising an iron control over it, aware only of the need for stealth and absolute silence.

He used the same cover that they did, not because he was following them blindly, but because it was the cover he would have used if he were himself making the stalk.

He watched the men, and he watched the wildebeest, and because he was also a hunter he was thinking along practically the same lines as the men, evaluating the situation in a similar fashion.

The bows in the hands of the men, the quivers on their backs, held no significance for him. He did not know how they would kill, but of their intentions he had no doubt: there could only be one reason for the way in which they were moving, and from the direction in which men and animals were travelling, there was only one point from which they could get close enough to make it.

He saw one of them pause in its grazing to lift a hoof and scratch. It was a good sign, because it showed him that they were unaware and unafraid. When the wildebeest turned and started back the way they had come, his tail switched in anger and disappointment, and then immediately after that he moved off to the right, falling back slightly as he kept to the line of cover, moving as swiftly as he could, intent on outflanking them and being in a position to strike from the other side of the pocket.

"That way!" Tsonomon whispered urgently. "We might be in time to get round them."

They moved off, travelling as fast as they could, in more or less the same direction that the lion had taken. At times they were on their hands and knees, and there were other times when they went flat down on their bellies and crawled again, but the wildebeest were moving more swiftly now, not hurrying, but pausing less and less frequently to graze.

The man and the boy threw themselves down behind a bush of white thorn. Their mouths were open and they were gasping, but even now they controlled their breathing so that there was hardly any noise as they sucked the air into their lungs and blew it out in quivering exhalations.

"They are moving too fast, we will never get a shot," the man whispered.

The boy nodded in agreement. He had been hoping that it might be quick and easy this time, but he felt no great disappointment that it hadn't been. Most of the times it was never easy, and he had become accustomed to work hard to get what he wanted. It was a simple and inescapable fact of life.

"We will have to take their spoor and see," the man said.

"Yes."

Tsonomon pointed. "That way, I think they'll come out there. Move, you child of a Bushman, you!"

Their eyes met, and they grinned briefly at each other, the excitement racing through them. The man went into a crouch, getting ready to move out from behind the screen of thorn.

"Father!"

The man stiffened, arrested by the raw urgency in the boy's voice. He glanced at the wildebeest, and their attitude made him freeze. They were at the far end of the open pocket, standing stiff and motionless, their heads thrown back.

An instant later the lion burst from cover. He sped towards them, as fast as he could go, but was hopping clumsily on three legs, and the man knew the lion didn't have a hope.

The animals whirled and broke into a gallop. Tsonomon felt an instant of terrible rage, but before it had time to really take hold he found himself clawing desperately for an arrow. He notched it to his bow, and out of the corner of his eye he saw that the boy already had his own arrow strung.

The wildebeest thundered straight towards them. They looked like small buffaloes, with their powerful forequarters, and the tufts of hair on their faces and their neck and dorsal manes made them look fierce and invincible.

They came to a sudden halt in a cloud of dust about forty yards from the thorn behind which the man and the boy were waiting. They turned slightly, to stare back at the lion.

The man and the boy rose as one. They shot together, and the twang of their bowstrings was drowned in the sudden roar of the lion. The arrows flew swift and true. The leading animal took both shafts in its shoulder.

For a moment it stood quite still, as if in disbelief, and then with a frightened snort it whirled away and broke instantaneously into a gallop. Its companion followed it, and second later they vanished into the brush at the opposite end of the pocket from which the lion had come.

"Now we have our food," the man cried, and there was a ringing jubilation in his voice. "Now let us work for it, to get our food."

He thought of the two arrows in the shoulder of the wildebeest, the poison already beginning to spread slowly through its body, and then in his mind he saw the shoulder, not as it had been, with the darker brown stripes running over it, but with the skin peeled back and showing the rich marbled fat and the red meat of the muscle. His belly tightened.

"The lion, he drove the game towards us," the boy said, wonder and delight in his voice. "He did it on purpose, and if he had not done it we might never have got close enough to shoot."

"You are dreaming a dream you want to dream," the man replied. "He was hunting for his own food."

"But he must know that he cannot hunt, with his foot as it is."

"He knows it now."

"It is not impossible," the boy persisted. "That he knew and drove it towards us."

The man fixed his eyes on his son. There was amusement in them, but it was not unkind. "Have your dream."

He went forward to where the wildebeest had been standing when the arrow struck it. They studied the spoor together, the man and the boy, fixing it in their minds as another would observe and remember the features of a face, noting each distinctive aspect of the hoof marks and remembering them so that they would be able to pick out this particular set of tracks even if it were amongst those of a hundred other animals.

They took up the spoor, moving at a steady lope. The woman trotted behind them, and behind her came the lion.

They were not perturbed that the wounded animal itself was not in sight. They were in contact with it all the time, through the marks its fleeing hoofs had made in the sand. The first of the detached arrow shafts they found before they had gone more than a few yards, and they found the second one a little further on. They picked them up, and after examining them briefly returned them to their quivers.

It was easy following the spoor of the wounded animal, and now and again they caught glimpses of the pair in the distance. For three and a half hours they followed the spoor, the slow heavy tension mounting within them with each mile they covered. They were tired, but they felt no weariness, only a steadily increasing anticipation.

They saw where the two animals had parted, the wounded one going straight on while its companion turned aside and left it.

"He knows that all is not well with his brother," the man commented. "He knows it and he has left him."

They saw from the spoor and from the depth of some of the prints where the tiring animal had lurched and staggered and then regained its balance and gone on. So well did they know their quarry and understand the destruction taking place in its body that they saw not only the hoof marks in the sand but on the screens of their vivid imaginations they could also see the heavy animal as if it were before their eyes at that very moment.

When finally they came upon it the wildebeest was standing motionless with its head down at a distance of about fifty yards. It scented them first and then saw them, and the scent of the smell was of man and lion, and both of those were danger.

It lifted its head, as if it were a great effort, and then it staggered forward in a series of lurching stumbles and then came to a halt again.

It turned to watch them as they closed in on it. It staggered forward a little way and then halted abruptly. It spread its legs wide, as if to steady itself against the rocking of the earth.

The moment it sighted the wildebeest, the lion froze. He sensed immediately that the animal was mortally stricken. He went into a crouch, flattening himself to the earth. He began to creep forward, restraining the impulse to whimper each time he had to put weight on his damaged leg.

He hadn't gone more than a few yards when he halted abruptly. The men were already closing in on the wildebeest, and there was no mistaking the deadliness of their intentions. It was apparent in their movements, in the hot tight aura of excitement which emanated from them. He flattened himself further, watching them, and his bright tawny eyes filmed briefly with the weight of his exhaustion.

Warily the two hunters closed in on the wildebeest. It stood four feet three inches at the shoulder, its massive body dwarfing the little dust-smeared golden men who approached.

It watched them, its eyes rolling in their sockets, and it was afraid. During the last three hours a strange and bewildering paralysis had crept into the once powerful muscles of its body, and it knew at that moment, with the certainty of its instinct, that it was almost finished now and done.

It lunged forward, in a last despairing attempt to flee, but there was no strength or co-ordination remaining in its numbed limbs. It stumbled and fell as its front legs buckled, and it hit the ground with a thud that jarred the earth.

The men closed in quickly. There was no excitement left in them now, only a vast relief and thankfulness that it was finally over. It showed on their weary faces.

"Finish him off," the man said. "Send him on his journey and thank him for his body."

He could have done it himself, with a greater swiftness and certainty than his son, but he wanted the boy to achieve the same efficiency as himself, and there was only so much that a man could learn by watching.

Pxui put down his bow. He walked up to the wildebeest which was lying on its side. He was poised and wary, because sometimes a stricken animal would lumber to its feet with the last of its strength and horn a man to death or crush and trample him beneath its sharp cloven hoofs.

The wildebeest kicked out, trying to get its feet beneath it. The boy watched, gauging its strength, but he saw that its movements were feeble and without true purpose behind them.

He moved right in, the spear in both hands. He put the point against the animal's chest, towards the left and inside the big blade bone of the shoulder. He thrust it forwards and up.

There was that first instant of resistance, a sort of pause, as if the motion of the shaft in his hands had been temporarily arrested, and then he felt the steadying grip of flesh around the spearhead and he rammed it deeper, putting more of his weight against the shaft and driving it in till it was so deep he knew it must have taken the heart.

The animal reared, its head and thick neck and even its shoulder lifting partly off the ground. It held the pose for long unending moments, its muscles and sinews stretched rigid and the big brown irises of its eyes glowed with a stark brilliance they had not possessed even in life.

The boy worked the spear in the wound, twisting and levering it from side to side to make the killing quicker. The sharp edges of the spear head cut indiscriminately through veins and arteries. The heart itself was lacerated in the process. The great muscle continued its rhythmic contractions, heroically and indifferently, until it could no longer perform its task and ceased to beat.

The animal reared higher. It stiffened, and then fell back to the ground suddenly. The light in its eyes flared even brighter, making them look luminous and transparent. But it was only for a moment, and they became opaque and dull, and whatever had been there was extinguished and no more.

Pxui put his bare foot against the chest of the animal. He braced himself and drew his spear smoothly from the dead flesh. Blood gushed from the gaping red flower, and it made a darkness against the desert sand.

The boy stepped back. His face had not changed, but now it looked old and seamed, as if it reflected some different state of being within him. He looked down at the slain beast.

"I am sorry to have killed you," he said softly, and it wasn't just a mechanical utterance, because he truly felt sadness at its death. "But I thank you, oh yes, how I thank you."

And having said this, he turned to his father and a sudden wide grin transformed his face. He laughed a moment later, from deep in his belly, the sound of it bubbling with happiness and a deep satisfaction. They had hunted, and they had worked hard at it, and this time it had not been in vain as it sometimes was.

The reek of the spilling blood reached the lion. It was thick and delicious in his nostrils, striking at him in wave after scarlet wave till all his senses were drowned in the overpowering scent of it. Saliva filled his mouth, and the emptiness in his belly became unbearable. It diminished his fear of the men, overcoming most of his caution. He started forward, limping heavily.

"Tsonomon!" the woman cried.

There was a tight urgency in her voice, fear also. The man looked up from his skinning, the boy too. They froze, crouched there motionless beside their kill, watching the lion as he came forward. The animal was fifteen feet away when the boy rose suddenly. He plucked his spear from the ground.

"Wait!" Tsonomon shouted.

The boy paid him no attention. He started forward, the spear in his hands. He knew intuitively that he had to stop the lion, and stop it now. Once the beast got to the meat they were finished, because even fire did not frighten him, and there would be no way to drive him off until he had filled his huge belly.

The lion had flattened himself to the ground at the boy's approach.

His eyes were discs of yellow fire and his tail lashed angrily. The boy came to a halt about ten feet away from him. The lion stared back, and then growled suddenly. It was a shattering sound that seemed to make the air vibrate.

The boy felt a sudden burst of fear, but then the fear in him was abruptly transformed into a cold anger that was in its turn supported by a vast indignation.

"Stay away from our meat!" he shouted threateningly, conscious at the same time that there was no real way he had of enforcing his order. "You helped us to kill, so we will share with you. But it was we who crawled on our bellies to get it." His voice rose to a shrill crescendo. "It is our meat, do you hear me? It is ours."

Unwinkingly the lion watched the boy. The sounds that reached him were meaningless, but he recognized the tone of voice in which they were uttered and he remembered the heat of the fire in his face.

His eyes flickered to the dead wildebeest. The air was hot and sweet with the smell of its body and its blood. It had been killed by the men, he had seen that, and like any other predators one of them was defending their kill. Even as he did.

He snarled, uncertain and afraid once more, then he settled down to wait and watch. Patience was something he knew about, even if it wasn't in this particular context.

"Stay away!" the boy shouted again, brandishing his spear.

He backed away, watching the lion. But the animal made no further move, and he felt a sudden sharp surge of relief which was followed by a mounting incredulity that gave way to exultation.

"He listens," Tsonomon exclaimed in disbelief. "It is strange, but he hears you and he listens when you speak."

"He should," answered the boy, a smugness creeping into his voice. "He was crying, and I licked his tears and now he does not cry."

The man glanced sharply at his son. There was a strange look in his eyes, surprise and uneasiness and something else, but he made no comment.

They went back to their skinning. The boy worked on the legs, peeling the tough hide from the flesh and fat, each stroke of his flying knife separating it further.

The man worked on the body. He made an incision all the way down its chest and right along its belly, careful not to cut into the paunch, and then he set to work, slicing and lifting and then slicing again, his flashing knife moving with such care and precision that only here and there was any of the red meat left attached to the skin.

While they were busy with the skinning the woman gathered wood. There wasn't too much of it around, and she had to forage far, but it was no particular hardship, because she knew just where to look and she had done it ever since she had been old enough to walk.

When they had finished peeling the hide from the wildebeest they paused for a moment. They resharpened their knives with a stone the man took from his satchel.

The wildebeest looked strangely obscene now, its hide spread beneath it like a mat, its bleeding carcass white with fat and the flesh so dark and red in places that it looked almost purple.

"Father, let us give him the guts and the paunch," the boy said.

"All of it?" the man asked, a little incredulous at such unthinking generosity.

"He helped us, he must have his share."

"It seems a lot, a waste."

"We have plenty."

"Yes, for now." The man was thoughtful a while. "And what of the paunch, the water?"

It wasn't actually water, but the half-digested grasses and leaves yielded a valuable and perfectly drinkable fluid when squeezed and pressed.

"He needs it more than we do, I think. He must be thirsty, and he must need it."

"I don't like it. He is taking the water from our lives. If he takes it, he also takes our life."

"He helped us to hunt," the boy reminded him. "We might still be crawling on our bellies if he had not helped us."

"Yes, I know, I still do not like it, but as you say, he—he helped us."

"Thank you, oh my father."

Their eyes met and held, the boy grateful, his face alive with excitement, the man dark with foreboding.

They opened its belly and tore out the guts and paunch. The strong rich sweetness filled the air. The lion lifted his head, and a strange moaning rumble burst from his mouth. He heaved himself to his feet, the smell of the food and his own great hunger crumbling the last of his restraint and caution. He started forward, snarling softly, and then abruptly he froze.

The boy was coming towards him, dragging the paunch and the guts of the wildebeest. The lion began to back away, growling softly with anger and frustration.

He backed a little way and halted. He sank to a crouch, his powerful back legs tensing as his claws dug into the earth. He would make his stand, he would back no further. He felt the strength coming back into his body as he tapped hidden reserves. He was still a killer, regardless of the crippled leg.

To his surprise and bafflement the boy also halted. He saw him drop the food he had been carrying, straighten up, and then after a moment begin to back away.

The lion watched him retreat, wary and puzzled. He eyed the food in front of him. The rich aroma of blood and tripe was overpowering.

He hesitated a moment longer and then started for it, saliva flushing his mouth. He paused to eye the men, but they were still and they made no move towards him. He grunted softly and then lowered his head and began to feed.

He bit into the mass of bulging bluish pink tubes. He tore off a mouthful and began to chew. He felt new strength begin to flow back into his body with each mouthful he swallowed. He interrupted his feeding once to stare at the boy. Far back in his golden yellow eyes there was a glow that might have been calculation or recognition.

It took them an hour to finish butchering the carcass of the wildebeest. When they had finished, the animal had been jointed and the meat cut up into manageable chunks. It lay in neat piles on top of the skin.

They were covered in gore when they straightened up from their task. With their knives they scraped the blood and flecks of meat and fat from their arms and chests and their legs, and then after that they washed their hands with sand.

They cut branches of thorn and piled it high round their meat. The sun was almost over the horizon by the time they had secured it, and all the land lay bathed in a pale orange light that made everything stand out stark and clear. But there was no more warmth in the distant winter sun, and the cold of the coming night was already beginning to strike at them.

The man used his sticks to make fire while the boy collected more wood. He sang quietly to himself as he gathered the kindling. He thought of Xhabbo and the lion, and he thought of the good red meat which would fill his belly later as he sat before the fire.

The first stars were just beginning to show when he was satisfied that he had collected enough to last them throughout the night. He was still singing softly when he sank down on the skin that had been spread beside the fire.

They feasted that night beside their kill, on the liver and the heart and on rare grilled meat which was sweet with blood. They ate till they were sated, with their bellies round and the skin stretched tight, almost to the point of bursting. Each one of them consumed approximately eleven pounds of flesh.

From his skin sack the man took a small bow-like instrument. It was strung with sinew, and the sinew was tied down to the bow at its centre, making a crude kind of jew's harp.

He placed one end of the bow in his mouth, and with a small stick began to beat on the string, and using his mouth as a sounding box he caught and shaped the notes.

They came out soft and muted, with a tonal monotony that created a hypnotic harmony by its repetition. The boy began to sing, the songs that were as old as his people—of the burning sun and the scorched earth which waited for the rain just as a woman waited anxiously for her hunter to return.

His mother beat the rhythm out, clapping the slightly cupped palms of her hands together softly, the sound of it hollow and reverberating.

From far out in the night a spotted hyena uttered its weird and mournful cry. It began as a low ghostly chuckle, then rose to a wailing shriek, and it floated eerily through the night, seeming to come from first one direction and then another.

They stopped their music to listen to it, and a few moments after the echoes of the tormented cry had died out and left the night strangely still the lion roared in answer and in challenge.

The thunder of his voice seemed to splinter the night, and they stiffened with shock and flinched involuntarily as they waited for the shattered pieces to come together once again.

"I do not think the hyenas will come sniffing for our meat tonight," the boy said at length. "He sits out there, and they will not come, for they know that he sits and waits for them."

He stared out into the night, at the dark shadows which lay just beyond the circle of firelight, and he saw the darker shadow which was the body of the lion; and as he stirred the eyes picked up the light and for a brief instant they flashed and glowed like burning orange coals. He wondered if the animal had looked for him.

The boy began to sing again. The woman started clapping, and then after a while the man reluctantly tore his gaze from the darkness where the lion lay and began to play once more.

14

IN THE MORNING they cut the meat into strips and hung it as high as they could in a thorn bush where it would cure in the shade and in the dry desert air. When they had finished only the neck and the ribs and the head remained with any meat on them.

Using a stick, Tsonomon scraped the ash and coals of the fire to one side, and then he dug a deep pit in the hot sand. Into it he placed the head of the wildebeest, covering it over with sand again, and then he heaped the burning coals back on top of it. It made a simple and efficient oven.

They grilled some of the neck meat for breakfast, and ate it with half-cooked chunks of the sweet delicious fat, which was one of their greatest delicacies. In addition to being highly prized as food, it was, in the harsh environment of the desert, an unrivalled source of energy.

The boy finished eating and plucked a sizzling piece of fat from the fire. He juggled it from hand to hand until it was cool enough to hold, and then he stood up and began to grease himself, squeezing the chunk of fat between his fingers to express the oil and then rubbing it into his skin.

He greased himself all over, and when he had finished he ate what remained, chewing it with relish and swallowing it down. He spread his arms wide and stretched. He rose up on his toes, and in that one brief instant before he slumped, when he was posed and motionless, he looked in the hard sharp light of the morning sun like a small shining statue cast in polished gold.

A small groan of satisfaction escaped from him as his stiffened body suddenly relaxed and his arms fell to his sides of their own weight.

He glanced over at the lion. The animal was in a different place to where he had been the previous night. He himself had slept so close to the fire that he had almost been inside it, and still he had been cold. He wondered how the big hunter had fared in that terrible coldness that bit so deeply in the small hours just before dawn.

"Father," he said, glancing quickly at him and then flicking his eyes away. "Let me give him the lungs."

"The lion?"

"Yes."

"Are you mad?"

"He helped us to hunt, and he should have his share," the boy went on stubbornly, and though he quailed at the sudden anger which lit the man's eyes, he forced himself to meet them. "He helped us to kill, and he has not had his share."

"He has had his share."

"The guts?" the boy asked ironically.

"Maybe not," the man replied grudgingly, because he was not without a sense of the fairness and rightness of things. "But when is it going to be our turn to be his brother? Will he feed us when it is our turn?"

"That I don't know."

For a while the man was silent, chewing thoughtfully. At length he said: "What is he becoming to you, this big beast? Has he stolen the sense from your head?"

The boy thought of Xhabbo and what she would think. He remained silent, but he felt a little bit ashamed, because truly the lion was eating their food. He mitigated his sense of distress by telling himself that the animal had, after all, helped them to kill.

"He sits there and waits," the man commented, throwing a bitter and scornful glance at the lion. "He waits to eat our food, and the food he eats is our life which he swallows."

"We have plenty."

"How much is plenty?" the man replied bleakly, and he remembered those times in the past when there had been no food, when the old and weak had died from hunger, and the pink spongy meat of the lungs which his son was proposing to give away would have given new strength to them and the courage to hope and endure a little longer. It was a narrow margin which divided survival and death.

"Let him have it, oh Tsonomon," the woman said.

"You too! Has he stolen your thinking strings as well?"

"He brought us luck," the woman pointed out. "He works his magic to bring us luck. To keep his magic strong we should feed him."

A strange and slightly troubled expression darkened the man's face, and then after a while he spoke. "Give it to him then. The lungs and nothing else, and he can eat it when he wants, because that will be his share and he'll get no more."

"And if he helps us to kill again?" the boy asked.

"He can have the guts again."

"And the lungs?"

Tsonomon debated it with himself, and then nodded reluctantly. "The lungs also."

The boy pushed aside some of the thorn barricade and picked up the lungs. They were cold and flaccid and an unlovely pinkish grey. He carried them towards where the lion was sprawled.

At the approach of the boy the lion stiffened, becoming immediately alert. Beneath the thick strong smell of the wildebeest fat and the smell of the lung meat he detected also the odour of man. He was getting used to it now, though deep within him there was still an instinctive fear.

He growled in warning, eyeing the boy and the meat in his hands. He was about to growl again when he saw the boy halt and drop the meat and then back off.

He rose swiftly and limped forward. His leg had stiffened, and the pain in it was terrible. He had licked it continuously for six hours through the night, but the hurt was deep where he could not reach it.

He sniffed at the lungs and then went down on his belly. He did it gingerly, sparing his injured leg. He ate ravenously, because now he was really hungry. Yesterday he had been emptier, but the emptiness had been so great that it had taken him beyond immediate hunger and into the realm of a dangerous lethargy. There was no lethargy now, only hunger, and his eyes became half-closed and the fire in them dimmed with the great pleasure and satisfaction that came from feeding.

When he had finished he licked his whisker-studded chops and his forepaws; then he went back to working on his injury. The hide on his flanks flicked and then shivered briefly. He lay there in the sun, feeling the warmth of it grow stronger, and the pleasant heat slowly thawed the night chill from his body. From time to time he lifted his head, and his gaze automatically focussed on the boy. The man and the woman were also there, presences to be accepted even more warily, but that was all.

"I will work on the skin," the man pronounced, indicating the hide of the wildebeest. "Will you get me the tubers, Pxui?"

The boy knew it was a command, not a request, but he knew also that such courtesy was a sign of respect, and all men felt better if they were honoured with it.

"For softening the skin of our brother, or for taking off his hair?"

There were many different kinds of bulbs which grew beneath the desert sands, and each variety had their own properties and uses. Some of them were acid, and some of them alkaline. He had no words to define their chemical composition, but he knew what they could be used for, and that was sufficient.

"For both," the man replied.

"I will get them."

The hides were a part of their living. Periodically one of their community would make the journey to one of the cattle outposts on the fringes of the desert, and there a parcel of hides would be exchanged for the iron they used on their arrows and spears, and for the tobacco which all of them loved to smoke.

The boy slung his quiver and his skin satchel, and then he picked up his bow and his spear. He set off eagerly, and because they had their meat for the next few days and the sharp urgency of survival had been taken from their lives, he felt like a child again, without worry or care. He remembered those times of long ago, when he had gone out with other children to look for wild plums and berries and succulent grubs, all of it a wonderful game, competing with each other to see who would find the most, tasting and munching as they went and then bringing back their spoils in triumph to receive the awed praise of the parents and their elders. It seemed such a long time ago.

He had gone about twenty yards when he paused and looked back. He called to the lion, and at the sound of his voice the animal turned lazily to stare at him.

"Come with me, big hunter," he called.

The lion studied him for a moment, then swung his head to stare at the hanging meat and the meat that was still on the skin behind the barrier of thorn, and then he turned once more to look at the boy and the yellow eyes were calm and regal and indifferent.

"Come, we will walk the desert together," the boy shouted. "Come with me!"

The lion looked away, and then rolled over onto his back, his paws up in the air, and began to purr loudly as he felt the warming sun on his belly.

The boy stared, surprised and a little disappointed. He felt the venom of resentment begin to creep into him, but then suddenly he laughed—at the way the lion had behaved and also at his own presumption.

He would not have expected gratitude and thanks from a human being for what he had done, so it was even more crass to want it from an animal. He had acted decently, and to have been thanked for the little he had done would have been an insult to him, implying that he had done something meritorious.

That was what he told himself, but just the same he wished that the lion had followed him.

He had been walking for a half-hour when his sharp eyes spotted two tiny leaves amongst the grass and scrub. They were each about an inch long, like a pair of small green ears.

He dug into the loose sand and pulled up the tuber. It was not one of the bulbs he had come looking for, but something for the thirst that was beginning to dry his mouth.

It was ten inches long, a muddy-river brown, looking something like a cassava root. He brushed the sand and dirt from it, and then pulled up a few tufts of grass which he laid on the ground. He squatted, holding one end of the root between his toes, and then using the grass as a board he scraped the tuber with his knife till all the pulpy white flesh had been shredded.

He stood up, and after a few moments searching he found the bush he wanted. He plucked three or four leaves from it and chewed them to a pulp, and then he hunkered down again before the scraped flesh and spat the chewed leaves and juices from his mouth onto the pile of grated white meat. The juice of this particular tuber was very bitter, and the leaves he had added to it would take most of that bitterness away.

He picked up a handful of the grated flesh. He tipped his head back and opened his mouth, and using his outstretched thumb to funnel the juices into his mouth he squeezed the watery pith and drank.

When only the squeezed pith remained he scooped up a quantity of it in both hands, and using it like a spongecloth rubbed it over his face to wash and refresh himself.

He moved on, over the trackless face of the desert, pausing now and again to dig up and munch an edible nut, slipping the choicest into his satchel so that he could share them when he returned.

There was nothing driving him, no urgency to what he was doing, and his progress was leisurely, almost dreamy. He read the sands as he passed, doing it without conscious thought: he was a hunter, and it was as much a part of his natural function as breathing.

He came across two wild tsamma, half hidden in the grass and scrub. He did not break the melons, but made a note of where they were so that he could pick them on the way back.

He went on, searching for the little leaves which would betray the hidden bulbs his father wanted. He had gone a little way beyond the melons when a flicker of movement caught his eyes just as he came abreast of a thorn bush. It was danger, and he knew it instantly, without having to confirm it with a good look.

The cobra reared, head flattened into a hood, its skin a dusty yellow-brown that shone dully in the sunlight and its eyes like beads of shining black glass.

It reared a little higher and lunged forward. The strike took it about three feet, but its gaping mouth with the forked and protruding tongue met only empty air, because the boy had sprung soaring to his left the instant he caught the first warning flutter of movement.

He landed five feet away and span like a cat. The snake was at full stretch on the ground where it had landed after its strike. It was rearing again when the boy darted in and with a vicious backhanded slash of his spear struck it and broke its neck just behind the beautiful spread of its hood.

Its sinuous vital body threshed and flailed the sand. The boy watched it writhing helplessly, his eyes fierce and glittering, the spear in his right hand lifted and poised to strike.

The moment he saw his chance he moved. He drove the spear downwards, driving it in just a little way behind the reptile's head and pinning it tight to the earth.

He watched it for a few moments, its struggles becoming weaker, and then he drew his knife and, holding the spear firmly, placed his right foot across its body and then cut its head off, sawing through the tough rubbery flesh and grinding through the bone.

The body stiffened and he felt the iron strength of its sinews through the sole of his foot as death galvanized it into one last furious and futile assertion of its life. The tail lashed forward and twisted round the calf of his leg, but he paid it no heed.

He finished severing the head, and then he freed the tight gripping coil from round his leg and pulled his spear free. The headless body writhed feebly, and he watched it for a while and then laughed.

He wrapped the head in leaves and grasses, and put it away carefully in his sack. Later he would take the venom from the sacs and dry it. This was one of the ingredients which went into the making of the deadly poison with which they smeared their arrow heads.

It was late afternoon by the time he got back, with the two melons he had picked and the bulbs and tubers required to begin the process of curing and softening the skin of the wildebeest.

On the way back he had begun to wonder about the lion, and whether he would still be there when he returned. He looked for it the moment he reached their camp, and to his great disappointment he was nowhere in sight.

"The lion!" he exclaimed. "Where has the lion gone?"

Tsonomon looked up, pausing momentarily in his work of scraping the skin. "He went into that thorn during the heat of the day. It was hot and he went there to hide and sleep. I don't know if he is still there, but it would be better for all of us if he has gone."

The boy said nothing, but his mouth tightened a little: it might have been pain, or resentment, or perhaps both of them together. He put down the melons and unslung his satchel. The bulbs for the skin he placed in one separate pile, the edible nuts in another.

"Will I help you with the skin, oh father?" he asked.

"I would be glad."

"Could my help wait a few moments? If it can wait, I would like to go and look quickly for him who limps."

"The lion, the lion, that is all you think about," the man said in disgust, but then his seamed face softened slightly. "Go then and look. Until you have looked you will be dreaming, and while you are dreaming a dream will be dreaming you."

The boy was surprised, but then suddenly his face split open in a delightful grin and he laughed happily. "Oh my father!"

He was about to turn away when another disturbing idea presented itself. He didn't want to ask the question, but he forced himself to do so, even if it meant facing the subsequent wrath of the man.

"Did you drive him away while I was gone? Did you drive him with fire or with your spear or your arrows?"

The man looked up: he stared bleakly at the boy, and behind his anger there was also indignation and sadness. "No."

"Forgive me, oh my father."

The boy turned swiftly and walked over to where the lion had been on his back in the sand when he left in the morning. He picked up the spoor and followed the pug marks to the thorn where he had lain. There was a small gap in the thicket, where the lion had entered, and he went down on his hands and knees and peered in and saw the marks of the body where the animal had rested in the cool shade. The lion himself was no longer there.

He circled the bush and picked up the spoor where the animal had left the thorn. He began to follow it, and a painful kind of emptiness grew in him, a feeling of loss. He knew that the lion was a wild creature, and truly owed him nothing, but just the same he felt a strange smothering sadness. He wished that the animal had at least stayed till he came back, not as a token of gratitude or anything like that, but just so that he could have seen him one last time before he went.

He thought of the melons he had brought, and how he had been planning to crack one of them open and give it to the lion so that he could suck the juice and get the moisture from it. The desert held no surface water, except for a few days after the rains, and only his own kind knew where to find it underground and how to suck it to the surface.

He wondered about the lion, and how he was going to survive. He could not hunt, and he would get weaker and weaker, from hunger and from thirst, and then the watchers of the desert would take up his spoor and help him on his way. It was a pity, because he must have been a great and fearless hunter.

He had been following the spoor for about a hundred yards, head down, when a flash of movement caught his attention and he froze.

One moment there had been nothing there but a patch of half-withered grass, but now the lion's head was lifted and visible above the feathery ends. It didn't seem possible that such inadequate cover could have concealed him, but he had been lying there flattened to the earth and it had.

After the first startled instant of surprise, the boy cried out in delight and ran forward unthinkingly. He hadn't gone more than a few paces when the lion rose and growled savagely.

He came to a dead halt, chilled by the ferocity he saw on the lion's face. The eyes were bright and terrible, glowing orbs of amber fire, and looking into them he felt as if he was falling headlong into darkness.

It seemed to him that he would never stop falling, but in actual fact it was no more than a few seconds before he recovered most of his composure. He wondered what had made the lion so fierce and hostile, and whether it was because he had moved so suddenly towards it.

"How can you be afraid of me, a mighty hunter like you?" he asked aloud.

He watched the lion carefully, and as he spoke he saw its ears twitch and take up a new position, as if it were intent on his words. He took a couple of steps forward, moving slowly and carefully. The lion remained alert, but made no move, and encouraged by the fact, he began to speak again.

"It was not my intention to anger you, but you were gone when I returned and so I came to look for you."

The fierce penetrating fire had left the eyes, and now the lion stared at him with that huge disdain he had come to know so well. He took another step forward.

"I come not to anger you, but to be your friend," the boy continued.

His voice was soft and cajoling, and the onomatopoeic clicking of the words he used had within it the music of the land which had given them birth.

He stretched his left arm out, the one without the spear, and then he started forward once again. The lion roared.

It was only sound, but it struck at him and shook him like the blast from an explosion. It froze him in his tracks, with his right foot poised in mid-air a few inches off the ground, and when the shock of it passed and his reeling senses were able to function again he backed away shakily, surprised that he was still alive.

When his immediate fear had passed he felt a burning resentment flare up in him. He had gone to him in trust and friendship, and the beast had roared at him in anger and hatred, he who had taken the steel from round his leg and suffered the wrath and contempt of his own father to feed him.

He filled his lungs, to scream and shout and hurl the most terrible insults he could think of at the lion when he realized that it would be meaningless to him. He snapped his mouth shut, staring at him morosely.

He was turning away when his father came to a skidding halt beside him. He had his bow in his hand and an arrow notched to the string and his spear was sticking out of his quiver.

"What happened?" he gasped. "What happened that he spoke with such anger in his voice?"

He threw a quick frightened glance at the lion and then stared intently at his son. He took in the pale face, no longer a shining apricot gold but a smudged bloodless grey.

"What happened?" he demanded again.

"I tried . . . to get near him."

"Fool!" the man exclaimed.

"I know—he does not really care."

The man studied his son for a moment, and a strange expression came to his face, of compassion and concern, and all the subtle shadings of emotion that came between.

"Come," he said gently, and he put his arm round the shoulder of his son and they walked away together.

The boy glanced back once. He saw that the lion was again following them. Remembering what had gone before, he didn't understand it.

15

THEY CAMPED by their kill for four days. They feasted and slept and woke to feast again. Their buttocks, which served them in the same way as a camel's hump serves it in times of privation, grew fat and sleek and rounded, plump and heavy with reserves of fat and carbohydrate on which their bodies would draw in leaner times.

The boy continued to feed the lion, but now he had to share his own food with him. He also gave him wild melons, which the lion broke open and devoured with obvious satisfaction. He derived no pleasure from his generosity, nor did he feel any resentment. He just shared, because he had come to think of the animal as his responsibility.

He still hoped that the lion would follow them to their permanent camp, because of Xhabbo and also so that the others would see with their own eyes what he had done, but these were no longer his prime considerations.

Tsonomon rebuked him for his foolishness, but he gave up when he saw that nothing would shake his son's determination. In the end he told him rather disgustedly that he could do as he liked with his own food, warning him not to complain when he found his own belly getting emptier.

On the fourth evening they dined frugally. When they had finished eating Tsonomon placed a little more wood on the fire and spoke his thoughts.

"We can carry the meat that remains. It is not too heavy for us now, because we have eaten of it well. Therefore we will carry it and begin back towards our water. We will begin when the sun comes back from his hunt."

"It will be good," the woman said, "to be back with our people again."

"Two days," the boy murmured. "If we are lucky enough not to kill."

"Not to kill?" the man inquired incredulously.

"It will be longer if we do."

"And that is unlucky?" the man went on in disbelief. "To have a full stomach?"

"I did not mean it like that."

"How did you mean it?"

"Just that it will be longer, till we get back to the people."

"What does it matter, how long it takes?"

"I think," the woman said slyly, glancing first at her son and then into the perplexed eyes of her husband, "that he wishes to make a very small bow."

"Ahh!" the man exclaimed softly, and his face lit up. "And who is it that he wishes to shoot with his arrow of love?"

"Have you been so blind, oh my Tsonomon," the woman chided him.

"A man has other things to keep him busy," he said defensively, and then after a slight pause, he blurted out: "But who is it, oh my son?"

"Xhabbo," the boy replied, and he was glad of the darkness, because he could feel the blood flushing hotly on his face.

The man was quiet for a while, and then he said simply: "She shines with the beauty of a lynx."

"Oh yes, father, yes!" the boy agreed happily.

In the beginning, the Dawn's Heart, who was the greatest hunter of all in the skies, had come down to earth and taken the shape of a man of his people. He had fallen in love, and he had taken as his bride the lynx, who in those far-off days was also a person. He had selected her, because of all the maidens she alone was beautiful enough to become the wife of such a great hunter.

"Yes," the man went on, as if he had read his son's thoughts, and now there was a sardonic dryness in his voice. "And can you measure yourself to the Dawn's Heart, with the lion following you like a hyena?"

The boy gasped softly. In that legend of long ago, the hyena, which was the symbol of evil and darkness, had taken the sweat from her armpits and mixed it with the ant eggs that Lynx ate. They were a great delicacy, and she ate them all, and because of the sweat that was mixed with them she fell under the spell of the hyena.

One by one her clothes fell from her body, and then her bead necklaces and her bracelets, and she ran away screaming to sit by the water, which is to say that the forces of darkness had entered the clean bright spirit of her consciousness and madness was approaching, and only near water, which was essential to all creation, could she hope to find any comfort.

But she fell deeper and deeper under the spell of the hyena, and one day it entered the hut of the Dawn's Heart while she was away, pretending to be Lynx in order to steal his love.

The great hunter had however been warned by Lynx's sister, who in the imagery of their thought was not a person but the essence of the true love of Lynx herself, and so he rushed at Hyena and drove her away with his spear, driving her back to the land of darkness and confusion from which she had sprung.

It was an old legend, and he had heard the story of it many, many times, and now it was a part of his being and his beliefs, and thinking about it the boy began to fear the lion in a way he had not feared him before.

That night when his mother and father were asleep he stole some of the hanging meat. He stole quite a lot of it, and he rubbed each piece under his armpit and then he fed it to the lion.

He wasn't quite certain in his own mind exactly what he hoped to accomplish, other than to get the lion into his power. The sweat of a man was a powerful thing, and a man baptized his own son with it as he himself had been baptized by his father.

The armpit of a man was the source of light and power and reason, for in the beginning of time the sun had come from the armpit of one of the early people.

In the morning his father discovered that some of the meat was missing. His first thought was that the lion had stolen it during the night while they had slept.

"The meat," he said, ominously, taking his eyes from the thorn bush and fixing them on his son. "That lion of yours has stolen our meat. He has followed you and done what I always suspected he would do."

"Perhaps he had a great hunger," the boy replied, and though he had known it would come to this he was not prepared for the sudden rush of fear he felt, for himself and for the lion. "We did not feed him, and therefore he was hungry and stole our meat."

"And does his hunger give him the right to steal our meat?" the man demanded savagely. "To steal the food which is our life?"

"Have we not stolen from their kills when we were hungry?"

"It was a chance we took with our lives," the man said bleakly. "And now he has taken that same chance for himself."

"What—what do you mean, oh my father?" the boy asked, and he felt a fearful apprehension, because in his heart he knew just what the man meant.

"I mean that he will have to be killed," the man said bluntly. "I will have to kill him, that is what I mean."

The boy was silent for a moment, staring at the grim, set countenance of his father. He got to his feet slowly, his heart beginning to beat harder. He had never dreamed that it would come to this.

"No," he said.

The man rose also. For a moment he was too shocked to speak, and then anger freed his tongue.

"You stand there in my body, in my own flesh, you who are me, and you tell me not to do what I have to do!" he shouted. "How can you speak like that?"

"Not that, oh my father," the boy whispered. "I meant he did not steal it."

He wanted to admit it and get it over with, but the wrath on the face of his father was terrible, and so he said nothing.

"What then?" cried the man. "Did the meat come together, and grow new legs and hoofs and a heart and head and gallop away into the night?"

"Such things have happened before. You told me the stories yourself."

The man paused, and a flash of uncertainty sparked briefly in his eyes, but then they became hard and opaque again. "Such things happened only in the time of the first people."

"Perhaps a hyena came in the night and stole it," the boy suggested.

The man gave a small start of surprise, and then he started purposefully towards the thorn bush. "We shall see."

"Father!" the boy cried. "Wait."

The man halted and swung half way round. "I wait."

"It was no hyena that took the meat," the boy said. "It was I who took it."

"You!" the man exclaimed. "Why did you not say so?"

The boy remained silent, his head bowed.

"I knew it would come to this," the man said angrily, and then his voice softening with sudden concern, he went on: "Were you that hungry?"

"It would be easy for me to say that I was, but I cannot do that."

The man frowned. "Speak."

"I gave it to the lion."

A look of stunned disbelief settled on the seamed and wrinkled face of the man. It was washed away a few moments later by a surge of black anger.

He turned slowly and paced over to where his son was standing. He studied him silently, almost trembling with his rage.

"Lift your head, look up at me."

The boy raised his bowed head. He felt a shiver run through him as he met the terrible eyes. It wasn't the morning cold.

He saw the blow coming, but he did not flinch. The hard hand of his father struck him across the side of his face. The force of the blow lifted him off his feet and hurled him sideways to the ground.

Through the ringing in his ears he heard the savage snarling of the lion. He sat up quickly, his head still spinning, his vision coming in broken snatches.

He saw the lion, only a few feet away. Its black lips were peeled back, the long yellow teeth laid bare. For a second he thought the animal was growling at him, but then he saw that his eyes were fixed not on him but on his father who was still standing a little way to his right.

The lion growled again, the sound of it full of fury. He saw him readying himself to leap, and he sprang to his feet and faced him.

"No!" he shouted, flailing his arms at it. "No."

Slowly he saw the animal relax, and the murderous intention left the animal's eyes as he watched the boy alertly. Pxui waved his arms at him again and shouted. The lion turned and limped away. He sat down a little distance off, his watchful eyes moving between the boy and the man.

"It was in him to kill me," the man whispered, his voice shocked but threaded with a wondrous awe. "I saw it in him."

"I bow my head, oh my father," the boy said softly. "I bow it in shame."

There was a wet glitter in his downcast eyes. It was the first time in his life that his father had ever struck him.

"Lift up your head," Tsonomon said quietly. "It seems you have another father."

They moved off an hour later, the two hunters in front and then the woman, and the lion limping and hopping after them. All that remained were the ashes of their fire and the clean picked skull of the wildebeest and its cracked bones from which they had sucked the marrow.

On the way to their permanent camp they saw game, but they did not make a kill. The march took them only two days.

16

THEY WERE a half-hour's march from their camp. The excitement had mounted slowly in the boy over the past two days, till now it was a hot breath-catching tightness that was almost unbearable. The evening sun drenched the desert in its golden light, and the tall grass moved in the wind like ripples running across the surface of still water.

They paused for a moment to rest, squatting down in the sand. They drank the last of their water, a swallow at a time, passing the ostrich egg between them, sharing it out meticulously.

"They will get a surprise when they see him," the boy commented, his eyes alight and sparkling at the thought.

"They know already," the woman said, tapping pointedly at her breast.

"I forgot," the boy murmured, dismayed and disappointed, but then he brightened. "But surely they will not know how he came to be with us?"

"That they will not know," she replied. "But they will know that a great beast of prey walks with us."

The boy nodded happily, and the feeling of anticipation which had begun to wither in him grew fresh and strong again.

They rested for about ten minutes and began walking again. In the distance ahead of them was a grove of tall camel thorn and iron wood trees. They grew on the sides of an ancient and dried-out river course, and their spreading roots tapped the same moist sand with its subterranean water that enabled them to survive. They headed straight towards it, and unconsciously, as if tugged by unseen forces, the man increased his pace.

There were seven small huts in the grove, fairly widely scattered. Each shelter was built against the trunk of a tree. They were crude and rough, the sides and roofs made of scrub wood and thorn and thatched in with grass.

At the moment there was a total of twenty-eight people in the small community. The number never remained static. Relatives dropped in from time to time, appearing out of nowhere from the glittering sun-bright reaches of the desert. They stayed a few days and then moved on, and sometimes, as Pxui and his parents had done, the established members of the group would wander away, occasionally vanishing for weeks at a time, driven by some deep inner compulsion to move.

They were there and waiting, all those who were in camp, from the smallest children to the old ones with the grey of their years and their wisdom in the tight little curls of their hair.

Tsonomon transferred his spear to his left hand and held his right arm out parallel to the ground, fingers open and palm up.

"Tshjamm!" he exclaimed happily, the click of the word like the flash and sparkle of sunlight on morning dew, the traditional and age-old greeting of his people. "We saw you looming from afar and we are dying of hunger."

"Good day!" came the murmured reply from a dozen throats. "We have been dead, but now that you have come we live once again."

The response was an indication of their innate courtesy, but the highly stylized greeting itself had been shaped by the brutal forces which opposed them and also by their own feelings of inadequacy with regard to their size. And so they spoke thus, denying the fact, and in doing so overcoming in some measure their own sense of shame at their diminutive stature. No one who was small could possibly be seen looming up from a great distance.

The lion came to a halt the moment the group of people came into view. The tension in them, the electric alertness, flowed to him like an invisible current through the ether.

Three short muffled grunts exploded from his belly, and then he lowered his head to the ground and roared softly, so that it seemed the noise was coming from far away. It was the same technique he used successfully to stampede a herd of animals, and his chest worked in and out like a bellows as he kept up the gurgling roar.

The lion lifted his head. To his surprise and irritation the people had simply drawn closer together into a more compact group. His amber eyes glowed transparently as he stared at the bunched figures. He watched them a moment longer and then his gaze swung slowly to focus on the boy.

Pxui turned to glance back across his shoulder at the lion. At that precise moment the animal sank to the earth and began to lick at his wound. Putting their own interpretation on the coincidence, a murmur of awe rose from the onlookers. One of them stepped forward, a wizened old man whose skin was like parchment that has been crushed and then smoothed out again.

"We knew of the beast, but we did not believe it," he whispered. "We see him now with our own eyes, for he is there to see, but how did such a thing happen?"

Tsonomon nudged his son. The boy straightened his shoulders, and his small golden chest expanded as he drew a deep breath. His eyes moved over them slowly. He saw and sensed their apprehension, their uneasiness and mistrust. His gaze steadied on Xhabbo, and he forgot about what he had seen on their faces.

She was wearing two necklaces. One of them was ivory white, the beads carved from broken fragments of ostrich egg shell, the other was of wood, the discs cut from the dark crimson root of a tree which grew only in certain places of the desert.

They hung between her smooth naked breasts, drawing his attention to their ripeness, the beads like jewels against the warm apricot colour of her skin.

He began to speak, his eyes holding hers, as if he were talking to her alone. He told them what had happened, and how the lion had followed him. He insinuated that this was no ordinary lion that would follow a man, seeking his companionship, and then he went on to describe the killing of the wildebeest, and the part that the lion had played. He mentioned how he had fed him, and by omission managed to create the impression that the beast was well disposed towards him.

He fell silent after that, and his eyes roved over the gathered people. They were silent for a long while, staring at him in a kind of trance-like wonder, and then abruptly the spell that he had woven broke and they sighed heavily like people reluctantly coming back to reality. They began to fidget uneasily, the murmur of their voices rising, one or two of them exclaiming more loudly than the others.

"Does he obey you then, this big beast?" demanded one of the young hunters. "Does he listen to you like a son to his father?"

Pxui was sorely tempted to claim it, but the knowledge that he might be asked to demonstrate his power made him hesitate. He was beginning to shake his head when his father interrupted his denial.

"Obey him!" he exclaimed, and there was a derisive and patronizing note to his voice. "That big beast eats from the hand of my son, and he rubs against him in the way that lions will sometimes do with each other when they have met after a hunt." He became confidential. "But it is only with him that he behaves thus. Not even with me, who is his father, but only with him who is my son."

The boy stared incredulously at the man. He was about to protest, but then he saw the expression of sudden pained guilt which came to his face as their eyes met and he shut his mouth tight, because he did not want to embarrass him by denying it.

He eyed the gathered people covertly. Many of them were staring at him with open-mouthed awe. It made him feel ashamed for a few moments, but then he got to enjoying the feeling of importance. He knew instinctively, with a half-understood knowledge, that the pretence might eventually cause him grief, but studying Xhabbo he pushed the thought aside, warming himself in the glow of her awed admiration.

"I think," he said modestly, "that he may be one of the old fathers walking the desert in the body of this great beast of prey."

The old man who had spoken before moved forward, stepping clear of the group. "That may be, but who will feed this big beast while he is unable to hunt? If we do not feed him it is in his nature to think of us as his food. He will kill us to eat us, because that is the way he will think."

"If he wanted to kill me, oh grandfather, he would have done that already. He saw me, and I was there, and he could have killed me."

"Perhaps his hunger was not great enough."

"I will feed him, till he can hunt again, so that never will his hunger be that great."

"If he ever hunts again."

"He will hunt," the boy said firmly.

"And when you have no food?" the old man went on. "And we have to share with you?"

If one of them went hungry, all of them did, and in those terrible times the only ones who had food in their bellies were the infants still at the breasts of their mothers. But ultimately starvation dried even that source, when the rains did not come and the game moved away.

"I will give him half of my share," the boy said quietly, and then his voice dropped even lower. "I gave him the chance to live. I gave it, and I cannot take it back now."

"And when that half-share could give some other life?" the old man went on relentlessly.

The barrage of words began to make the boy feel like a driven animal. "That is my business."

He had been forced to say it, but just the same he uttered the words reluctantly. To begin with they were discourteous, and they also made him an outcast, placing him in a position beyond the concern and mercy of others.

There was a long hushed silence, and then the old one spoke again. "So," he breathed softly. "You would give life to the big beast, and giving him life you would take it from one of us?"

There was no anger in his voice, only a troubled curiosity, because he too was looking into the days ahead, remembering those times of thirst and starvation through which he himself had so often travelled.

"He will be no burden," the boy said flatly.

"Let us drive him away!" exclaimed Gumkoo, stepping forward to stand beside the old man. He was a great hunter, a young man of twenty who was not as yet married. "Oh Pxui, this is a madness that has taken you. Who will sleep in the night, with a beast like that watching from the darkness? We will not sleep in peace, knowing that he watches us."

"Who will drive him away?" the boy asked contemptuously. "I have tried it, and even fire does not frighten him."

"There are many of us."

"He will not go, and in his anger he will kill."

"Let us kill him then, before he can kill us."

For a while no one spoke. The silence grew, till the quiet was like pain, a trembling empty stillness.

"Kill him!"

One voice, hesitant and a little uncertain, but then the cry was taken up, and the sound of their voices rose and beat against his ears and he was afraid of what he heard.

The lion came quickly to his feet. The sudden swelling roar of their voices startled and electrified him. Fear followed it swiftly.

He lifted his head, and with his mouth wide open and the black lips framing the red hole of his mouth he burst into a full-throated roar that seemed to shake the very earth. A stunned silence followed. Pxui let it stretch, and then he spoke, his words falling like stones.

"If you kill him, you must take my life first," he cried. "You must kill me, for I have licked the salt of his tears."

This they understood. They stared at him in a frightened and resentful silence. Some of them began to nod, while others began to converse in hushed whispers.

"Oh my Pxui!" Gumkoo called out, and the others fell silent immediately to hear what he would say. "You have married yourself to a lion, and when he finds out you are not a lioness he will bite you where it matters, and you will no longer be one of us, the qhwai xkhwe."

There was a subdued titter of laughter. The boy felt his face flush, but he could think of no suitable retort. Qhwai xkhwe was the name that the Bushman had given to his own race, and it celebrated the fact that he, of all the people on the earth, was born and lived with his penis in a state of semi-erection. He had been made different to other men, he knew, and this further distinction added confirmation to the fact. He accepted it with dignity and gratitude, marvelling at his God who had seen fit to make him so unique.

"And if you were the lion, Gumkoo!" Xhabbo cried out. "Would you have had the sense to realize your mistake?"

A startled silence followed her outburst, and then pandemonium broke loose as they understood the implications of what she had said. They laughed uproariously, and some of them were so overcome that they flipped over onto their backs and kicked their legs in the air in squirming helpless mirth. Gumkoo was one of them. When they had recovered, their earlier animosity had vanished entirely.

"Will you take the shells?" Tsonomon asked his son. "We have no water."

"Yes."

They started forward, heading for their own small shelter which was some fifty yards ahead. The lion hesitated, torn between fear of the massed humans and the knowledge that the man on whom he was coming to depend for survival was moving away.

He watched the boy a few moments longer, and then started forward abruptly, alternately limping and hopping, his warning growl deep and savage with his own fear.

The people scattered hastily to let him pass, and they stared after him, mesmerized by the sight of him at such close quarters and awed by his size. He stood three feet eight inches at the shoulder. The tallest amongst them was a bare five feet and two inches, and with his head up and alert his glowing eyes were sometimes on a level with their own.

When they reached their shelter the boy unslung his satchel. He took the empty shells from his mother, and with three others from the hut he bundled them into a skin and set off towards the dried-out water course.

His return had not quite been the triumph he had anticipated, and he felt disappointed, somehow cheated. He saw that some of the people were watching him, uncertain and still a bit afraid.

He glanced behind once, and he saw that the lion was following him again. The strange thing was that he didn't care very much now whether the animal followed him or not.

He had only gone a little way when Xhabbo stepped out from behind some scrub. Her sudden appearance startled him, and then his heart began to pound with excitement.

"I saw you from afar," she said.

"You did not think you could hide behind such a small bush, did you?" he responded politely. "A big person like you?"

Her black eyes sparkled briefly. "Where are you going?"

"To fill our shells."

"Let me carry your sack, for I would come with you."

He was simultaneously surprised and delighted. She had always seemed so shy to him before, that he had been half-afraid even to talk to her in case she used her quick tongue on him and ran away laughing.

He passed the bundle to her without a word, and she slung it on her back and they started off again, side by side. She glanced back, looking at the lion, and then she looked at him. He was conscious of her scrutiny, but he pretended otherwise.

"I must thank you," he said.

"For what?"

"For making them all laugh at Gumkoo."

"We would have laughed at you too, if you had been in his place."

"Not that."

"What then?"

"In laughing, they forgot about the lion," the boy said. "They laughed, and they did not think of wanting to kill him any more."

She met his eyes for a moment and then looked away, vaguely unsettled by the expression she saw in them. She threw a glance across her shoulder at the lion which was following them. It looked huge and sinister, moving through patches of light and shadow, and she felt a sudden burst of uneasiness she could not understand.

"It cannot be true," she said abruptly.

"What?"

"That you took the iron from around his leg and set him free."

"It is true, whether you believe it or not, and I say it on the head of my father."

"Then I believe you."

"Good."

She was silent for a while. "But why did you set him free?"

"I told you, when I told all the people."

"Were you not afraid?"

She was watching him, with a calculating curiosity. He was tempted to deny it for a moment, but then his innate respect for the factual overcame his desire to impress her.

"In all my days," he said, "I have never been so afraid."

She nodded quickly, imagining what it must have been like, remembering the sound of its mighty roar. "And were you angered when he followed you?"

"In the beginning."

"Why only then?"

"Because the hunters were coming, and I had robbed them of their prey, and I was afraid of what they would do to me. But then they went away, and I became happy that he was following me."

"But why? Did you not realize that you would have to feed him, that in feeding him he would be like a tick upon your back, sucking your blood and your life?"

"I did not think of that then."

"Then why were you pleased?"

The boy was silent for a while. He kicked at the sand as he walked, scuffing it with his bare feet. He looked up suddenly, meeting her eyes.

"You will not laugh?"

"Why should I?"

The boy felt it in his belly then, the same kind of tightness that came when he was flattened to the earth and nearing the end of his stalk.

"If he had not followed me, no one would have believed my story. But he did follow, and now they know that I walked up to a lion and did a thing no other hunter has done before."

"Yes," she commented, and there was a dry irony in her voice. "And now you will have to feed him, for the pleasure of that one moment."

"I wanted you to know it as well," the boy blurted out. "To know that I was a great hunter."

"You will still have to feed him," she replied laconically.

She held his alert and anxious gaze for a few moments. He felt incredibly exposed, and he began to wish that he had never spoken, but then just before she looked away the expression in her eyes changed suddenly. He couldn't define it, but it looked as if she had smiled secretly deep inside herself in those places that no one could see.

They reached the old water course. Pxui bent and retrieved from beneath some bushes a length of pipe about five feet long which had been made by reaming out the pith of a soft-cored stalk.

They went down the shallow bank and into the sandy bed. It was pocked with many small craters, where others had dug for water long ago just after the rains.

He walked into the deepest part of the river course with Xhabbo. He signalled to her and they halted. She unslung the sack from her back, and putting it down took the empty shells from it.

The boy went down on his hands and knees. He dug into the sand, like a dog digging a hole, throwing the moist sand up between his legs. When he was down to his armpits he took the hollow stem and wrapped one end loosely with the dried grass Xhabbo handed to him. It was necessary, to prevent the fine sand blocking the hole in the pipe.

He inserted the stem in the hole he had dug. He pushed it a few inches deeper, and then when it would go no further he filled in the hole and stamped the sand down, tamping it tight round the pipe.

He cut himself a thin stick from one of the bushes on the bank, and then he wedged the empty shells upright in the sand around the tube.

He went down on his hands and knees. He placed one end of the thin stick in the corner of his mouth, and the other end in the hole in the top of the first shell to be filled. He began to suck on the pipe.

From the top of the bank, the lion watched the operation, intent and highly curious.

The boy continued to suck. His chest heaved and his shoulders quivered with the strain, and the veins of his neck became so gorged with blood that they looked like knotted cord beneath the skin.

He sucked for perhaps two minutes without any result. He was beginning to feel light headed with the sustained and total effort he was applying when he felt the first faint easing of the pressure on his pumping lungs.

A bright drop of crystal-clear water appeared at the corner of his mouth. It clung there, trembling, and then it ran down the stick and into the shell. The drops came faster and faster, till eventually they came so close together they merged in a thin but continuous trickle. He filled the shells one after the other till all of them were full.

When he had finished he straightened up. He was gasping and fighting for breath, and the perspiration was streaming down his face and chest.

"Pxui!" the girl cried.

There was a note of urgency in her voice, and alarm. He brushed the sweat out of his eyes and looked up. The lion was hopping across the bed of the water course, coming straight towards them. Instinctively he plucked his spear from the sand and turned to face him.

The lion halted a few feet away. The boy gripped his spear tight, his heart beginning to hit harder. In the open river bed the beast looked even more huge.

"He will kill us," the girl whispered. "Now that we are alone he will kill us."

He couldn't bring himself to believe it, but at the same time he could not dismiss the possibility even now. He felt her hand on his arm, and he knew she had come close to him for comfort.

The lion grunted softly. The boy was about to back away when he noticed the direction of the animal's gaze, and at the same instant he saw the broad fleshy nostrils pulsing in and out. In a flash he thought he understood.

He thought frantically for a few moments, and then it came to him how he could do it. He dug a shallow excavation in the sand a few feet to his right and away from his precious shells. He placed the skin sack on top of the hollow and pressed it down, and then into it he poured water from one of the shells.

He was still decanting it when the lion moved forward eagerly, a guttural moan bursting from the half-opened mouth. The lion halted again, just beyond the apron of skin. In the late evening light his amber eyes looked almost transparent, and behind the shining, electrifying intelligence Pxui thought he saw the gleam of anticipation.

He felt a sense of relief flood through him, and also a feeling of elation that he had been correct in his evaluation of the animal's actions.

"Xhabbo," he said quietly, "pass me two more shells."

He took them from her, and he felt the tremor in her hands as she passed them to him. He poured out the water and then picking up the empties he straightened up slowly and backed away.

The lion moved forward instantly. He sank down on all fours and lowered his head. He began to lap at the water, his white chin hairs just touching the surface and his big shoulder blades jutting from his body and looking like stubby wings.

"He only wanted water," the girl said, incredulously, and then turning to face Pxui, she asked, "How did you know?"

The look of awe and wonder in her eyes was disturbing and gratifying. For a moment he was tempted to exploit her ignorance and so enhance his prestige, by telling her he could read the mind of the lion or something equally spectacular, but he couldn't bring himself to embark on such a deception.

"His nose was jumping," he replied. "The smell of the water came to him, and so he smelled it and looked at the shells. It was not difficult to understand."

She nodded silently, studying the lion, and the fear that she had felt a few moments before began to lessen slowly.

"It is true then," she remarked eventually. "I did not believe it in the beginning."

"What?"

"That he eats out of your hand and he rubs against you as if you were his brother."

He was pensive for a while, the temptation to deceive her about it coming to him again. He wouldn't even have to say anything. All he had to do was remain quiet and she would believe him.

"I tried to touch him once, but I will never try it again," he said. "He would have killed me, I think, but I saw the warning in his eyes and I heard it in his voice, and I did not try it."

"Why did your father say such a thing?" she asked, puzzled.

"I do not know," he admitted. "Perhaps it was to make my shadow taller."

Their eyes met briefly, but she looked away hastily, confused and thrilled and a little frightened by the terrible alertness she saw in his gaze.

"I am glad that you told me," she said softly.

"What?"

"The truth."

His breath caught, and there was a tremble in his voice when he spoke at last. "Why should it matter?"

"Your shadow is tall enough already."

He gasped softly. "Xhabbo!"

He reached for her arm, but she edged away, because she had already said more than she wanted to. Just then the lion finished the last of the water. The animal licked at the skin for a while and then lifted his head.

"Look!" she exclaimed softly. "He looks just like an old grandfather, with the white hair round his mouth and chin and——"

She drew a sharp startled breath and fell silent as the large yellow eyes focussed on her with an impact that made her senses reel, so deep did they seem to probe.

"His eyes glow like yellow stars," she breathed. "And glowing softly, they look like stars."

"You should see them when he is angry," the boy said, and there was a possessive note of pride in his voice. "The red fire in them turns your belly into water."

"I can understand that," she commented. "He is huge, and in his rage he must be terrible to behold."

The boy picked up one of the full shells. He offered it to her, but she refused politely, saying she had already drunk. He tipped it up and drank himself. It contained almost three pints of water, but he finished it without any difficulty. He wiped the back of his hand over his mouth and then went back to the pipe in the sand.

He began to suck at it again. The effort to start the water flowing once more was almost too much, but he persisted doggedly, and in the end the first drops began to appear like coruscating jewels at the corner of his mouth. He filled the four shells he had emptied and then pulled the pipe from the sand.

He plugged the holes in the top of the shells with their stoppers of wadded grass, and then he straightened up. The lion hadn't moved, and Pxui eyed him contemplatively. He was still belly down, and his massive forepaws were resting on the rim of the skin sack.

Pxui glanced at Xhabbo, and he saw that she was watching him. There was a curiously guarded expression on her face, and he knew that she was also wondering what he was going to do. He began to wish that he hadn't given the lion any water, because he didn't really know how he was going to get his sack back. He was afraid, and uncertain, and he didn't want her to see his fear.

He took a step forward and waved his arms at the lion. The animal stared back at him, and the expression in the eyes changed, as if he wished to understand but could not, and they were no longer as clear and transparent as they had been, but opaque with anxiety and a budding apprehension.

"Go!" the boy cried softly, keeping his voice low and waving his arms again. "I want my skin, big hunter."

The lion grunted softly, his eyes fixed unwaveringly on the boy, but he did not move.

Pxui glanced at the girl again. Her face was grave but otherwise without expression. He felt his embarrassment mounting.

He went forward very slowly, a step at a time, watching the lion every moment. He bent down and began to inch his hand out, sliding it over the sand towards the skin. His fingers closed on it. The eyes of the lion were no longer on his own, but fixed on his hand. He began to pull gently at the skin.

The lion struck at his hand with his left front paw. As swift as the animal was, the boy was swifter, because he had been watching for just such a move. Had he been watching the eyes instead, he might have been surprised. There was no mistaking the glint of mischievous enjoyment in them.

But he did not see it, and he snatched his hand back and sprang to his feet. For a moment he was paralysed with fear, but then he felt a sudden burning rage take hold of him. He had fed him, and given him water, and he was returning his kindness with a sneaking attack.

He bellowed at the animal, in a sudden burst of fury and righteous anger. The abrupt threat action surprised the lion. For a moment he was too stupefied to move, but then he lurched awkwardly to his feet and backed away, grunting and growling softly.

The boy darted forward and snatched up his skin. He backed away and began to fill it with his shells. His hands were trembling so badly that he almost dropped one of them. The girl did not miss it.

"You should have killed him long ago," she said bleakly, and then as if she were seeing something far distant in the future, her voice became sombre and full of a heavy foreboding. "He will cause you grief, for he must, because a man and a lion can live under the same stars but not under the same roof."

"You have seen his eyes," the boy replied. "How can you kill him when he looks right into your heart the way he sometimes does with those eyes of his?"

He slung his sack on his shoulder and picked up the water pipe and his spear. He climbed out of the river bed and pushed the pipe away out of sight beneath the bushes where it was always left.

They walked back the way they had come. The winter cold was already creeping into the evening air. They walked in silence for most of the way, and then just before they reached the first of the small shelters the boy halted.

"What is it?" she asked, puzzled that he had stopped.

He remained silent for a long while. He stared deep into her eyes, with the same concentration with which the lion had gazed at her. She began to feel uncomfortable.

"What is it?" she asked again.

"I am glad," he said, "that you came with me."

"It was nothing."

"I have seen you before," he went on. "But this is the first time you have seen me."

"I was afraid of you before. I saw you, but I was afraid. There was always a great fierceness in your eye when you looked at me."

He was astonished, because he had felt only timidity and apprehension. "But I also was afraid of you."

She stared at him intently for a moment, and then suddenly she laughed. "It happens."

"And now you are no longer afraid of me?" he inquired.

"Who could be afraid of you after seeing your face when Gumkoo spoke of your marriage to the lion?" she retorted. "It was a face to make a woman lift the child to her breast."

"I am not a child," he said hotly. "I am a man, and one day I will be the greatest of all hunters."

"If you miss your aim I will sing a prayer to a star for you," she said. "I will ask him to take your arm, with which you miss your aim, and to give you his own arm."

"Thank you."

She did not miss the stiffness in his voice, the note of indignation, but she let it go by. "They are saying already that the lion is an evil one. They say it, because no beast of prey would eat from the hand of a man."

"That is not true," the boy exclaimed sharply. "He was hurt, and he came to me that I might take the hurt from him. It is a natural thing."

"A lion?"

"If you had seen his eyes."

"Perhaps you should tell them, that he does not eat from your hand, that he is just a wild beast."

He was silent for a while. "I cannot."

She heard the anguish in his voice. "You will still be known for having taken the bracelet from his leg."

He shook his head: it didn't seem very important now. "My father," he explained. "The skin would tighten on his flesh, and tightening it would shrink his shadow."

"I had not thought of that."

"Will you—speak of what you know?"

"I would not hurt my father either," she said, and then after a pause, as if speaking of the matter had triggered another thought: "His heart is sad enough for his own father."

"Forgive me," the boy said quickly, contritely. "How is he?"

"He is old," she replied. "And for that sickness there is no root or flower to help a man."

He nodded, but it was difficult to feel sad, because he was young and he couldn't even imagine what it felt like to be old and wrinkled.

"Come, I must take the water to our place," he said. "They wait for it, and I have been gone long already."

He hitched at the sack on his shoulders and they started forward. After he had gone a little way he looked back. He saw that the lion had risen and was following him again.

"I wonder if he will always follow me?"

"You have fed him, have you not?"

"Can it only be that?"

"A babe does not seize its mother's breast out of love," she replied gently, compassionately.

"He is no child," he retorted defensively.

"He is as helpless as one."

"That is so."

There was a note of gloom in his voice, and then after that he too began to see for the first time the pattern of the days which lay ahead. He felt a momentary resentment, but then he remembered the way the lion had looked at him when the steel was round his leg, and the wonder came into him again and he marvelled at the extent of the trust the animal had shown.

17

FUNCTIONALLY IT ACTED like a shuttle-cock, but the resemblance ended there. It was made of a single ostrich feather tied to a five-foot-long leather thong which was attached at the other end to a heavy sanganyamma nut.

It was in the air now, descending rapidly, the thong a straight line against the backdrop of the blue evening sky. Pxui leaped forward, sidestepping to avoid Gumkoo, the long, whippy rod held high in his right hand and poised ready to strike.

He sprang, soaring like a jumping cat. The lashing rod swept through the air horizontally. He felt the momentary jerk as it slashed across the leather thong. The force of his strike held it captive for a moment, and then with a cry of triumph he whipped the rod and sent the shuttle soaring into the air once again.

The game continued, sweeping from one side of the clearing to the other, the players laughing and shouting with the excitement of the chase.

From a little way off, at the edge of the clearing beside a clump of mokalong thorn, the lion watched the darting figures. There was a glow like fire in his amber eyes, and a tight hollow emptiness in his belly.

They had killed yesterday, the little men who were now hunting that strange bird that dropped from the sky only to soar incomprehensibly once again the moment it came within reach of their striking arms.

He had fed on the offal, and also on the scraps which had been thrown to him by the gorged hunters. Some of them had laughed and jeered at him, the king accepting alms with the eagerness of any beggar, but their derision held no meaning for him. His was an unperverted reality, where food was food, and the means by which he obtained it in his present condition would have left him indifferent even if he had understood. He was still hungry.

His wound was mending. The flesh had grown together, the broken bones were knitting slowly, and daily he was able to take more and more of the weight of his great body on the leg which had been smashed.

Watching the soaring shuttle and the frenzied activity of the men he felt an old excitement begin to mount in him. His amber eyes glazed briefly, extinguishing the light that was in them, and then an instant later, when they came to life again, they burned with the deadly concentration of purpose. His tail twitched and then grew still.

There were women watching the men at play, and a group of children to one side leaping and prancing and imitating the movements of the men. The most active of them was a young girl.

Her movements caught the eye of the lion. He glanced once again at the shuttle, and then his eyes returned to the child. She was ten years old, her body delicate and beautifully formed, her small breasts like the promise of budding flowers.

The excitement that had come to life within him from watching the shuttle was still there, but the shuttle was no longer the centre of his interest. His tail twitched again. It quivered briefly and then became still. He flattened his belly to the ground and began to stalk her.

One of the rules by which they played the game was the absolute avoidance of all physical contact between the players. The origin of the rule was lost in antiquity. They obeyed it now religiously and mindlessly, unaware that it had stemmed from the days of their peril and the harsh brutality of their environment that demanded a physical fitness of all the hunters unimpaired by needless injury. Now it was a rule that they adhered to, some of them vaguely sensing the nature of the seed from which it had grown, none of them curious or concerned enough to even begin to try and make the identification.

The lion continued to inch forward, his eyes on the young girl. Proximity to humans had dulled his instinctive fear of them to a certain extent, and the remnants of it were now swamped beneath the excitement that had sprung from watching the hunting of that strange single feathered bird. The fragile beauty of the naked girl held no meaning for him. His heart began to beat harder, the pumping blood feeding strength to the massive muscles of his body.

Tsonomon struck at the shuttle. He feinted to the left, and then with a quick twist of his wrist sent it flying in the other direction. Pxui had anticipated the move, and before the shuttle left his father's stick he was already moving away from the rest of the players. When he saw that his guess had been correct, his satisfaction came bursting from him in a shout of triumph.

The lion heard his voice and froze. The sound of it smashed through the barrier of his concentration. He felt a sudden spurt of fear shoot through him as his eyes singled out and held the boy, and the memory of smoke and flame fled frighteningly through the charged alertness of his mind. His fear was also accompanied by the warmth of a special recognition.

In that same brief instant of time his attention was once again captured by the flight of that strange bird. He exploded from the crouch in which he had been and shot forward. Out of the corner of his eye Pxui saw the charging lion. He froze in petrified disbelief, as did all the other players.

To his astonishment the lion went past him, missing him by no more than a few feet. He saw it leap into the air and clout the descending shuttle.

The lion came down awkwardly, stumbling before he regained his balance. He pounced on the shuttle and bit into the seed.

An expression which was almost human in its incredulity replaced the savagery in his eyes. He tongued the broken remnants of the nut from his mouth.

He turned to stare at Pxui with a look of haughty disdain, and then he limped off with his head held high and flopped down beside the thorn bush in the warmth of the evening sun.

A moment of hushed silence followed his departure. The hunters stared at him, and then they turned to stare at each other in silent, wide-eyed wonder.

In the days which followed, no one was able to decide who had been the first to burst into laughter, or who was the first to fall over onto his back and squirm and thrash the air with his legs in the helplessness of mirth.

18

WITH HER GRUBBING stick of iron wood Xhabbo deftly unearthed a dark brown nut. It was about the size of a golf ball. She brushed the sand and dirt from it and held it out to Pxui.

He took it from her and cracked the thin shell and stripped it away from the flesh. They were delicious when roasted, but even raw they were tasty. He bit into it, savouring the nutty, slightly bitter flavour, and then he passed it back to her.

The winter was gone, and the heat of the summer was on them. Even now, in the evening, the earth and the sky still trembled from the assault of the burning day.

The boy glanced about, but he could see the lion nowhere. He had taken to calling him just before feeding him, imitating the sounds made by the hoofs of the eland.

It was a creature of the desert, the eland, and when it walked its toes spread, the hoof flattening and becoming wider to prevent it sinking too deeply into the sand. When it lifted its foot, the toes snapped together with a characteristic click.

The boy stretched his mouth, and working his tongue against his palate gave a perfect imitation of the sound. Moments later the lion came into view from behind some scrub. The animal advanced to within about fifteen feet of him. He studied the boy, his eyes alert and alive with curiosity and anticipation, and then after a while he sank down on his haunches and then slowly flattened right out.

The wound had healed slowly, and there was no pain now, but he still limped, as he would limp for the rest of his life. The delicate metatarsals which the trap had broken had mended, but they had knitted crookedly.

He could walk now, and he could run, but the great frightening speed of his charge was a thing of the past, and his movements no longer had their old grace and power and rhythm.

"I see it with my eyes, and they tell me it is so," Xhabbo said. "But even with my eyes, I cannot believe it."

"I have fed him, and that is why he follows me when I call."

"And have I not fed him as well?" she demanded. "Yet he does not come when I make the eland sound."

"Perhaps he knows me better," the boy murmured, and then quickly changing the subject: "Let us rest a while."

He sank down in the shade of a small bush, and he lay on his side. He was only barely aware of the girl who came to rest beside him. He was thinking of what he had just said, about the lion knowing him better. If the animal did, that was the only indication he ever gave. He had tried as the days went by to get close enough to touch him, but always the lion warned him off with that savage note in his voice which he had come to recognize so well.

Thinking about it he felt puzzled and a bit resentful. He had gone hungry some days to feed him, and other times when both of them were empty he had trapped the small sand plovers, moving one of the brown speckled eggs outside the ring of leaves on the sand which was its nest. In pushing the egg back within the circle with its beak, the bird sprang the small noose through which it had to insert its head to reach the egg. They weren't much to eat, for a lion or a man, but it had been better than nothing, and the hungry animal had devoured them with relish.

While his leg had been healing the lion had taken to a dense thicket of thorn, lying up there during the heat of the day and sometimes right through the night, emerging every evening to wait patiently in the hopes of being fed.

When the bones in his leg mended and he could walk without pain he sometimes took to following the boy again, but there were days when Pxui made the eland sound in the hopes that he would follow him and the lion merely sat and stared at him with his far-seeing eyes that seemed to be gazing blindly into the distances of the desert but which were in fact missing nothing.

"How long has he been here now?" the girl asked.

"Two moons."

It didn't seem that long to her. The days had passed with the speed and radiance of a shooting star laying its trail of blue fire through the heavens.

"I hope the rains come soon."

"They had better," the boy said ominously. "Each day it becomes harder to suck the water."

He glanced out across the desert, at the burned and withered land. If their water failed, it would be a time of suffering, because even now the tsamma and the tubers were becoming more and more scarce.

Into his mind there came a picture of the swamplands. He had been there once as a child, and it was very far back in his memory. But it was a place of fever and sickness, of red and black strangers, and they had never gone back again. He pointed unerringly to the north, seeing again in his mind the vast stretches of reed and water.

"Have you been there, far, far to where the big water lies?"

"I have heard of it, but my eyes have not seen it."

"It is beautiful, but a strange and frightening place, and in the deep waters live they-who-scatter-their-dung." He was referring to the hippopotamus.

"Why do they do that?" she asked.

He was incredulous. "You do not know?"

She shook her head. He stared at her, as if she were a person of very strange appearance, as if he could not believe what he saw.

"Tell me," she begged him, for she dearly loved all stories.

He cleared his throat and sat up, and thinking about the wonder of it his own eyes sparkled and lit up. He cleared his throat again and began to speak.

"In the beginning, the hippopotamus asked if he could live in the water. To live——"

Interrupting, she said, "Whom did he ask?"

"Dxui, of course," he retorted scornfully, and then went on again. "To live in the water was his greatest desire. He loved that water more than anything else on this earth, more than the stars he loved it, more even than the sun. But Dxui told him that such a thing was not possible, because he had such a great mouth, and eating with a huge mouth full of big teeth he would soon kill all the fish.

"He promised to eat nothing in the water, and in his promise he swore to come out each night and eat of the plants and grasses that grew near the water, but still he was not given permission to live in his beloved water, because God knew that the temptation to eat the fishes would be great, and in the water, being hidden deep in it, no one would know whether he had eaten the fishes or not.

"Then the hippopotamus had an idea, and he said he would come from the water each day and scatter his dung with his tail, so that all creatures could look to see if there were fish bones in his dung, or whether he had kept his promise.

"And Dxui gave him permission to live in the water. So he does it now, even as he has done it from the beginning. He comes from the water and scatters his dung, so that scattering it, all might know that he has kept his word."

For a while she stared at him in wonder, like a person confronted by something so mysterious and majestic that it was beyond mere words. After a while she began to nod slowly.

"His works are many," she murmured, and looking about her she saw the mark of his hand on everything her eye fell on and she came to marvel at it all over again. "And they are——"

She broke off suddenly and turned to stare at him in startled surprise as she felt his fingers biting deep into the flesh of her upper arm. The protest in her died before it could take shape. His forefinger was against his lips in a command for silence. She stiffened and peered in the direction which had riveted his gaze.

She saw nothing at first, but then the movement of its long delicate ears caught her attention and she made out the shape and form of the little steenbok. It was a hundred and twenty yards or so distant, as still as a statue except for its ears, and in the soft broken shadows of the bush beside which it stood it was perfectly camouflaged and almost invisible.

"Stay here!" the boy whispered.

He checked the direction of the wind, powdering a blade of dried grass between his thumb and forefinger and tossing it into the air. The buck was upwind from him, but there was not enough cover to enable him to make a direct approach. He glanced about quickly, taking in the lay of the land, and he saw immediately that he would have to circle out to the right and then close in on it.

The steenbok waggled its ears again, and then, head held high, it stepped out daintily from the concealment of the shadows. It walked a few yards and then paused to graze on the burned grass.

The boy was about to move off when he darted a quick look to where the lion had been resting. He was no longer there. He searched for the animal frantically, and just when he was about to dismiss the thought of him from his mind he saw him moving out from behind a small bush, inching his way forward to the next bit of cover, his belly hugging the ground. The lion was making his own stalk, moving on the opposite arc to the one the boy intended travelling.

The beast was already about half-way to his objective, and at first Pxui was horrified and dismayed lest he should spoil his own chances of making a kill. But then it came to him that the lion was himself a hunter, and he felt a thrill of excitement shoot through him. It was, to his knowledge, the first time that the lion had set out to kill since his leg had healed.

With a final glance at the stalking animal he set off at a crouch. He said a few quick words in his mind to the Steenbok Spirit, asking him not to stand behind him and spoil his aim when he shot by pulling at his arm. They were small and beautiful creatures, too innocent and trusting by far, and so to protect them they had a very great magic, and this magic was in the shape of a person who stood behind the hunter and spoiled his aim. He knew it was the truth, because he had shot at them so many times and missed for no apparent reason.

The lion crept forward. He worked from one bit of cover to the next, inching his way closer. He moved as silently as a shadow through the grass, and an old excitement began to grow in him.

The heat of the earth was against his belly, and grass stubble and scrub pricked and clawed at him, but he was totally oblivious to the discomfort of it.

He was doing again what he had been born and trained to do, killing to survive, doing what his strength and the terrible armament of his teeth and claws had been fashioned for.

He slid into position behind the last bit of cover that was between himself and the browsing steenbok. A small swarm of flies buzzed round his head, but he paid them no heed. His big yellow eyes glowed, and the deadly concentration in them was frightening to behold.

The muscle in his haunches moved and tightened. He launched himself. He went straight over the small bush behind which he had been crouched, and the sudden explosion of his steel-sprung muscles catapulted him more than thirty feet forwards in a single bound.

He hit the ground, and even as the great propulsive muscles in his back legs were bunching to hurl him forward again over the last few yards and onto the back of the little steenbok, his crippled leg gave way beneath the weight of his body and he stumbled and went down.

For a moment the steenbok stared in blank and paralysed astonishment, then it whirled and fled. It ran about fifty yards, a fawn brown blur like a shadow dancing over the land, and then it halted and turned to look back, its delicate pointed ears standing straight up and alert.

It heard the startling twang of the bow. It was swivelling to face the direction from which the sound had come when it felt a blow against its neck and a heartbeat later the shearing burn of steel slicing into its flesh.

It screamed, a kind of bleat, the sound so human that the boy felt his hair stand on end. It took a step forward, its legs already jellied. Through its glazing eyes it saw the hunter ten feet away. It turned instinctively, but its movements were uncertain.

It fell, but it wasn't really aware that it had fallen. Its legs kicked and thrashed for a while, and in its dimming mind the desert sand fled beneath its dainty drumming hoofs.

The boy strode forward and paused beside his kill, looking down at it. There was no excitement in him now, only the relief that it was over, that he had shot well and shot truly and could return with the hunter's gift.

"Pxui!"

He heard the warning in her voice, the fear and agitation. He spun about. He saw the lion coming towards him at a fast trot. The black tufted tail was stiff and stretched out horizontally. The rounded ears were laid back against his head, and his eyes were hot and savage with frustration.

The boy plucked the spear from his quiver. Fear struck at him, knotting his belly. He didn't have a chance, and he knew it. He wanted to turn and run, but he held his ground. It was his kill, and no one else had the right to it.

"Get back!" he screamed, fear and anger distorting his voice. "It is mine."

He saw the lion halt a little way from him, and as he met and stared into the fierce glowing eyes a change came over the animal that was so startlingly abrupt that Pxui wondered at first whether it was a trick of his mind and his imagination or whether it had really happened.

The lion started forward again. The ferocity in his eyes had been replaced by a definite warmth and recognition. The boy was still in a state of shocked and disbelieving ambivalence when the huge head lifted and rubbed against his shoulder. He felt the wash of his breath against his face, and his nose and throat filled with the stinking carnivorous stench of the breath.

The head continued to rub against his shoulder, and he felt the stiff bristles of the whiskers scratching against his own smooth skin.

The force of the caress almost pushed him off balance. For a few moments he was too stunned to think or move, but then he reached out and ran his fingers through the coarse mane.

He heard the sudden loud rumbling purr start up, and then the animal was moving past him and Pxui felt the vibrations of the lion's pleasure drumming through his leg as he brushed past and rubbed himself against him and then turned to stand and stare at him with a look of anticipation in his eyes.

He drew his knife and bent swiftly. He opened the belly of the steenbok with one quick pass of the knife. He gutted it rapidly, taking out the guts and the stomach, the lungs, the liver, the heart and everything else. He scooped up the bloody mass and heaved it all to the lion, and then he picked up the small carcass and backed away.

The lion fell on the offal and began to feed instantly. He watched in silence, and then after a while he became aware of Xhabbo who had walked up noiselessly to stand beside him.

"Did you see it?" he breathed. "Did you see it with your own eyes, the thing that he did?"

"There was fear in my heart, for I thought in my heart that he was going to kill you."

"I thought it too." He was silent for a while, and then he went on, his voice rising with excitement. "Did you see him jump? Oh it was pretty, oh, oh. He leaped from the grass where he was down on his belly, and he went as fast as an arrow from my bow."

"I saw him fall."

"He stumbled a little," the boy said. "It could happen to anyone."

She eyed him curiously, and then her face hardened. "He tried to kill, and he could not."

"No, no," the boy protested. "He drove the game towards me, as he has done before."

"It was only by chance that the little buck ran to where you were," she went on remorselessly. "He tried, but he could not kill."

"I tell you it is not so."

"One day you will go hungry," she said bleakly. "He will try to kill and frighten the game away, and your belly will be empty."

"He will learn about his leg," the boy said stubbornly, but he was unable to meet her grave and penetrating stare. "It is only a matter of learning again."

She shrugged and returned her attention to the feeding lion, not bothering to reply. The boy bent and pulled the arrow head from the slender neck of the carcass. He fitted it back to the shaft and returned the arrow to his quiver.

"Will you speak of it?" he asked abruptly.

"What?"

"That he—stumbled."

A look of compassion came to her face. "Not if you do not want it so."

"Thank you," he said, and then after a pause he went on hesitantly: "Perhaps—we could even say that he killed the little buck himself. There is truth in it, because in a way he helped me to kill it."

"And hearing such a thing, do you think others will feel more nicely towards the beast?"

"I do not care how they feel," he said harshly.

"Then why do you wish to make them believe that the honey bird does not like honey?"

"It is for him."

"What does he know or care?" she asked scornfully. "As long as his belly is filled."

"You do not know. He feels, he understands, that he is not liked or wanted. In his eyes you can see it, in his beautiful eyes it is there to be seen."

"He has stolen your shadow," the girl wailed softly, and there was a superstitious fear in her voice, and also a vein of disgust.

"Will we say it?" the boy persisted doggedly.

"And the wound of the arrow?"

"I will cut."

"No one will be deceived."

"The neck and the head, from behind the wound of the arrow."

She was shocked and indignant. "You would waste all that meat?"

"It will not be wasted, I will cut the poison away and feed the rest to him."

She stared at him incredulously for a while and then shook her head in a gesture of defeat. "Do what you will."

"And you?"

She saw how bright and alert his eyes were, and with the sure unerring instinct of a woman she knew that it involved more than just
the deception about the lion. Her resolution wavered and then broke,
and in that lost moment of its breaking she experienced again a brief
and black foreboding.

"I will say," she said quietly, and she saw his lips part as he hung
on her words, as if he were in pain, "that I saw the lion kill."

She saw the tension run out of him, and the look he gave her was
overflowing with gratitude. She watched him draw his knife, and
then squat beside the body of the buck and take it by the pointed
ears.

19

DAY AFTER DAY the earth shimmered and danced and seemed to
writhe in upon itself in an attempt to escape from the fire of the sun
which burned malignantly and without mercy in the heat-shocked
sky.

The tsamma were all gone, and the tubers and bulbs were scarcer
and more difficult to find. The game began to move away, and more
often than not the exhausted hunters came home empty-handed to
throw themselves down and recover in the shade.

Daily they searched for signs of rain, but the cloudless skies mocked
them with their emptiness. They watched for the lightning, but it did
not come.

A nameless unease grew steadily, deep within them, and the suffering of the scorched and thirsty earth became their own anxiety and
pain. Their hidden water held, but it was becoming more and more
difficult to suck to the surface.

The boy sensed the desperation of the land, but he did not feel it
too deeply within himself. He was busy carving a bow. It was about
six inches long, and he carved it painstakingly and carefully from a
sliver of springbuck bone.

He worked the bone beautifully, with all of his skill and love and
talent, ornamenting it with rings that he notched into it and stained
black with the juices from a root. He strung it with a length of sinew,
and then after that he busied himself with the arrows.

He made four of them altogether, although he only needed one for
his purpose. But he was a hunter, and he had to keep faith with his
knowledge and his spirit.

The arrows were made from the dried stems of a grass that grew in places by the water course. These too he decorated elaborately, and when they were as beautiful as he could make them he fashioned a quiver for the minute shafts from the hollow quill of a porcupine.

Like the bow with which he hunted and killed, the miniature he had made would also be used to hunt. Not to kill however, but to make his declaration and, if it were accepted, to go on from there and create.

In his mind and his imagery he thought of himself as a bow strung by the woman of his choice, the pair of them together shooting the arrow into the distances to create new life, the arrow which was the slender shining spirit of his male self.

It was an arrow which was lost forever, but only in that loss, in that dying, could life be created, just as the full moon had to die before it could be reborn in the shape of a strung bow.

All he needed now was the courage to use the little bow he had made with so much care and love, and an auspicious moment in which to send the tiny arrow to its mark.

That moment came two days later.

20

THEY HAD KILLED a young eland cow in the early morning, a group of five hunters and the lion which had refused to be driven away and had followed Pxui. If it hadn't been for the lion, they would have had to spoor the wounded cow for hours on end, waiting for the poison to do its work.

They had closed in on the herd, four of them, a young bull and three cows. Two of them had managed to creep silently to within range and shoot. One of the arrows found its mark.

The herd had panicked and thundered away, the bull in the lead. The wounded cow had passed close by where the lion lay crouched. He had exploded from the brush and landed with his forepaws over her withers in a single bound. He had dragged her to the ground and bitten into her throat. She was still kicking and floundering and dying slowly under the stranglehold when the hunters came up and finished her off with their spears.

In their mutual excitement, both men and the lion had forgotten about each other. When the eland was finally dead, the lion became aware of the men once more. He growled furiously, his ears laid back and his eyes alight with a black savagery.

They shouted and screamed at him, but he would not move. They tried fire, but he held his ground in snarling defiance. Thinking that the animal might heed him, the boy went forward alone.

He thought he saw a recognition in the eyes, but it was difficult to be certain, because they were still ablaze with a savage fire.

The body of the eland separated them. He was a few feet from the carcass when the lion sprang at him and knocked him over. The impact drove the breath from him and jarred every bone in his body.

He lay there on the ground, looking up into the snarling face of the lion. He thought he was going to die, and in the hot breath of the animal which washed against his face he smelled the stench of decay and death.

He was dazed, numbed with shock. The lion's mouth was open, the lips peeled back in a fearful snarl. He saw the teeth, the three big yellow fangs and the one that was broken. There were hair-thin lines in it like the cracks in old china.

The lion lowered his head. The boy steeled himself for the bite. He felt a tongue rasp roughly over his face, and then with a low grunt the lion lifted from his chest the paw with which he had pinned him down and moved away. The beast did not return to the kill, but sat down some way from it.

Pxui struggled up off the sand, and the others helped him to his feet. There was awe in their eyes, and fear. He was shaken, but not really hurt. There were claw marks on his chest. They seeped blood, but they were shallow. When he thought of what the animal could have done to him, he could only marvel silently. He began to love him then as he had not done before, this lion that could have taken his life.

They gutted the eland quickly, and fed the offal to the lion. They butchered out the meat, and then leaving Pxui and the lion to guard the kill they carried home the first load, their legs rubbery under the weight.

A little way before they reached their camp they heard the voices of the women and the children lifted in a song of praise. For the hunters who had killed the eland, and for the kindness of the animal which had given them its flesh. They had known already, with the telepathic perception that plucked the waiting chords within their breasts and set them trembling into images, that their hunters had killed an eland.

The women and the children followed the hunters back. They helped to carry the meat, and making one trip after another they eventually brought it all back.

That night they danced the Eland Dance. In the centre of the clearing they had made, a fire blazed. The women were gathered on one side of the clearing, the men on the other, the musicians in the centre, a little to one side of the fire.

Tsonomon was one of them, and he played his jew's harp. There were two others: one with a three-stringed lyre that had for its sounding-box the shell of a desert tortoise, and the last of the trio with a flute made from the reeds which grew by the river courses just shortly after the rains.

The women began humming, beating time to the rhythm of the music with their feet and clapping with their hands. They moved forward from the edge of the clearing, advancing slowly, and the firelight glittered on their oiled skins and on their necklaces of egg shell and wood.

Their bodies swayed and quivered, and the pounding of their feet grew faster. The men also began to dance and sway, but they moved with a deliberate restraint, very slowly, mocking the women and exciting them to a greater frenzy.

But no sooner had the men started forward than the women began to back away, to the edge of the clearing and then beyond it where they were hidden from sight. And from the darkness their voices rose in song.

The music rose and fell, a challenge and a capitulation. The women came from the shadows again, swaying and writhing, and the men in their turn backed away into the darkness beyond the light of the fire.

The tempo of the music increased, beating faster and faster, the notes thin and stretched, and then with a sudden ecstatic moan the men burst from the darkness and surged forward in a mindless wave, their feet pounding with a rhythm that made the ground tremble.

When the spirit of Dxui first quickened the earth, he took the shape of a praying mantis. In the beginning he was an egg, in the hot bed of the earth. The egg hatched, and the crawling grub was miraculously transformed into the beautiful creature of long legs and transparent mottled wings.

And then Mantis himself began to create, and of all the creatures he made he loved Eland most dearly. He had made the greatest of all antelopes, the strongest of them all, but he was also more noble and gentle than the others, and for these qualities and for his regal beauty, the Bushmen loved him.

When Mantis had finished creating, he mated, and after he had mated he was devoured by his wife and died. And after his death came his children, who themselves went on to create. The circle was complete, perfect and without contradiction.

The dance continued, and it pantomimed the life of the great antelope and also their own lives. They showed him as a member of the herd, with his cows and his children with him. They danced him as he courted, and Pxui, with his face frozen in an expressionless mask, began to circle Xhabbo.

The eland disappears with his cow to mate alone in the fastness of the bush, away from all eyes. So did Xhabbo move out of the circle of fire and into the shadows in the same way that the eland did.

Pxui followed her, drawing the little bow from the pouch at his waist. He had stained the tips of the diminutive arrows with a special love potion. He fitted one of the arrows, and as he swayed ecstatically to the music there in the dark broken shadows he fired the shaft into her rump.

She squealed in startled surprise. She whirled, and she saw the boy crouched two feet from her with the miniature bow in his hands. He was as tense as a leopard waiting to spring.

She reached for the arrow in her rump. She plucked it out, and a pin point of blood flowered and then broke to course a little way down her gleaming flesh.

She stared at him, their eyes locked in a tense and mutual appraisal. She smiled suddenly, radiantly, and put the small arrow away inside her own loin skin.

The boy breathed out raggedly, almost shattered with relief. She had accepted him, and not broken and destroyed the arrow which was his spirit and his longing.

The dancers moved back into the clearing, and the mime enacted the twilight of the bull, when he became old and lost his strength and was challenged by the younger bulls of the herd.

He was driven away, out into the night, the symbolic banishment. The women watched, their faces mask-like and in a state of shocked suspension, but then the young men came forward, and with a great tenderness put their arms around the shoulders of the women, and the fear left them, because they knew that this was the justice of all life and nature, and that only the young could take it further forward.

The musicians paused for a few moments, resting, gathering their strength, and then they began to play again. It was a strange urgent music, and as it drove its beat into the night three of the young hunters danced into the middle of the clearing.

It was a new dance, a ballet of improvisation. For a few moments the spectators were puzzled, but then they understood, and their voices rose in a murmur of awe and appreciation and then died out into silence.

They watched in rapt concentration as the lion pulled down the eland and throttled it. They saw the hunters assist with the killing, and then the lion roared and drove them from the kill.

The music grew softer and softer till it was almost inaudible. It started up again, hesitantly at first, growing in volume and confidence.

Watching the dance, Pxui once again saw himself walking towards the lion. It was so real that he felt fear clutch at his heart, and then there right before his eyes he saw himself being knocked to the ground, with the lion savage and omnipotent above him.

There was a shocked stillness amongst the spectators, and then abruptly they sighed with relief as the man who was taking the part of the lion tossed his head and walked away.

After a few moments of stunned silence he heard their voices lifting in praise and adulation. He was conscious of their eyes on him, and he felt a great exaltation surging through his breast. He knew then that he would be immortal, as long as the memory of his people lived, as long as they continued to sing and dance.

It filled him with a sense of god-like power, but at the same time he experienced a strange humility that was combined with a vague uneasiness.

They began another dance, all of them, and this time only the men moved away, their small bodies swaying ecstatically as they danced their way out of the firelight and into the deep shadows of the night beyond the clearing.

The music became solemn, and the flute played alone for a while. The notes sounded like the cry from a pierced heart. Slowly the women began to sway to the hypnotic pain-filled lament of the flute, and then they began to sing, their voices soft, filled with the same pain and a deep desperate longing.

> "The heat of the sun
> Burns the earth dry,
> I sit by the fire,
> Alone I cry.

> All through the day
> For the rain to fall,
> All night my heart cries
> For my hunter to call
> And take me away."

There was a dead silence after they had finished singing, and then from the darkness the voices of the men rose, swelling with a gentle triumph as they came from the shadows.

> "Listen to the wind,
> Woman by the fire,
> The rain is coming
> You must not fear,
> Listen to your heart
> Your hunter is here."

They joined hands, and they moved round the fire, their almost naked bodies gleaming like burned gold. They lifted their eyes, searching the star-studded heavens. But there were no clouds, and no lightning flickered anywhere.

21

THE NEXT NIGHT they lay side by side, the boy and the girl, in a shallow depression she had scooped in the sand, beyond the reach of firelight. The night sky seemed to throb and pulse with the light of the African stars. On the ground beside the boy lay his spear.

His left arm pillowed her head, and his right arm lay over her belly, holding it tight. He rubbed his cheek against her face, and he moaned softly with the heat of the fire that was in his loins. She turned, pressing herself to him, and he felt the female softness of her body, strange and wondrous and so different to his own. The rain and the withered desert was only a memory in his mind.

She pressed her mouth to his, and she licked his lips and then his face, and he felt her tongue hot and velvet smooth against his closed lids.

"Come, my hunter," she whispered. "Give me the arrow of your body, before the heat in my heart burns it to white ash as the fires turn the wood to nothing."

He drew her closer, trembling, a great aching for her in his body and in his mind. For a moment he was tempted, almost yielded to the fierce urge, but then he shook his head and drew away from her slightly.

"Oh Xhabbo, oh, oh," he murmured. "We are not yet man and wife."

"What matter?" she cried softly, driven by the urgency of her own desire. "You are the bow, and I the string which will drive the arrow of ourselves into the days beyond. For you there is no other string, for me no other bow."

"I know it," he said softly, his breath coming in short gasps. "But it is not right."

"How can you say that, oh my Pxui?" she rebuked him hotly, "when you will be my hunter, and I will be your woman."

"The duiker," he whispered. "I haven't yet driven the duiker to your place."

There was a tremor of uncertainty in his voice. If others had done it, so would he, but until he had actually gone through the ordeal himself, he could never be absolutely sure.

It was the custom, as old as the people of his tribe, that before a man could take a woman for his wife, he had to prove both to her parents and to her that he could provide. The proof involved running down a duiker, spooring it over the burning desert sands, keeping on its heels till time and terror exhausted it and the hunter was able to drive it staggering to the place where his prospective bride waited. Sometimes it took days, and he had seen the looks of blank and numbed exhaustion on the faces of others who had run the terrible race.

She was silent for a few moments, chained and made fearful by the bonds of a tradition that was as old as the beginning of time, but then she spoke again, driven by the urgency of her ripened body.

"Are you not the hunter who has faced and freed a mighty lion? No other proof is needed."

"The people would not think that. And I do not know, and so I must drive a duiker to your place, so that in my heart I can be sure that we will live."

"You live now, you are already a great hunter. What need is there to wait?" She drew a quivering breath, and gathering her courage she uttered the blasphemy. "I have never believed that it is the true way. It is but a game which the hunters play to prove their manhood to themselves. It means nothing."

For a moment he was shocked, but then in a flash of sudden intuition he saw through the ritual to the heart of the matter.

"If it proves it to the hunter, that is enough," he said. "His spirit draws strength from it, like green wood does from the fire. The desert is like the fire, and I am still wood that is green."

"I do not wish that we wait, oh my Pxui," she said softly, stubbornly.

He shook his head, and there was a finality in the movement which she did not miss. "I cannot," he said simply, and there was a longing and a sadness in his voice.

She sat up suddenly. Her words were filled with despair. "The rains do not come, the game has all gone. Where will you find a duiker to drive to my place?"

"We will wait."

Xhabbo sprang to her feet, stood glaring down at him, her body trembling with her anger and her unreleased tension. "Then you will wait forever."

He reached out, and he took her by the hand, and with one swift jerk he threw her to the ground and pinned her body with his own. She struggled fiercely, but after a few moments her body grew limp and motionless beneath the iron of his own. He rolled off her and cradled her in his arms.

"The desert is a long time, oh Xhabbo," he whispered. "Let us be patient."

"And if the rains never come?" she breathed, her heart beginning to beat a little slower.

"They always come," he replied.

They lay in silence again, looking up at the cloudless skies, the stars mocking them with their clarity and brightness.

22

AS THE DAYS passed and the rains did not come, the sun-blasted land took on an aura of desolation. The parched and withered earth seemed to cringe before the daily onslaught of the sun, and the desperation of her plight communicated itself to her children.

They became listless and apathetic, and their bellies were never full. The game came, but it moved on swiftly without lingering, because there was nothing to keep it there.

One night lightning flickered far away, low down on the western

horizon. The next morning, a group of eight of them had vanished.
They departed silently, picking up their meagre belongings and leaving, drawn inexorably towards the lightning and the promise of its
rain.

Tsonomon felt the magnetic pull of it, but he curbed the growing
hunger of his spirit. It had only been a small lightning, and very,
very far away.

The next night lightning flared again, and in the morning there
were another eight souls less. They had said their farewells quietly
in the night, and the next day they were gone, swallowed up in the
burning sea of the desert. They would survive somehow, and perhaps
some of them would die, but they had lived all of their lives against
such odds, and that made it easier. The desert was not an enemy to
them: it was simply an environment. They knew what it could do
for them, and also what it could do to them.

"Let us go to the lightning, oh my father," Pxui urged. "It is
there, and it pulls me, and I see on your face that it has also eaten
of your flesh."

"We will wait, for it is still far, far away," the man replied, and in
the rising inflection of his voice there was mirrored the vast burning
distances of the wasted earth.

"If the lightning comes tonight again, Xhabbo will be leaving,"
the boy said. "Let us go with them."

The man smiled, not unkindly. "Do you know how far it is, the
nearest place where we can drink the water from the sands?"

"Eight days."

"Fast walking."

"We will live," the boy said confidently.

"And struggle."

"But Xhabbo and her family wait for the lightning," the boy protested. "If it comes, they will go."

"Let them."

The boy was silent for a while, and then he looked away, out into
the desert. He began to speak, but he could hardly hear the words
for the pounding of his heart.

"I made a bow, and I shaped it with my hands and with my
love. The arrow that I shot, it did not miss. This arrow with which I
did not miss my aim, she pulled it from her flesh and kept it.
Xhabbo has it, this arrow that I touched her with from far away."

The man was incredulous for a moment, but then he smiled and
put his arm around the shoulder of his son. "I did not know."

"If it comes tonight, let us follow it in the morning with the others."

"Let us wait and see," the man replied. "Let us see how far it is, and if it is strong enough to try and frighten the eye of a man who looks into it."

There was no lightning that night, or the night after, but the next evening, when the still murderous heat of the day had passed and Pxui was down in the river bed with Xhabbo and some of the others who were also filling their shells with water, what they had feared for so long became a reality. The water gave out.

After the first shock of fear had passed they dug frantically up and down the river bed, but nowhere could they suck up any water. Pxui still had three empty shells to fill, but they remained empty.

When the realization finally sank home that the water was truly gone, there was a moment of naked dread as they searched each other's eyes. But then that passed, and it was followed by resignation and acceptance. All of them had known thirst before, and most of them had survived.

There was a tension in their music that night, but still it eased the clutching anxiety in their hearts. After a while it made them forget entirely about their pedicament, and they sang and played late into the night.

They made no plans, for there were none to make. They had been through it before, and the coming ordeal did not hold the paralysing poison of terror.

They set off in the morning, when the skies were still smudged and formless with the pre-dawn light. The men in front, the women and the children behind. There were eleven of them altogether. Pxui and his parents, Xhabbo and her parents, and the old, old man who was her paternal grandfather. And there was Exxwa and his wife, the woman with a babe on her hip and her six-year-old son walking beside her.

They set off in single file, into the waiting desert. In its generosity it was lavish, but periodically it called a reckoning. Then they had to pay the price, and the coin in which they paid was life itself. They knew this.

Behind the men and the women and the children, about forty yards to the rear, limped the lion. He also knew the desert intimately.

PART TWO

I

JANNIE WAS feeling pretty good when he came out of the Station Bar. He wasn't drunk, but he wasn't feeling any pain either. He paused for a moment, just inside the doorway, reluctant to leave the shade and face the inferno of the dusty sun-blasted street.

A car went past, lifting a swirl of dust. He glanced at his own pick-up, half tempted to drive it across the street and down the few yards to the store. He changed his mind and began to walk, because he knew it would be even worse behind the wheel, an oven of metal and scorching fabric.

He heard the north-bound mail train whistle from the railroad yard just the other side of the street. It was a long-drawn-out whistle, full of metallic impatience. A short period of silence followed the demand, and then a moment later the whistle blasted again, a staccato hoot of triumph that was drowned in the hiss and roar of escaping steam as the train began to pull out and in the clank of the con rods on the big driving wheels.

He stepped out into the sunlight. He felt the sweat beginning to pop on his back under his shirt, and he hurried down the street and into the store. It was roofed with corrugated iron, and it was almost worse inside than it was out, except that it was a heat without the oppressive weight of the sun behind it, and that was something to be thankful for.

He paused a moment, letting his eyes adjust to the gentler light. He sniffed appreciatively once or twice. The compound odour of hides and grain and iron mingled with the smell of the human sweat which had produced it. He strode to the counter, some of the Africans greeting him, moving aside to let him pass, others who did not know him staring open mouthed.

"How's it, Barney?" Jannie said.

Barney Wierzynski glanced up from the ledger he was working on, peering over his spectacles suspiciously. The habitual wariness of his face gave way to a delightful smile.

"Aggh, Jannie," he exclaimed, in the thick guttural accents that not even forty-five years of the Protectorate had erased. "What you doing in this beautiful city of ours, hey?"

They shook hands across the counter, two men who were pleased to see each other again. They weren't friends, in the normal sense of the word, but there was an indefinable empathy between them, based on a mutual liking and respect.

"Making it more beautiful, what else?"

"Ja, Ja," chuckled Barney.

He took a handkerchief from his pocket and wiped the beading moisture from his forehead and shining scalp. He folded it again carefully and put it back into his pocket.

"When is the rain coming, tell me that?" he went on.

"It's bad," Jannie agreed. "I can't remember when it was worse."

"We always say that, every time the rains do not come, but this time I think it is the truth," Barney said. "Your water, how is it?"

"I'm still pumping, thank Christ, but the grass, Barney, it isn't there any more. They're mostly feeding on scrub now, and that doesn't put any fat on them."

"It's terrible, terrible, no money anywhere, everyone waiting for the rain."

"We'll just have to wait and hope."

"Ja—and now, Jannie, is there anything I can get for you?"

"I want two boxes of .375," Jannie said. "Solid and soft."

"You going out to the desert again, to hunt?"

"In this weather? I'd have to be crazy."

"What for you want the ammunition then?"

"I'm almost out. I like to keep a stock in hand."

Barney stared silently at the younger man. The sprawling store might have been empty except for the two of them, so intense was his appraisal. He began to shake his head. The simple gesture conveyed a depth of sadness and concern.

"Ach, Jannie, you are not thinking again of that lion that got out of your trap?"

"He's dead by now, that's for sure."

"But inside you are still wondering, not so?" Barney persisted softly. "You are asking yourself about it all over again, still hoping that you will find out."

"I've forgotten about him," Jannie said flatly. "Long ago."

"So you say," Barney went on. "But there is nothing there now in the desert, for man or beast. Only the heat and the dust and the flies."

Jannie raised a hand and fingered the right side of his face. He did it without knowing he had done it. "I told you, I'm low, Barney, that's all."

"All the time you spend out in the bush," Barney remonstrated. "Go to Johannesburg, Bulawayo, the bright lights. Get yourself a girl and forget about the desert at this time of the year."

Jannie grinned. "What's wrong with our own fair girls?"

"Nothing, nothing, you understand me," Barney said hastily. "I would be the last one, but sometimes a man needs to meet a nice girl, his own kind."

"You're getting old, Barney. You're starting to dream."

"For myself I am too old to dream. I dream for others now."

There was a moment of sadness on his face, as if he were remembering, thinking of things which might have been. It was there only an instant, but Jannie did not miss it. He punched the older man lightly on the shoulder.

"Go and dream up those boxes of cartridges," he said.

Barney shook his head, as if he were coming back from a long way off. "Jannie, Jannie."

He pronounced it Yannie, and the way he said it, it was a benediction and a lament. He went to the big old-fashioned safe inside the glass-partitioned cubicle that served as his office. He unlocked it and swung it open. He took out the two boxes of ammunition, and marked the withdrawal in the ledger which he was required to keep by law.

It was another bit of foolishness. In the old days a man didn't have to keep records of every cartridge he sold. He sighed philosophically and locked the door of the safe. He walked back, limping on his left leg.

"I will write it down for your account, Jannie?"

"You might be taking a chance."

Barney frowned, his eyes narrowing and becoming alert. Behind the banter he had detected the gravity it was intended to hide.

"For what?" he asked. "For what will I be taking a chance?"

Jannie smiled. "On your money, Barney."

"On my money? How is it that I take a chance on my money with you? Some people, yes, but not with you."

"You know how it is when you're hunting," Jannie went on, teasing him, trying to keep a straight face without much success. "Anything can happen, you know that."

For a moment the old man was shocked, but then he laughed. "You make sure nothing ever happens. I am a Polish Jew, and you know what I am like for collecting my debts. You would not want to be haunted by a greedy old man, would you?"

"No, and I won't give you the chance."

The old man nodded happily. He wrapped the boxes of amunition in brown paper, and then taped the folds flat. He edged the parcel across the counter, reluctant to let go of it, because he wanted to talk some more.

"Money, money, money," he said. "The older I get, the more I want. That is madness, no? Maybe it makes an old man feel safer. It is a lie, but it helps." He sighed heavily. "I should have had it when I was young, that is the time for a man to have money."

Jannie slid a hand across the counter, towards the boxes of amunition. "The bright lights?"

"Ja, Ja, the bright lights, the pretty girls. They blind a man, the lights and the girls, but what is life for, if it is not to allow yourself to be a little blind at times?"

"You're right," Jannie replied, but he wasn't thinking of it one way or the other, and his inching hand closed over the paper-wrapped parcel. "I'd best be getting along, Barney. It's a long, hot road."

"It's just terrible this heat." Barney relinquished his grip, and there was something forlorn in the way he watched Jannie pick it up and heft it for weight in his big hand. "Did I thank you for the last bag of biltong?" he asked abruptly.

"No."

"Jannie!"

"But someone delivered a case of Viceroy to my place by mistake."

The look of anxiety on Barney's face was replaced by one of mollification. "God, good, I would not want anyone else to be lucky."

"Okay, Barney, I'll be seeing you again."

"When will you be in?"

Jannie shrugged. "Two weeks maybe. I don't know."

"Go slowly."

"I will."

Jannie turned and walked out the door. For a moment, just as he stepped out onto the street, it seemed to Barney that the sun silhouetted his broad stocky figure in a blaze of light, and then he was gone, past the open doorway and out of sight.

Jannie glanced into the back of the pick-up. He checked over the various purchases he had made earlier in the morning. He inventoried them for a few moments, trying to remember if he had forgotten anything.

"Hey, mister man!"

The voice came from right behind. It startled him, and he threw a quick glance over his shoulder to make sure he hadn't been hearing things, and then seeing her there he turned slowly to face her.

"Jesus!" she exclaimed softly.

Involuntarily she began to back away, but she forced herself to halt. She couldn't keep her eyes off his face. She stared at it in awed fascination. The right side of it seemed to be slightly lower than the left, as if it had dropped somehow. It hadn't, but the puckered shiny scar tissue created that impression.

"Pardon me?" he said.

She had enormous eyes, and they were filled with a shocked and disbelieving incredulity. They were a greenish blue, and in the hot bright light the colour seemed to alternate, blue one moment, green the next, and in that first startled instant of mutual appraisal it was the only thing about her that registered with any force.

"Did you fall off a house, or what?"

He stiffened, almost imperceptibly. Unconsciously his right hand began to lift, but he checked it before it had moved more than an inch or two. His eyes bored into her, cold and bleak.

"No."

She tilted her head to one side, appraising his features with an undisguised and shameless frankness.

"No offence, mister man," she said eventually. "But it looks pretty awful."

For an instant he was shocked and angry, but then it passed and he found her directness refreshing. Most strangers politely and studiously ignored his disfigurement, making him even more conscious of it, or they embarrassed him with their patent uneasiness. He was aware that she was watching him with a nonchalance that concealed a poised alertness.

"It does, doesn't it?"

He grinned at her, and his face really became hideous, the shiny tissue stretched and twisted. She stared at him a moment longer, and then she smiled suddenly. It was a crooked sort of smile, but for a brief moment it transformed her face, making her look somehow young and vulnerable, but then it was gone, and the transition was so swift that he wondered whether he had imagined it all.

"How far are you going?" she asked.

"Ramabana."

"Where in God's name is that?"

"About forty miles after Serowe."

She shook her head. "I'm still no wiser. Where I want to get is Rhodesia, and then north again after that."

"That's a long way off," Jannie mused. "Why don't you get a train? You'll have to wait till this evening, though. The north mail pulled out a little while ago."

"Trains cost money, mister man," she informed him. "I've done okay so far lifting my thumb."

Jannie shrugged. "I'm sorry, I can't help you."

"You're not going north at all?" she asked. "As far as the next— town or anything? Every bit helps, and I don't much like staying still."

"I'm going west from here."

"Oh well——"

"I'm sorry."

"Thanks anyway," she said.

She gave him a sudden brittle smile just before she began to turn away, and in that moment he was struck by the weariness that showed briefly in her face.

"Wait!" he said, speaking impulsively, the word out before he had time to stop himself.

She stiffened slightly, then relaxed and swung back to face him. "Something troubling you, mister man?"

"If you like, I'll take you into Palapye," he said quickly. "It's the next station north, you might be able to pick up a lift to the border at Plumtree from there. Quite a few travellers stop overnight at Pala-pye."

"I thought you were going west?" she said, and her voice was dry and ironic.

"It'll only take me about forty miles out of my way. I can cut back into Serowe from there."

"Thanks, but I don't want any special favours."

"I just thought I'd try to help," Jannie said, and he shrugged and turned towards the pick-up.

"Mister man."

He paused, his hand on the door. "Yes?"

"Is it all right if I change my mind?"

He hesitated, but only because he was surprised. "Of course," he said quickly, and then after a moment: "Where's your luggage? Is it at the station?"

She hefted the small zipper bag she was carrying in her right hand. "This is it."

His eyebrows lifted fractionally, and he saw the crooked smile flit across her face again. He opened the door for her and held it. She noticed the other scars then, on his right arm and on his right thigh and leg. She got in and sat down, dumping her bag between her feet. A moment later she yelped in startled surprise as the plastic seat covers burned the underside of her thighs.

"Christ up a tree!" she swore.

"The seats get a bit hot," Jannie said apologetically.

He turned the ignition key and held it down. The engine turned over and caught almost immediately. He shifted into gear and drove forward.

In a few minutes the sprawl of the town had fallen behind. The road ahead was straight, the white gravel surface blinding in the sunlight. He kept the needle hovering round the fifty mark, but even the rush of wind through the windows didn't make much difference, because the air was hot and dry and heavy with dust.

"You really got chewed up, didn't you?" she commented.

"Yes."

"What happened, mister man?"

"The forge," he said. "I had an accident in my forge."

"You a smith?"

"It's a hobby, I like making things."

Behind the speeding truck the dust storm of its passage corkscrewed up into the air and was whipped backwards, completely obscuring visibility from the vehicle.

"It's hot and dry," she said, looking out the window, "but I love it, the emptiness, the miles of nothing on either side of the road."

"Ahh," he said softly. "You should see the desert."

"What desert?"

"The Kalahari."

"Who's interested in deserts?" she remarked. "Miles and miles of sand."

He shot a quick glance at her, full of hurt incredulity. "The Kalahari's not like that. It's got sand, certainly, but there's grass, miles of it in some places, all open, and then in other places there's bush so thick you couldn't get through it with a tank. It's got everything."

"That's a funny kind of desert."

"It's not really a desert, the way people think of one, miles of end-less sand dunes. It's just that there's no surface water there."

"So what's to do in this desert, that makes you so happy about it?"

She was so direct that he found it easy and pleasant to talk to her. "Well, I like to hunt, but it isn't only that. There's so much space out there, you get a sense of—freedom, as if nothing has changed in a thousand years."

Her laugh was ironic, almost harsh. "No one's ever free, not in this old world."

"I don't know," he replied. "Whenever I'm out there, I feel pretty free."

"Good for you."

He stole a glance at her. She had a fresh-looking mouth, as if it had been crushed and bruised into swollen life, but now it was twisted sardonically. He guessed that she couldn't have been more than about twenty, and it was somehow disturbing to see an expression of such cynical and ancient wisdom on her youthful face. He found himself becoming curious about her, against his will and his better judgement.

"Do you have much trouble getting lifts?"

She shot him an amused look and then laughed. "Not much. A man's always got ideas about a woman, so you can usually get a ride. You have to be careful, that's all."

"You could say the same thing for a woman."

She stared at him, a little surprised, and then she laughed again. "I guess you could, at that."

"Why did you change your mind?" he went on. "I mean, about coming with me."

"I told you, a girl has to be careful."

Her smile was mocking him, but he wasn't annoyed. If anything, he felt a little sorry for her, this ancient child who was also a woman.

"Aren't you, well, frightened, taking lifts from strangers, people you don't know?"

"Mister man, I'm always frightened. You tell me who isn't fright-ened in this bloody world. Still and all, you just carry on. That's what it's all about, isn't it?"

"It's not that bad, is it?"

"You're right," she answered abruptly, but the smile she flashed him was very brittle. "I was just kidding you on."

"I thought you were," he exclaimed, and for some reason he felt happy that it was so.

He had his eyes on the road, the speedometer needle steady on sixty-five, and he didn't see the wry amusement on her face, the sardonic curve to her mouth.

"Where are you from?" he asked.

"From where you picked me up."

"No, I meant——"

She cut him off. "I know what you meant. You're a straight kind of guy, I think, so I'll give you a straight answer."

"Yes?"

"I never answer questions like that, and a lot of other questions too."

For a moment he was startled by her blunt declaration, and then confusion and embarrassment followed. "I didn't mean to—pry."

"Stop playing with that mashed up face," she said abruptly, and there was a harshness in her voice. "You want to make it worse than it is?"

He snatched his hand down, angered by her rudeness. He shot a quick seething glance at her. The hot words died inside him. Her eyes were very steady, huge in her small face, mocking him, but gentle too. He returned his attention to the road, even more confused.

"So what's your racket, mister man?" she asked conversationally. "Besides shooting up all the elephants in this desert of yours?"

"There aren't any elephants out there," he replied stiffly.

"Oh, oh!" she exclaimed softly. "The man's got his knickers in a twist."

"I've what?"

"I mean you're angry, sitting up there all stiff and starched on your big white charger. Isn't that right?"

There was the barest hint of a smile on her lips, and in the face of it, he found his annoyance somehow ridiculous. And then he found himself smiling, mostly at himself.

"So what do you do?" she went on.

"I never answer questions like that."

"Touché!"

Her impudent grin somehow got through his defences. "I've got a farm, at Ramabana."

She glanced out the window, at the scorched scrub land which stretched as far as she could see. "You mean you can grow things, in this country?"

"You can, when it rains. But no, I mean cattle."

"Oh—a ranch."

"Same thing."

Off the road, in the bush, the first of the adobe rondavels began to appear. The walls were brown with mud wash, and the roofs were of thatch. Further on, the first of the European houses came into sight. Jannie braked, beginning to slow the truck.

"I'll turn off here to the right," he said. "I'll drop you off at the hotel. You might be able to pick up a lift, if you can't you can always stop over for the night."

"Is it expensive?"

"Three rand a day."

"Is that with meals?"

He nodded. "Good food, and all you can eat."

"Sounds like the place I've been looking for all my life."

Jannie slowed, swung the wheel hard over and turned off the road and then accelerated again. The road now was red earth, and it was inches deep in dust.

"What's your name?" Jannie asked.

"What do you want to know for? You'll never see me again."

He shrugged. "You're a person. It's nice to remember someone you've met by—a name."

She was silent for a while, and then abruptly, as if she were doing it against her will, she said, "Carol."

"I'm Jannie."

She shrugged indifferently, peering out through the window. He made a right turn again, just in front of the fenced railroad yard and brought the truck to a halt opposite the Palapye Hotel. He switched off the engine, and it was suddenly and startlingly silent, with the heat beginning to accumulate again.

She reached for her bag. She took it by the straps, but she did not lift it. "Well," she said, and there was something hesitant about the way it came out as if there were doubt and uncertainty in her now.

"I'm sorry that I'm not going any further," he said.

She smiled wryly. "Which being translated means, 'I've already gone out of my way for you, so get out and let me get on.'"

"No, I meant it."

"So why don't you take me to the next town, if you're all that sorry?"

He bit his lip. "Well—I've got quite a bit of work to do when I get back."

"You see," she said, but her voice was gentle. "It's just like I told you."

He stared at her pensively, somehow reluctant to let her go. "Okay," he said abruptly. "I'll take you into Francistown. Your chances of a lift should be even better from there."

For a moment her eyes softened, but then she grinned at him, wry and mocking and yet with a sadness buried somewhere beneath it all. She reached for the door, clicked the latch, pushed it open.

"There's just no way I could let you do that."

"It's no trouble, truly. I'd like to."

"Don't play with the face, mister man."

When he had guiltily lowered his hand she held her own out. He took it, and it felt very small and warm inside his own, a small animal in the cave of his fist.

"Thanks for the lift," she said, and then she withdrew her hand firmly. "And good luck with those elephants."

She climbed out of the truck. She stood there, her auburn hair picking up the hot reflections of the sun, staring at the quiet, lifeless hotel. There was no one to be seen anywhere. A mangy mongrel passed by, paused at the white-painted picket fence. It sniffed, cocked its leg, squirted a jet of urine and then hurried on.

"What time does it open?" she asked. "Or does it ever?"

He stared at her helplessly, a lost kind of feeling in him that he hadn't felt in many years. He glanced at his watch.

"Half an hour," he replied. "But you can go in and wait in the lounge or on the stoep. The manager should be up soon."

He opened the door on his side and got out. He walked round the high bonnet of the truck. He stopped in front of her.

"It's like a morgue," she said.

There was something lost-looking about her. "Do you have to be in Rhodesia soon?" he asked suddenly. "I mean, do you have to be there soon, on a certain day or—or anything?" His voice trailed away helplessly, and only the heat remained.

She shook her head absently, staring at the deserted stoep of the hotel. It was in gloom, behind the screening of gauze mesh.

"Christ, it really is a morgue."

He took a deep breath and then blurted the words out. "Why don't you come with me? I'll show you my place, where I live. You can spend a few days there, and I'll show you around. It's not much to look at now. It's dry, you see, but it's still beautiful, and——"

He broke off when he realized he was babbling. He felt suddenly very exposed and vulnerable, and he didn't like the feeling.

"The face," she said. "Leave it alone."

She started forward, past him, went through the white-painted gate and up the short walk to the stoep. She flipped open the spring-loaded door and vanished into the gloom.

He stared after her for a moment, and then he walked round the truck and got in behind the wheel. He sat motionless for a while, staring blindly into the sudden emptiness that had sprung up within him. He sat there for quite a while, lost in the deep silence of himself. He was reaching for the ignition key when he heard the door of the stoep slam. He turned his head quickly, looking out through the window. She came down the short path, halting in front of the sun-white gate.

"Mister man?"

He just stared at her.

"Mister man, can you hear me?"

"I—yes."

"Is it all right if I change my mind?"

"I don't understand."

"About—coming with you."

He stared at her in astonishment, his mouth open, unable to say anything for the bursting inside him. He smiled suddenly, radiantly, and she opened the gate and pushed through. She walked round the truck, got in and shut the door carefully.

"You shouldn't smile, mister man, it makes you look even worse."

"You'll like it, I think," he said softly. "Out where I live."

He turned the ignition key over and held it down. The engine caught with a burst of sound that was startlingly loud in the still flat heat of the afternoon. He reversed, backing up to the left, and then he spun the wheel over and drove out the way he had come.

"You mentioned," he remarked casually, "that you were going north."

"You going to start asking me questions again?"

He threw a startled glance at her. There was a wry mocking curve to her mouth, and the denial he had been about to make died inside him.

"You'd make a good mind-reader," he said instead.

She flicked a swift curious glance at him, as if she were seeing something she had not previously suspected might exist.

"You always ask so many questions?" she asked drily.

"Well, it's not every day you meet a girl wandering around on her own, especially in this part of the world."

"And that makes you curious, because I'm a girl?"

He glanced at her briefly, and his blue eyes were very steady. "I'd still be curious, even if you were a man."

He slowed for the main road, changed down, swung onto it and then accelerated. She studied him in silence for a while, as if she were trying to make up her mind about something, and then she spoke abruptly.

"I guess I owe it to you."

"Owe me what?" he asked in surprise.

"To satisfy your curiosity, mister man."

He felt embarrassed, somehow on the defensive, as if he were an interloper, a prowling marauder violating the territory of another.

"I don't bite," she remarked, breaking the growing silence. "At least not at this time of the day. The heat does something to my digestion."

The smile on her face again, mocking him but somehow also gentle. It gave him the courage he needed.

"Where are you heading for," he asked, "in the north?"

"Just north."

"But you must be going somewhere," he protested. "You must have some destination in mind, you can't just wander like that."

"Who says you can't?"

He tried to understand, but it didn't make sense. "You're just—travelling? You're not going anywhere special?"

She smiled briefly at his mystification. "Maybe I'm escaping."

"From what?"

"There's always a man to escape from, isn't there?" she said.

She saw the quick startled look he gave her, and her mouth curved in a dry smile. "Or maybe I'm escaping from myself," she went on.

"That doesn't make sense."

"It wouldn't—unless you've been to there yourself."

Her mouth curved again, enigmatic and mocking, but far back in her eyes there was a darkening, as if a memory of pain had come to life to hurt her once again.

"What—what work do you do?" he asked at length, when the silence between them had begun to take on a life of its own, heavy and suffocating.

"I wondered when you'd get to that?" she remarked wryly.

"It was you who said that you owed it to me," he commented, and there was an edge to his voice.

"That's right," she said easily, "so I'll tell you. What I do is try to stay alive."

"That's not what I meant."

She was silent for a while, looking out of the window, the dry heat of the wind on her face. She turned back to him after a few moments.

"I used to be a—dancer."

It took him by surprise, and then he wondered if he had imagined it, or whether there had been a certain emphasis on that last word, a cynicism and a contempt.

"But what are you doing here, in Africa?"

"It's a long story."

"Tell me."

"It would take a long time, because that would just about add up to the story of my life."

"It's a long drive," he said, his voice neutral, not pushing her, not backing away either.

The vehicle began to vibrate and tremor abruptly as they hit a bad stretch of corrugations. Jannie pushed his foot down on the accelerator and as the truck responded and gathered speed the hammering grew less intense, and then they were over the worst of it and the vehicle rolled smoothly once again.

"I was in New York," she said, her voice sounding weary, as if she had told it before and was bored by the recitation, or afraid to waken old ghosts. "I answered this ad. I should have known better, because it was an ad that got me there in the first place. South America was fine, but we found out that it wasn't only dancing that we had to do. That would have been fine too, but me, I don't like getting conned. We were broke, but I got the first boat out. It happened to be heading for Cape Town, so that's how I'm in Africa." She paused for a moment, and her mouth curved ironically. "And from the Cape, there's only one basic direction you can go, unless you want to swim. Now you know, mister man."

"But you said you were broke," he exclaimed. "How did you manage to get a passage?"

He threw a quick glance at her, and the bitter mocking knowledge he saw in her eyes made him sad and angry both at the same time.

"How'd you think?" she replied, grinning at him, but it was a smile without light.

"I'm—I'm sorry," he said, looking away quickly and giving his attention back to the road.

"What kind of shit is that, mister man?" she asked mockingly. "People always got to pay for what they get, and mostly they get just what they want."

Her language startled him, shocked him even a little. He was about to remark on it, but there was a knowing grin on her face, as if she were just waiting for him to comment so that she could hit him with the counter punch. He kept his mouth shut, and sat forward, trying to ease the sweated shirt from his back.

"Incidentally," she remarked after a while, "all dancers are born liars."

He turned his head to stare at her, puzzled again, but her eyes were steady and level, and he could read nothing in them. He looked away, the road again, correcting his drift, and he was even more mystified than he had been a few moments before.

"What do you want me to believe?" he asked at length.

"Whatever you want to," she replied.

He heard her laugh quietly, but he couldn't hear any mirth in her voice.

2

SHE ATE the last slice of canned peach and then spooned her plate clean of the cream. She pushed her chair back a little. She glanced across at him, and then stroked her belly, as if she were caressing something separate from herself, a final act of gentling and gratification.

"I can't remember when I last ate that good," she remarked.

"You enjoyed it?"

"You bet."

She leaned back in her chair. The kerosene pressure lantern hanging from the ceiling fascinated her, the glowing white orb of the mantle and the subdued hiss of sound that came from it.

A cricket began to sing outside. She glanced out through the copper mesh gauze that enclosed the stoep. In the distance she saw three small fires burning, and from somewhere close by she heard the sound of a drum beginning to beat. She shook her head, slightly incredulous, as if she couldn't believe any of it.

"Who'd have thought it?" she commented.

"What?"

She waved her arm vaguely, the gesture taking in the house and the night which lay all around it, a heart within its protective body.

"That I'd be here, in a place like this. I didn't know Africa could be like this. It's really like out of the movies."

He found himself inordinately pleased by her appreciation. "You'd get bored with it, after a while."

Her eyes mocked him. "You trying to do my thinking for me?"

"Pardon me?"

She sighed, simulating a vast exasperation. "How'd you know I'd get bored with it?"

"Well—there isn't much to do really, for a woman."

"I don't notice you getting bored with it. In fact you looked real happy to get back."

"It's different for me. I've lived here ever since I can remember. And besides, I like the bush."

"Can't blame you," she said. "There aren't enough people to screw it up."

He coughed, a little embarrassed by her forthright choice of words. "Would you like some coffee? A brandy with it?"

"I'd love."

"Mary!" he called.

She padded silently onto the stoep in her bare feet. She had big high breasts, thrusting out from under the cotton dress. She was young and ripe, about eighteen, and she moved with a wild sinuous grace. Her black face was expressionless as she came to a halt beside Jannie.

"Morena?"

"Bring some coffee, Mary," he said in Setswana. "Two glasses and the brandy, the KWV."

She threw a quick glance at Carol, and then she nodded and departed as silently as she had come.

"Let's sit down there," Jannie said, indicating the two Morris chairs. "We'll be more comfortable."

The coffee came, and the brandy, and they sat in silence while the table was cleared. She leaned back in the chair, her legs stretched out comfortably, sprawled apart. She had changed to a pair of shorts after her shower. They were tight, leaving just a little bit to the imagination, and he found his glance straying involuntarily.

"They're maybe a little thin," she remarked, sipping at her brandy, her eyes steady on him. "But not too bad, or so I've been told."

"Pardon me?"

"What do you think?"

"About what?" he asked, perplexed.

"My legs."

"I—I haven't really looked at them," he stammered, after he had got over his surprise and embarrassment.

"Come on, mister man," she chided him gently. "You've been using your eyes."

"I——"

He had been about to protest his innocence, but it seemed to him that her steady level eyes were peering right into his mind. He smiled, a little hesitantly.

"I don't think that, well, that they're too—thin."

"That's better." She nodded approvingly. "You're pretty shy, aren't you? What're you so shy about?"

"Have some more brandy?" he asked quickly, and before she could say whether she wanted it or not he had refilled her glass.

She picked it up, and there was a quiet amusement in her eyes as she studied him over the rim. She sipped at the drink and then held the tumbler cupped in her hands.

"She's got a great body, that Mary of yours," she commented.

"She cleans the house," he said quickly. "She does my washing, and well, looks after the place generally."

She nodded, as if she believed, innocently, and then quite casually she said: "You've slept with her, haven't you?"

He was too startled and surprised to dissimulate. "How did you know?"

"Oh, mister man, a woman can always tell, because she's being sized up for competition," she reproved him laughingly. "That's what the whole world's about, isn't it? Competition, climbing on backs till you get to the top because that's where you think it's going to be safe and you won't be frightened any more of someone trying to get on yours. But there's always someone."

He frowned, and there was a look of pain on his face, as if he had been hurt, not by what she had said so much, but by what it implied of her experience of life.

"It's not like that," he protested.

"Isn't it just?"

She smiled at him pityingly, as if he were some kind of mad and saint-touched innocent. She waved her arm again, that all-encompassing gesture that took in the world which surrounded her now.

"You've got it made, you're already a king."

"I had to work for it," he said. "It took a long time, but now I've got what I want. I'm not rich, but I live the way I want, and I don't want to climb on anyone's back."

"Sure, everyone has to work, but in some places people go for the jugular," she said. "You want to hit New York, with twenty bucks in your pocket and a dream. It turns into a nightmare."

"I'm sorry," he said, not really knowing why he felt sad.

"You crazy?" she exclaimed. "Never feel sorry for any bastard."

"You shouldn't swear like that."

"Why the hell not? It's just a word, like any other. It has a meaning, hasn't it?"

"Yes, but it doesn't—doesn't *do* anything."

She laughed. "What's the matter, were you real close to your little old mummy, or something?"

The muscle bulged briefly along the line of his jaw and then it flattened again. "I didn't know her really. She died when I was still a child."

She downed the rest of her drink in a gulp. It seared her throat, and then she felt the heat spreading back up from her belly.

"So maybe the old man taught you to respect women and all that sort of jazz."

"Is there something wrong with that?"

"Man, you just don't live in the real world, do you? I'm talking about reality."

He found himself copying her gesture, waving his arm. "This is reality, for me at any rate."

He saw her mouth tighten, the full bruised lips, and it seemed to him that a shadow fled across the brightness of her eyes.

She said, softly, "Keep it that way, mister man," and then she gestured at the bottle. "You mind if I help myself? It's good booze, that."

"Forgive me."

He lifted the bottle and poured for her. He offered her a cigarette, lit it and then lit his own.

"Tell me," he said, curious. "How old are you?"

"I don't answer questions like that."

"No—really, I'm interested."

Her mouth curved, mocking. "I'm not jail bait, if that's what's worrying you."

"Pardon me."

For a moment she thought he was trying to ridicule her, but then incredulously she realized he didn't understand.

"Forget it," she said, and then she laughed, feeling the hot warm brandy fumes wrapping her mind in a soft cocoon. "I could really take you, mister man, you're so goddam dumb."

He laughed, fascinated by her and at the same time saddened he didn't know why. "You're very bitter, aren't you?"

"Realistic."

"No—bitter."

She sat up, drank from her glass, smiled at him. "Okay, we'll talk about realism. If you don't mind, that is. Do you?"

"Not at all."

"Okay, why did you ask me to come along?"

"I——"

She grinned crookedly. "Spit it out, mister man."

He stared at her, and he knew what had been at the back of his mind, but he couldn't bring himself to say it. Not because he was too embarrassed by it, but because there was so much more than just that.

Her grin grew wider. "Okay, I'll tell you. You said to yourself, well here's a split, a woman, so maybe if I can get her along with me I might get into bed with her. Right?"

He was silent for quite a while, troubled by the look of triumph on her face. "It's natural, isn't it," he asked at length, "for a man to be attracted to a woman?"

"Sure it is, providing the cards are all on the table. Just now you couldn't lay them out."

"I didn't force you to come," he said defensively.

"Oh, mister man," she exclaimed, and there was something sad about the way she looked at him. "I'm a woman too, you know."

He busied himself stubbing out his cigarette. He didn't know why, but suddenly, glancing at her, he began to think again about the lion that had got out of his trap. For some reason he didn't understand entirely, he began to tell her about it.

"You know, I was last out in the desert about four months ago. I trapped a lion, and it got away. Don't ask me how, but it did. The unbelievable thing is that, from the spoor, it was a man, a Bushman, who took the trap from the lion's leg. I still can't believe it really happened."

"A lion!" she exclaimed, sitting forward with interest, flashes of half-remembered pictures going through her mind, the magic of the king and the legend surrounding his name firing her imagination.

"Yes."

"Why can't you believe it?"

"A wild lion, in a trap?" he breathed incredulously. "It's impossible, no man alive could get near him."

"And you're hoping to find this lion again?" she asked, and there was a shrewd and curious alertness in her voice.

He shook his head. "Not a chance. He's probably dead by now, and even if he wasn't, the Kalahari is a big place."

"Why dead?" she asked, strangely saddened by the thought.

"My trap probably smashed his leg up a bit. They do you know. He wouldn't be able to hunt. He'd get weaker and weaker, and the hyenas would pull him down in the end."

"What for? Don't they like lions?"

"They don't like anything that lives," he replied. "While their bellies are empty."

Her mouth puckered, and then she nodded, and he saw the shadows in her eyes again. "Just like people, huh."

"I wish I knew just what happened," he went on softly, as if he were speaking to himself or the brandy glass that he was turning endlessly in his hands. "I don't like a lion to get away from me, especially a wounded one. But we lost the spoor, and I had to leave and come back. I didn't want to leave, but I had to. I wish I knew exactly what happened that day. I've often wondered whether he's still alive."

"Maybe you'll be lucky," she said. "Perhaps you'll see him one day and he'll chew your goddam head off."

He was startled at the vehemence in her voice, but he was too deeply engrossed with his own thoughts to pay it much heed. He shook his head doubtfully.

"As I said, it was a long time ago," he went on. "Three months and twenty-three days, that's a long time."

She regarded him with a curiously alert expression on her face.

"What you got against these lions, that you want to go killing them?"

His right hand began to lift. He checked the movement, and after an infinitesimal pause he continued it smoothly in another direction. He picked up his glass and put it to his lips. He tossed the brandy back and set the empty glass down. She missed none of it.

"You get money for their skins."

She nodded, as if in agreement and understanding, but the pene-trating alertness did not leave her eyes. "That's what makes the world go round," she affirmed lightly, and then, settling deeper into her chair, she went on with a dry amusement in her voice and said: "You know, I don't believe you give a damn about the money."

"What do you mean?" he asked, his eyes narrowing watchfully.

"I mean, what really happened to your face?"

He felt a momentary tightening deep inside him, but he checked it before it could grow and forced himself to relax.

"Why do you want to know?"

"Just making talk," she answered, shrugging carelessly. "Tell you the truth, I couldn't care less."

It was her simulated indifference which partially penetrated the armour of his guard. He poured himself a drink and took three or four quick sips, feeling the beating of his own heart.

"There's not really much to tell," he began quietly, and then he went on, in a sudden rush, the words tripping one over the other, as if that which had been dammed within him too long had finally breached the last of his reticence and was now spilling in an uncon-trollable torrent. "I used to hunt and trap with a—friend. We used to like getting up really close to them when they were in a trap. Lions, leopards, anything. They go berserk, and it's really something to see. We'd go up to them together, one of us with the rifle, the other empty-handed, sort of naked, if you know what I mean. We took it in turns, to be—to be without the rifle. It had to happen one day, and it did. A leopard got loose and—and I lost my head and . . . and ran. I had the rifle that day." He paused and drew a shaky breath. "When I came to my senses she—my friend, that is, she was already dead and the leopard was coming for me."

She stared at him in shocked silence, at the hand which lifted to his face and the blunt fingers which stroked the scarred skin.

"Oh Christ!" she gasped softly. "I'm sorry."

"Forget it," he said harshly. "I don't want your pity."

She studied him in silence for a few moments longer, and then nodded brusquely. "What time did you say we were leaving for this cattle post in the morning?"

"About five-thirty."

"Christ," she said, and then: "If you don't mind I'll crawl into my bed. Otherwise I'll never make it."

He stood up quickly. "Of course."

"You don't have to stand," she said. "I'm no lady."

She grinned at him mockingly, but he said nothing, just stared back at her, a slightly troubled expression on his face.

"Goodnight, mister man," she said abruptly, and she turned and walked into the house and through to the spare room which Mary had fixed for her earlier.

He sank into his chair again and poured himself another drink. For a while his mind was a pleasant blank, but then he heard the sound of her washing, and a little later the creaking of the springs as she settled herself, and he began to think about her.

She was difficult to understand. Her face conveyed the impression of innocence and vulnerability, but after a while he came to the reluctant conclusion that it was no more than a misleading physical accident on the part of nature. He wondered what impulse had driven him to make the invitation to her. He remembered the way she had looked, standing there outside the hotel. She had looked like the loneliest person in the whole world. It had touched him somewhere inside, because he knew that feeling too.

He remembered what she had said, about a person putting their cards on the table, and the expression on her face, mocking and ironic, and he felt the embarrassment he had felt then rise to shame him all over again. There was truth in what she had said, but it was only a part of the whole.

He didn't want to think about the other parts, so he finished his drink and poured another. He was half way through it when he found himself thinking of her again. He wanted to look at her once more, into her incredible eyes, and see if there was any meaning written there that he could understand.

He fought the desire, through that drink and the next one. Maybe it was the drink that helped, he didn't know, but when his glass was empty once again his earlier apprehension seemed to have melted away. It was, after all, his house. He did have the right, just to look at her, didn't he?

He tiptoed to her room. The door was open, the heat still heavy. There was a small lamp burning on the bedside table, the flame turned down low.

He saw her and froze. She was lying on her side, her back to him, naked except for her pants, her left arm stretched out and her right thrown carelessly over her head. In the frail light of the lamp her skin was white and gold.

She turned suddenly, onto her back, and she turned her head. Her eyes were wide open, staring at him.

"I wondered how long it would take you," she said.

"What?" His voice was a choked whisper.

"You want to go to bed with me, don't you, mister man?"

He shook his head, a man fighting something, drowning perhaps, but he couldn't keep his eyes off the dark secret aureoles of her breasts.

"Come on," she urged him softly, taunting him now in his confusion, enjoying his discomfort. "I always pay my way, mister man. That's what you have to do in this world. You have to pay, one way or the other. That's what it's all about."

He gasped suddenly, like a man who has finally found air. "I didn't invite you to come with me for—that."

"Oh no?"

"No."

She laughed at him, still lying easy on the bed. "What's the matter? You want it with love and all that? Is that what you want, mister man? Love, the big conquest, the big deal with the caviare and all the fancy wines, the big schnock handie-holds to take you on that great ego trip? Is that what you want?"

He shook his head, fighting the drowning again. Her voice had been calm and conversational, but her eyes were terrible.

"You don't understand."

"Sure I understand. We can play it that way if you want, but it's an awful waste of time."

He stared at her, beginning to feel afraid, not of her but of the madness and sickness within her which was reaching its tentacles out to him in invitation. He knew instinctively that they were the heralds of death, not life. He began to edge away, very slowly.

"You're like a wounded lion, you just come," he whispered, and the sequence unreeled in his mind, because it was a world he knew intimately. "You've been shot, and you're afraid, and you attack me, just like the smallest little animal, when you put him in a corner."

She reared up on the bed, her breasts full now and quivering with her movement or her raging breath, not flat as they had been before when she was lying down, almost boyish, but woman now, caught in the frightening tempest of her own fury.

"Now you know," she breathed. "Now you know we're no bloody different."

He stared at her a moment longer, into the drowning depths of her eyes, not afraid any more, but in pain, for himself and for her, and also maybe the whole world. He turned and walked away.

She watched for a moment, and then she lay back, trembling. After a while she turned over onto her belly. She buried her face in the pillow. Her shoulders heaved, but she didn't make any noise.

Skeletal images began to flit and dance through the black shadows of her mind. She fought them violently, but they took shape and clothed themselves in flesh.

All skinny long legs and awkward arms but the legs made for walking and strong like her pride I'm glad to get away from that stinking adobe house all beginning to fall down which wasn't clean like the bush and the little button bead eyes of the rock chucks with the foresight like a frown between them and the blast of the rifle and the old man's voice bitching as he sat sprawled in his chair with the chuck lying dead.

What the hell you want to clean in there the froth scumming round his soft wet lips as he lowered the glass of beer with his fat gut belly pushing out his bib when it's like a hog pen and you know it's not my whining fault as if I care about fault shmault and if I want it clean where I sleep I can scrub it with my own hands I'm not asking you to do it taking another pull at his glass of beer and belching before asking if she thought she was better than all the rest of them I went on cleaning doing it for myself you don't care about any of us just yourself if you're so goddam proud and high and mighty why don't you clean everywhere I had always done it but they dirtied it everywhere and I did it again and again but they went on fouling it up not caring and then I did it once again and after that she didn't do it anymore.

The happy shouting laughter all those boys and girls playing children's games at school and how happy I was when I was there and running free as a child I don't know when she grew up it wasn't a day or a month or a year that I can remember only the eyes began to look at me in a different way the boys as if they knew a dark secret that I didn't showing in their guilty eyes which touched and slid away to make me feel unclean about my body which was clean and beautiful and gave me only pride in the way it moved and obeyed and did the things I demanded that it do.

Eyes transformed to hands and the hot shocking electric thrill of lips against her own and you've been in the bushes with Pete so what makes you think you're so good that you won't come there with me I wasn't *hiding* there with Pete because I was ashamed of kissing him it wasn't anyone's business but my own to show him that I saw in him the things I honoured the same way he held his head and walked with pride and tried to do the things that had to be done never complaining but just doing them the best way he could others panting to get a kiss from me that I could not give because I couldn't see any meaning to a giving of that kind trying to make me feel unclean about something that was beautiful slut living in a tumble-down shack on the outskirts who do you think you are trying to keep it clean which was the feeling I had about herself. She.

The summer sun in the sky or was it a grapefruit I used to love picking those ripe swollen suns from the green-leaved trees and many of the pickers coming from far away in places that had magic names like Eddie on that first day that she saw him I watched him working out of the corner of my eye the swift sure hands and the quiet dignity in his bearing not like so many of the others trying to make you believe by word and gesture that it was beneath them.

He had a beaten-up old Ford but when he got behind the wheel it became as new and clean and shining as himself the wind rushing in her face and blowing my long hair in his hands as he kissed me in the dark with the starlight in his eyes took me out tomorrow and have a night in the town he wanted to pay for everything he said it was his pleasure but I also get pleasure being able to pay my own way in such a beautiful place he took me but didn't get angry when I paid for what I'd had but laughed his golden summer smile and understood that it was all a lie and he the spider I the fly caught in a timeless snare I read that somewhere or is it my imagination wondering what it would be like in New York the pain aieeee and then the warmth of his body and his arms holding me so gently like a mother holding its child she said before she died in my arms that I had to try and look after them all older than me who is she it is me.

His belly getting fatter and wondering if it would pop one day like the springs on the chair popped up bare when he heaved himself up to get another beer when she came in that night studying her with a strange crafty expression puzzled by the steady light of new pride in her eyes that said she was a woman now.

You filthy slut all the people talking go and get those food stamps and her head bowed as she exchanged them for groceries feeling filthy and unclean and wondering why the purity of offering her body in salute should not make her feel the way people said she was supposed to feel about those stamps there was something wrong with words that tried to change and distort reality and manipulate me instead of trying to understand my mind.

Waiting for the letter I knew with all the knowledge I had that it would have to come and thinking when it didn't that he must have got hurt or been killed because nothing else could prevent him from keeping his word otherwise why would he have said it unless he wanted to make her believe that which wasn't a fact and then when it never came I began to think so hard it hurt her head to find out why and the only answer she got was that he tried to make me believe what wasn't real and she couldn't understand that either because I would have given myself to him even if he hadn't promised to send for her in New York I didn't love him because of that something surely must have happened.

The soft wet beery lips tightened as she waited for the letter making her father look human and then when it never came pulping into slackness again with the slyness of a smile that was happy telling me that she was no better than him with the righteousness of half the world giving strength to words which made me feel evil so that she had to fight it each moment of the day or else let it destroy the reality of my own perception how tired I got thinking all the time and fighting to stop herself believing I cannot be evil when it only made me happy.

Getting worse and worse at home the sly insinuations were what she couldn't stand his eyes smearing her the way they slid over her body in a drooling invitation to commit the unspeakable crime of hiding that which should have been her pride and screaming at him with all the strength in her body I'd give that to you too if it was what you wanted and needed if there was anything in you that could make me hold her head up high and what is that spark that sets alive the kindling of my soul the ugliness in his eyes replaced by the blind terror of seeing himself and quickly picking up another beer to dim the vision of that awful moment that was transformed into blank irrational hatred.

The ad in that paper it was left behind by some diner who was he I wonder where he went it started there when I picked it up and here I am the hole in the ground where I had hidden the money she had saved from all those summers picking suns I bought the ticket for New York wondering if she would see Eddie it was only a dream she didn't believe to pass the time away on the speeding Greyhound feeling sometimes as if it wasn't moving or was it she who felt I wasn't moving wrapped in the terror of the waiting unknown as a continent swept past the window of the standing stranded bus in a dream she woke when it slid into the roar and stink of the Lincoln Tunnel her heart lurching and trembling those ivory-coloured tiles shining wetly in the fluorescent lighting with the cops on the walkway making her heart skip a beat walking slowly up and down they can't be looking for me and a sudden exhilarating sense of freedom as she got off the bus my legs were so stiff at the Port Authority Terminal.

Dodging the clothes racks on Thirty-first Street between Sixth and Eighth when she went to work each morning from Evangeline House or was it Angeline I can't remember the song how did it go pretty little Angeline or Evangeline working at the sewing machine I'm glad she taught me how to use one before she died.

I was so nervous and excited when the super came and asked me if I could help out with the trade display the clothes so new on my body shining like the spirit inside me as the buyers watched and noted the men and women with their eyes undressing me as if they could reach the thing inside which was myself beneath the flesh is all they thought about when what they saw came from deeper than the skin which covered it and left the sewing machines for good I'm glad that girl was sick that day not happy at her sickness but at the chance that it gave me to find out that the sickness she had run from was everywhere the man in charge of all the girls who did display telling her she was good she had a flair and all the hours she spent before the mirror working to perfect the art.

And later telling her *slow down you work too hard* he told her which made me work even harder *I want to keep this job* it was the kind of behaviour I had lived by expecting praise *that's not the way to keep it* with a strange half-bantering smile *how else can I earn the right unless I do my best* in simple puzzled wonder that funny smile again *you know* enigmatically *I don't* fighting against permitting herself to understand the monstrous *slow down anyway that's an order if you want to keep your job* and later hinting that he had done her a favour by not making her work as hard as she had wanted and intimating that she owed him something in return after having forced her to accept that which she did not want in the first place how can people try to change reality by juggling with words and then I understood that they were trying to wreck my mind to get at the flesh which covered it the easy way. Scum.

She learned to play them at their own game it was a better job that second one I let him think what he wanted to believe of me and then he found out that he couldn't play a game where non-rules were wishes that turned into rules by wishing that they would.

Looking for Eddie all the time not in the flesh but in the name of the spirit which she had glimpsed in him and which was the essence of all the good that was within herself I had to hide it deeper and deeper because she found out in a terrifying leap of understanding that it was not my flesh but my spirit or whatever it was inside me that they were trying to violate as if it could be done through the instrument of her body I buried it so deep that I don't even know if it's there anymore or what it is I remember now that Angeline was the name of the girl in the song she was pretty dancing on the village green little angeline in Greenwich Village.

And then I met Eddie oh not the same one who picked those golden suns with me I was so happy then but with another name in whose person was the same spirit and slowly she began to show the things she had hidden till she heard a whisper which she thought was the soft sweet sigh of love and looking into his eyes she saw it wasn't that but the hiss of air against the falling blade of a guillotine. I ran for my life.

Jannie lowered himself carefully into the chair. He poured himself a drink. He felt a sudden rage pour through him, thinking about her. He downed his drink at a gulp and then filled his glass again.

After a while he got up and went into the lounge. He took the tuft of black mane hair from the display cabinet against the wall. He stared at it blindly. A sudden blistering surge of pain ran through him. He cursed horribly and tossed the piece of fur back into the cabinet. He whirled and strode back to her room.

"Are you awake?" he demanded.

She was lying face down, a blur in the half-dark. He heard the beating of his own heart, and then the rustle of her moving body.

"Yes." Her voice was muffled, coming out of the pillow.

"I've changed my mind," he said. "I'm going hunting tomorrow, out in the desert."

"Good for you."

"You can come with me if you like, or you can stay here till I get back."

The silence flowed again. "Why not? It can't be any worse a place than this."

He opened his mouth to speak, then snapped it shut abruptly and spun on his heel and walked off. There was a tremble in his hand as he lifted his glass from the table.

3

WITHIN THE THICKET of thorn were the guts and the left shoulder of the old hartebeest ram Jannie had shot on his way into the desert that morning. All the natural entrances into the thicket, except one, had been sealed off with more thorn that they had cut.

From a nearby bush Spartala lopped off a thick branch of scrub. He wired it to the end of the chain on the trap. Preparing the site had taken them half an hour. Now they were ready to set the first of the traps.

Jannie scooped a hole in the sand just inside the entrance. He dug a small circular pit, six inches in diameter and four inches deep at the centre, the depth decreasing towards the circumference of the hole.

Over it he laid the brittle twigs which Spartala handed him, making a platform which he then covered over with dried grass. He buried the chain after that, and then using the sole of his boot to immobilize one of the jaws of the trap, he prised the other one open.

Spartala, crouched beside him, quickly fitted the sear and held it in position while Jannie eased back very carefully on the jaw in his hands. The sear lifted against the trigger notch of the firing pan. The moment it was holding Jannie nodded. Spartala hastily withdrew his hands. He remained there in a frozen crouch, eyeing the armed and now lethal trap.

Jannie lifted his foot gingerly, his eyes riveted on the pan, and then he breathed out with relief. He picked up the trap, handling it from underneath, and placed it with great gentleness on its waiting bed.

When it was in position he camouflaged the jaws with grass, and then scattered sand over the grass and the pan, layer after fine layer, till suddenly there was nothing there but wind-blown grass and desert sand.

He stood up and backed away, and using a branch whisk Spartala brushed the sand smooth in front of the trap, dispersing the taint of their smell and removing the evidence of their murderous preparations.

Carol stared incredulously. A few moments before the trap had been visible, but now there was nothing, absolutely nothing to indicate that death lay there and waiting. She wasn't even sure where it was any more. She felt a shiver run down her spine.

"Christ," she breathed softly. "What if a man walks into that—that thing?"

"There's no one out here."

"What about these Bushmen you were telling me about?"

He laughed. "They wouldn't be fooled by that," he said, and there was a note of pride in his voice. "Come on, we've got two more traps to get out, and it's going to be dark before we know it."

They piled into the Land Rover, Jannie behind the wheel with Carol in front with him, and Spartala and Tsexhau in the back. He started the engine and drove forward through the trackless wilderness.

She stared out through the open window. There was something frightening about the vast sun-scorched desolation which lay all around in every direction. It made her feel small and insignificant, and she was glad she wasn't alone.

"It's awful big," she commented. "And empty."

He nodded silently, concentrating on his driving.

"How do you know where you're going?" she asked. "Do you ever get lost out here?"

"Sometimes."

"My God, what happens then?"

"You go back, and you try to pick up your own spoor, and then you start off again from there."

"Spoor?"

"Tyre tracks."

"And if you can't find them?"

He shrugged. "If I really get lost, there's Tsexhau. He can always find his way back to where we started from."

"But how? There's nothing out here, nothing. It all looks the same. I was already lost a hundred yards out of the camp."

"It might look the same to you, but it isn't really. Every tree, every bush, each one is different, and they remember where it was, where they saw it. I myself, I have to pin-point and remember a landmark consciously. With them it's instinctive."

"You mean like animals?"

He laughed. "An animal learns its territory the same way, by observation and memory."

Wrapped once again in the magic of his beloved desert, explaining it to another, he had forgotten about last night and was happy again.

"But that's not—instinct."

He frowned, glancing at her in surprise. "I suppose it isn't," he admitted. "Not in the way we usually think of the word."

"I don't know," she said dubiously. "I don't know how anyone can find their way around here."

"You sort of get a feel for it."

He halted the Land Rover a little further on and after a consultation with Tsexhau set the second trap. They worked meticulously, and once again when they had finished she experienced that same sensation of cold dread.

The third and last trap Jannie set up in really thick bush. There were big trees and plenty of thorn, ideal leopard country. For bait he used the half-eaten carcass of an ostrich. He had driven the vultures from it earlier on and taken it aboard. He wasn't sorry when he got rid of it, because even to his own hardened sense of smell it was stinking pretty high.

"That's a relief," she exclaimed, when they were on their way again. "That dead bird was just about turning my belly inside out."

"Why didn't you tell me?" he said quickly, concerned.

"What difference would that make?" she asked. "You had to use it, didn't you?"

He glanced at her, and he saw the mocking curve of her mouth. The memory of last night came back again, and he felt himself begin to withdraw.

"You're right," he said, a little stiffly, but at the same time he had to acknowledge it as the truth, and that in itself thawed him again, because he liked honesty, or thought he did.

The sun was a huge red ball hovering just above the horizon when they got back to camp. It flooded the land with a light that was softly translucent.

*   *   *

Huddled on the other side of the fire, the Africans were shapeless bundles beneath their blankets. She stared at the stars overhead, big pears of light that seemed as if they were hanging in the branches of the trees. She pushed herself up on one elbow. She stared across at Jannie, and then she lit a cigarette.

"You asleep, mister man?"

He turned his head. "No."

She drew on her cigarette, the glow lighting her face. "About last night," she said. "Don't take it to heart."

"Don't worry about it," he replied. "It was just one of those things, you probably had too much to drink."

"Don't try and make excuses for me," she said. "I'm not trying to make them for myself."

He met her cryptic, quizzical stare for a while and then shrugged. She was trying to tell him something, but he couldn't work it out.

"Would you like a cigarette?" she went on.

"I wouldn't mind."

She lit it for him and passed it across. She had to stretch to reach his own outstretched hand. Their fingers touched briefly, and then the contact was broken.

"You know that animal you shot this morning, the big brown one?"

"Hartebeest."

"Yes," she said, and then: "It was so quick, wasn't it. That bullet, the sound that it made as it hit, and then it just took one step and died. It was kind of sad."

"We ate some of it tonight."

"Sure, I know, but it was still sad."

"That's life."

"Do you—do you like shooting them?"

He frowned, puzzled by her question, wondering where she was trying to lead him. "I like hunting, the same way other people like doing other things," he said. "That means killing an animal."

"That's what I mean, killing," she said quickly. "Do you like to kill?"

He studied her, in the flickering light of the fire, and his frown deepened. She was watching him a little too intently for comfort.

"Don't get me wrong, I'm not knocking," she went on hastily. "It's just that I'm—curious."

"I've never thought about it much," he said. "I've always hunted, and I've always liked it."

"I know you eat the meat and all that, and use the skin, but doesn't it make you kind of—kind of sad to kill something that didn't do you any harm?"

He tossed the butt of his cigarette into the flames. He thought about what she had said, and he wondered if he should try and explain it to her. The trouble was, that unless a person had hunted themselves, they never really understood. He decided to try.

"Everything has to die, sometime or the other," he said. "And when you kill an animal, with purpose and intention, in a way you give it life."

"Are you out of your mind, mister man?" she asked softly. "You give it life by killing it?"

It did sound rather strange, when she put it like that, but he knew there was so much more. He tried to marshal his thoughts, to express the feeling he had about it all, this land of his, and of the men who lived as close to it as did the animals themselves. He looked into the fire, and he began to speak again, taking the images from far back in his mind where he had stored them.

"As I said, everything has to die, and the way that most of these animals die out here isn't pretty. Sometimes it's quick, when a lion or leopard kills, but not always even then. Other times it's not nice to watch, like when a bunch of hyenas pull down a sick animal, or a pack of wild dogs go after their dinner. They're eating before the animal's dead even."

"But what's that got to do with you killing them and giving them life?"

"I'm trying to explain it to you," he said patiently. "The way I feel."

"Surrender," she said. "Go on."

He turned away from her, and he looked back into the fire, remembering some of the different times he had killed, trying to isolate the essence of the experience and its accompanying emotion.

"They all die out here, sometime or the other, but there's no one to remember that they ever lived, that they were strong and beautiful in life," he explained. There was a sadness in his voice, and a subdued elation too, and his eyes were wide and slightly puzzled with the enormity of what he had only vaguely sensed before but had never clarified and defined in words. "When I kill an animal, it's as if I give it life, because it stays alive in my memory."

"You could do that with a camera."

"I suppose, but death is in a way more final, it fixes it in your mind. It would have died anyway, and no one would remember. I always remember, the way it was running, the way it looked, the kind of day it was, even the clouds. There isn't one that I don't remember about."

She thought she understood, but the contradictory nature of the premise still puzzled her. "I still think you could do it all with a camera."

"I prefer a rifle."

"With a camera you could let them live a little longer, and preserve them for ever," she persisted. "For other people as well."

"These are my memories," he said. "They're not for other people."

She stared at him, her eyes searching, and then she began to nod slowly. "I know just what you mean."

Jannie lay down again on his sleeping bag. "You'd better try and get some sleep. We'll be up pretty early."

"Those traps?" she said.

For a while the question hung in the air between them. "What about them?" he asked at length.

"They must hurt, don't they?"

"You've seen them," he replied tersely.

"Why'n't you just shoot them, instead of trapping them?" she asked. "These lions and leopards."

"You could spend a month out here and never see one. I could perhaps sit by a bait and shoot one, but I haven't got the patience for that, so I trap them."

"It's kind of unfair, wouldn't you think?"

He laughed, and there was a harshness in the sound. "He goes after the meat in the trap, he takes his chances. I do the same when I go after him."

"I guess," she said hesitantly. "I guess you're right, but still——"

"Let's get some sleep," he said bluntly, cutting her off.

She eyed him curiously, alerted by the raw edge in his voice, but then she decided she had imagined it, and she lay down and stared up at the black vault of the sky which was so full of stars. For a moment she let her imagination run, thinking of them as peepholes into some hidden mystery beyond, but the light that came through them was so bright that it blinded her and she could see nothing.

4

THERE WAS a certain magic about a trap that filled Jannie with an even greater anticipation than an ordinary hunt. You set it, and it exploded in the dark, and it was like a lucky dip, because in the light of the next day you never knew what you'd find on the draw.

"You didn't eat much breakfast," he commented.

"This early in the morning I'm not even human."

The Land Rover bounced over pot-holes and crashed through the scrub in places. She glanced out of the open window, taking in the desolation of the land. It was burned and dry, and even in the soft morning light it looked tired and beaten.

"Is it always like this?" she inquired. "So—so dead."

"Oh no!" he exclaimed. "You should see it after the first rain. They come up almost over night, well, in a day or two. They really do, the Namaqualand daisies and wild mimosa, primulas and Bauhinia and all sorts of flowers I don't even know the names of. It's like waking in a different world, all new and beautiful, and you don't want to hunt or kill, you just want to loaf around camp and maybe get drunk and feel happy about being alive." He shook his head in wonder and fell silent for a while, remembering how it could be. "It's as if the desert had gone mad with life, but if the rains fail it doesn't last. The sun comes up and just flattens it all out again."

She stared in disbelief at the sun-blasted wilderness, unable to visualize it as he had described it. "How far is the first trap now?"

"Not too far."

"Do you think we'll find something?"

"Keep your fingers crossed."

"What sort of animals get trapped?"

"Lions, leopard, sometimes you get a hyena."

"I didn't know hyena skins were valuable."

"They aren't."

"Then why do you trap them?"

"I don't. They come for the meat and they get caught."

"But what do you do with them?"

"Kill them and re-set the trap."

"Can't you set them free, or something?"

He laughed shortly. "A trapped animal? It would bite your head off if you went near it."

"It seems kind of a—a waste," she murmured.

He shrugged. "I can't put up a sign, lions and leopards only."

"Don't lose your cool, mister man," she said. "I'm only asking."

"You ask too many questions," he snapped. "For this time of the morning."

"Oh wow!" she exclaimed mockingly.

A few minutes later he slowed the vehicle. He peered out uncertainly through the windscreen, and then out through the open windows, first on one side and then the other.

"Now where am I?" he muttered.

Around them was a sea of scrub and sand and burned out grass stubble, and all of it was frighteningly the same. He brought the truck to a halt. He studied the harsh landscape for a while and then shook his head in defeat. He popped his head out of the window and called back.

"Which way, Tsexhau?"

Without any hesitation the half-breed Bushman raised his hand and pointed. Jannie nodded in acknowledgement. He pushed the clutch in and a moment later they were rolling again.

About ten minutes later Jannie heard the staccato double-tap on the roof of the cab. He braked and stuck his head out of the window. Tsexhau pointed silently.

Jannie swung the wheel over and drove forward slowly. He had gone about twenty yards when he recognized the thicket of thorn in which he had set the first of his traps. He braked and killed the engine, his body tightening with anticipation.

He stared into the black shadows of the thicket, his heart beginning to race, but he could see nothing. And then his eyes picked up the marks of the drag, which were cut deeply into the ochre red sand.

"I hope it's a leopard," he said. "A leopard or a lion."

Through her own mounting excitement she heard the charged bleakness in his voice. She stared at him in surprise, but his face was impassive, and she wondered whether she wasn't beginning to hear things.

Jannie started the engine again and drove over slowly to where the spoor first began. He glanced at the prints in between the wavering furrows cut by the branches of the drag. He began to curse just as Spartala began laughing from the back of the Land Rover.

"What is it?" she asked, curiosity struggling with her apprehension.

"Strandjut," he said disgustedly.

"What's that?"

"A brown wolf, a hyena."

"Is it dangerous?"

He shook his head absently. He breathed out heavily and the tension drained from him. "Well—that's the luck of the draw."

He meshed the gears and drove forward. It was easy following the drag marks. Five minutes later they came up with the hyena. It was about thirty yards away when Carol first glimpsed it, moving slowly and heavily, dragging its trapped leg. The branch scraped along behind it, like some determined parasite. She felt a spurt of excitement, and revulsion.

Jannie halted the vehicle. The hyena paused and glanced back. For a moment it stared incomprehensibly at the monster behind it, and then it whirled and began to run, driven by its fear, the pain in its leg now secondary to the terror in its brain. The drag held it back and slowed it, and there was something grotesque about its hobbling run.

Jannie drove forward, swung wide and then cut in towards it, herding it towards a patch of thorn. It ran past, but the drag got caught and tangled up in the brush and held the animal fast. It jerked frantically once or twice at its imprisoned leg, whimpering and yelping at the pain, and then it turned fearfully to face the men who came bursting from the vehicle.

"Are you going to shoot it?" she asked.

He shook his head. "It's a waste of a good cartridge."

"But what are you going to do?"

"Look," he said.

Spartala and Tsexhau approached the animal warily. Each one of them had a spear in his hands. The shafts were seven feet long, made of teak, and the broad flat heads were of iron, eight inches in length, with a cutting edge on either side. They were formidable weapons.

"Give it to him, Masarwa," Spartala said, grinning in anticipation. "Let us see if you can use a man's spear."

Tsexhau darted him a swift look that burned with animosity, and then his eyes became expressionless once again. He hefted the spear, getting the weight and the feel of it. He drew his arm back, and then he danced forward suddenly and hurled it.

A branch deflected it slightly. It struck the hyena, going in just forward of the left flank, but it didn't go in deep.

The hyena yelped in pain as the steel bit. It bared its teeth and cowered backwards from the men, jerking its right front leg spasmodically and whimpering with the pain.

"Hau!" Spartala exclaimed in derision, and he stepped forward chuckling to himself.

The hyena backed away from him, but its movements were restricted. The shaft of the spear caught against a branch. The knock tore the head loose, and the spear fell to the ground.

The bright blood poured suddenly from the gaping wound. It looked almost black, and the parched land gobbled it up there in the white, drenching sunlight of the hot desert morning.

"Come on, Spartala," Jannie urged. "Finish him off."

"A nice clean bit of butchery," she commented from beside him. "Why don't you shoot it, for God's sake?"

"I told you."

Spartala grinned and closed in. The terrified hyena jerked furiously at the trap round its leg. When it found it could not get free it crouched and turned to face its tormentors again. The eyes, fashioned for night vision, peered myopically and pathetically at the man.

Spartala feinted at it with his spear, trying to get it to move so that he could get an unobstructed throw. It shrank back, baring its teeth. He feinted again, and the animal leaped at him. He jumped back nimbly, laughing happily, and the enormous crushing jaws snapped shut on empty air.

Carol stared at the animal, feeling a little sick. It was an unlovely creature. It had a long hog-like mane, and its front legs were longer than its back ones, raising its shoulders and giving it an ungainly appearance. The greyish black fur was matted in places, and it stood there peering dismally at its attacker with its flanks heaving and the blood seeping slowly from its wound. For all that, there was something noble about it.

Spartala leaned back, and then with a sudden guttural explosion of his breath he launched the spear in his hand. It took the hyena just behind the shoulder. The impact rocked it and threw it off balance. It stumbled and fell. For a few moments it lay there on its side, froth at its mouth and its chest heaving tumultuously as it fought for air.

It lay there a little longer, as if it were resting, and then it kicked out suddenly, trying to get its feet beneath it. But the effort was too much, and it lay back again. The huge jaws opened and closed as it continued to gasp for breath.

It rolled and kicked out again, got its feet beneath it and came up off the sand. It stood there, its great head hanging and its limbs shivering. The desert was hot and silent, but there was the sound of wind in its ears, the rush of a far-away storm.

It took a step forward and pitched to the ground. It kicked out feebly once or twice, and then it stiffened and became still and limp. Whatever had been there was gone for good.

It hadn't been much in life, and now in death it looked like a worn and discarded rug.

"That—wasn't very nice to watch," she said quietly.

"You get used to it."

"The pain," she said. "It must have been terrible."

"That's life."

Spartala tore his spear from the body of the hyena. He cleaned the blood from it, wiping it off on the fur. He prised the jaws of the trap open and drew it clear of the leg. With Tsexhau helping him, they threw the carcass into the back of the Land Rover.

Jannie drove back to where the trap had been set in the beginning. They threw the hyena into the thicket, fresh bait for the next hungry animal, and then re-set the trap.

He unhooked one of the water bags from the bonnet of the vehicle. He pulled the stopper and gave it to her. She drank eagerly, surprised at the coolness of the water.

A few minutes later they were rolling again. The next trap was empty, and there was no sign of any spoor round it.

In the back of the Land Rover, Tsexhau and Spartala leaned against the top of the driving cab, taking the jolting and bouncing on wide-spread legs. They stared straight ahead at the approaching forest of scrub which surrounded the deepest part of an old water course.

Spartala nudged the small half-breed beside him. Tsexhau turned his head, his eyes questioning.

"What do you see?" Spartala asked.

His own eyes were good, but the eyes of a Masarwa, even a half-breed, were the best eyes in all of Africa.

"Nothing, but I feel something."

Tsexhau tapped his chest significantly, and Spartala nodded and leaned forward, his eyes straining. He could see nothing, but he did not doubt the tracker, because he had never yet been wrong in his predictions. He didn't know how they did it, but all of them seemed to have this strange ability. He thought it was maybe because they weren't human, like an African or a white man, but something sub-human and closer to the animals. It was a well-known fact that one animal could sniff the presence of another from a great distance. But that was puzzling too, because Tsexhau did not really sniff them out, and when he had tried to explain the only answer that he could give was that he felt it as a sort of tapping within his chest. Still and all, he had come to know and respect Tsexhau over the years, even if half of him wasn't even human.

Jannie wheeled the vehicle into the thickening scrub. He knew exactly where he was this time, and no mistake about it. Thorn and brush scraped against the battered wings of the Land Rover, scratching them and laying the metal bare.

He picked up the spoor of his own wheels from the day before. He followed the tyre tracks as far as they went, and then brought the vehicle to a halt.

He stared into the gloom of the sun-dappled brush, searching the scrub where he felt certain he had positioned his trap. But he saw nothing, and disappointment began to creep into him.

"Morena!" Tsexhau hissed.

Jannie froze, his hand half way to the gear shift, electrified by the sibilant whisper. He snapped his head out through the window. He followed the direction of Tsexhau's pointing arm.

He had been looking too far to the left, where the trap had been set originally, and that was why he hadn't seen it.

He saw the torn-up vegetation first. The brush was smashed and flattened, and two saplings as thick as a man's calf had been torn down, the ends of the stumps shredded and splintered.

But still he saw nothing. He was about to speak when he drew a quick startled breath, and his stomach turned over and tightened into a hard, cold knot.

Even now it was difficult to discern, standing there with its head up and watching them, blending so perfectly with the light and shade that it looked like a sun-speckled shadow.

"Leopard!" he breathed softly.

He took his eyes from it for a moment as he turned to whisper to her, and when he looked back it took him a few seconds to locate it again, so motionless and ethereal was it.

"Where is it?" Carol exclaimed, craning forward to peer out through the window. "I see nothing."

He reached forward and switched off the ignition. The engine died, and in the sudden silence which followed the sound of his breathing was startlingly loud.

The leopard spat at them. It was a single shattering explosion of concentrated sound, filled with fury and hate. The inarticulate intensity of it was shocking and overpowering. She saw it a few moments later.

"They're not going to try and spear that, are they?" she whispered.

"Are you out of your mind?" he retorted tensely. "That's a leopard."

She was quiet for a moment, watching the tension in him mount. "I didn't figure they would," she said wryly.

"That's a leopard," he said again, and there was a tremor in his voice. "A leopard!"

He glared at her, and then he turned and lifted down the .264 Winchester with the Redfield scope from the rack at the back of the cab. He was reaching for the handle of the door when she spoke.

"Is it all right if I get out?"

He hesitated, and then nodded. "Get out and get up in the back of the truck. And don't slam the door."

He slid out, closing his own door noiselessly behind him. Out of the corner of his eye he saw her being helped into the back of the Land Rover by Spartala. He started forward, moving slightly to his right from where he could get a clearer field of fire.

The leopard saw the man-shape detach itself from the background of the vehicle. It spat again and erupted in a savage snarling uproar. It thrashed from side to side as it struggled to tear free from the trap, clawing and biting at everything within its reach.

She watched it in awe. It was as if some terrible and demonic power had been unleashed, some evil and hate-maddened force so shocking and primeval that it did not seem it could have originated in mortal flesh and blood.

It tired after a minute or so, and once more it stood statue still, head up and watching.

From the back of the vehicle, Spartala studied the leopard. There was fear and a wary admiration in his black eyes.

"A devil that one," he whispered. "Truly he is the son of the devil."

There weren't many things that he was afraid of, but a trapped leopard was one of them. They went berserk at the sight of a man, and sometimes they broke free from the trap, especially if they were approached. He shuddered.

Jannie lifted the Winchester, his face pale beneath the tan. He worked the bolt and cocked the rifle. He stared at the leopard a moment longer, his eyes cold and hard, and then he snugged the rifle deliberately against his shoulder. He felt the firm, smooth warmth of the stock against his cheek. The leopard sprang into sudden focus as he peered through the 4X scope. It looked so close that he felt he could reach out and touch it.

But its eyes were what drew and held his attention. They were overflowing with madness and hate, and as he stared into them he felt a sudden surge of primal fear.

He centred the triangular tip of the reticle post against the thick muscle-heavy neck. He breathed out slowly, and when his lungs were almost empty he froze his breath and began the gentle squeeze on the trigger.

"You're missing out, mister man," Carol called softly. "You could have had a lot more fun with one of those spears."

He stiffened at her words. His vision blurred, and through the roaring in his ears he heard another voice from long ago.

When his mind cleared again his hands were shaking so badly he couldn't hold the rifle steady. The tip of the post kept moving, wavering on and off the target.

He gasped, as if he were fighting for air. He pulled the rifle in tighter against his shoulder, but he just couldn't keep it steady.

The post continued to waver. He took a deep breath and let it out. The sight steadied a bit. He snatched frantically at the trigger the moment the tip of the post was centred against the leopard's neck. Even before the rifle had recoiled against his shoulder he knew he had missed.

The bullet clipped through the branches above the animal's head. The high-velocity slug was deflected, and it ricocheted with a shrill whine that could be heard distinctly above the flat whipcrack of the rifle.

The leopard exploded in a fresh paroxysm of rage. It leaped into the air. The chain on the trap tightened with a click of the links and the leopard was plucked out of its flight in mid-air and smashed back into the ground. It sprang instantly to its feet, snarling and spitting. It lunged furiously from side to side, turning a complete circle and then threw itself forward.

It lurched as the chain snapped taut, and it staggered forward, and then a moment later it was back up on its feet and staring at them motionlessly.

Jannie slammed another cartridge into the breech of the rifle. He put his eye to the scope again. Through it he saw the cat's lips peel back in a silent snarl, and he saw the yellow teeth laid bare.

He found himself staring straight into its jewelled eyes. They glowed with hate and a single-minded concentration.

He tried desperately to steady the rifle. He was trying once again to pin the post to its neck when the leopard lowered its head and licked at its foot. Involuntarily his eyes followed the movement.

Terror swept through him. The trap was no longer round the animal's leg. For a moment he was paralysed, bound by the chains of his own fear.

"Even I can shoot better than that, mister man," she called out.

He started at the sound of her voice, and then he felt the wash of something flow through his body, swift and cleansing. He pulled the rifle in against his shoulder. It was steady in his hands. He centred the tip of the reticle against the spotted neck. He squeezed the trigger, slowly and deliberately.

The silence of the desert morning was shattered once again by the crack of the rifle. Through the scope he saw the puff of fur and dust which exploded from the neck of the cat, and an instant later he heard the solid slap of the striking bullet.

The leopard stiffened, and then it crumpled, exactly where it had stood, as if it had suddenly grown tired and had settled down to rest.

Jannie ejected the empty cartridge. Smoke wisped from the breech and the cartridge case span away to the side. He closed the bolt, holding the trigger down as he did so.

They approached it warily, the four of them, Jannie in front with the rifle ready, Spartala and Tsexhau carrying their spears. It was quite dead, and for a few moments all of them stood and stared down silently at it. Dead now, it looked somehow small and insignificant.

She found it difficult to reconcile the limp nothingness of the spotted body with the magnificent and furious savagery it had displayed only a little while earlier. She glanced around incredulously at the devastated vegetation. She was about to comment on it when she heard Spartala's shocked exclamation.

She followed the direction of his pointing spear. The lacerated paw, with the pad almost torn right off and the tendon gleaming yellow, held no significance for her. It was horrifying, that was all.

"What is it?" she asked.

"He got himself free of the trap."

"You mean it was free, before you killed it?"

"Yes," Jannie replied.

"Why didn't it run?"

"It was waiting."

"For what?"

"For me to miss again."

Her eyes widened momentarily, and then her gaze was drawn once again to the mangled leg.

"It must have been in terrible pain," she remarked quietly. "Do you suppose that they feel as much pain as—people?"

"I hope so."

She started, frightened and shocked by the black fury in his voice. She saw his hand lift half way to his face before he checked it.

"You told me it was an accident," she breathed, startled and stunned by her intuitive certainty. "You told me it happened in the forge."

"Shut up!" he shouted at her. "Shut your mouth."

He became aware of Spartala and Tsexhau watching him in open-mouthed astonishment. He swung on them, his anger finding another target.

"What the hell are you staring at?" he shouted in Setswana. "Get on with the skinning."

They hastily dropped their spears and bent to the carcass, each one of them drawing a knife.

"Why?" she asked softly, puzzled and pleading. "Why did you tell me that?"

"Mind your own business," he said curtly.

Her eyebrows lifted, and then she smiled mirthlessly. "You trying to get back at someone, killing these cats?"

He started, but then he grinned, the smile twisting his face up and making it look hideous. "I've always hunted, always enjoyed it."

She flinched inwardly, but it didn't show. "Doesn't look like you're enjoying it much these days," she commented sardonically.

He glared at her again, his eyes darkening. "Who do you think you are, talking to me like that?" he demanded. "You're just a bloody useless woman."

"So," she drawled softly. "So that's the way it is."

"What's that supposed to mean?"

"It means you shouldn't swear, mister man," she said, ironic and contemptuous and somehow feeling a little sad at the same time.

Jannie turned away from her, and he lit a cigarette with trembling hands. He smoked in silence, watching the skinners at work. When the leopard finally yielded up its skin it looked naked and somehow obscene.

Tsexhau cut off its testicles and penis, and he stripped some of the thick fat from the carcass. It was all powerful medicine. He rolled it up inside the wet hide where it would keep in safety.

They tramped back to the Land Rover in silence, taking the trap with them and the ripe-smelling remains of the ostrich.

"Are you going to put that trap out again?" she demanded.

"Yes."

She nodded, digesting the information. "How much longer we staying out here in this desert of yours?"

He thought he detected a note of sarcasm in her voice, but he wasn't sure. "Five or six days. Why?"

"That'll be about six days too long for me."

He opened his mouth, shut it, then opened it again and spoke very quietly. "Too bad."

He opened the door of the Land Rover. He fingered two shells from the box on the shelf beside the dash. He reloaded the rifle and then racked it and climbed in behind the wheel.

He fired the engine and revved it. He swung the vehicle hard right and then reversed. He followed his own spoor out through the bush.

5

THEY DRAGGED themselves wearily into the scant shade of a thorn bush. The sun was almost directly overhead. It beat down on them, implacable and indifferent.

They were thin, their lips black and cracked, their sunken eyes dimmed and dulled with fatigue. Of them all, Pxui was in the best condition, the natural resilience of his youth and the vitality of his strong young body still working for him. The old man, the grandfather of Xhabbo, was not far from the end. He knew this.

They unslung their packs, propping themselves against them. For a while they sat motionless, dazed, and when their eyes met the fear and uncertainty passed from one to the other and back again like the endless flowing of the current in a cool stream.

The lion had found his own shade a little further back. He dug into the earth with his claws, and he lay belly down on the freshly exposed sand which was a little cooler, his mouth open and his flanks heaving. There was hunger in him, and thirst, and his amber eyes stared unwinkingly at the group of people and beyond them into the shimmering furnace of the desert.

Exxwa's wife stirred. From her skin sack she took a root and passed it to her husband, and then she swung the babe in her arms to her shrunken breast. The infant began to suck. She felt the tug of his hungry mouth, and she knew that a little more of her life and her strength were being drawn from her starved body.

Her husband scraped the root she had given him, an equal portion into each waiting hand. They squeezed the crushed meat, drinking the bitter, milky-white juice. It quenched the thirst, but that was all.

"We have one root left," he said, when he had drained the last drop from the crushed pith. "What else remains among us?"

"I have two," Tsonomon said, giving the accounting of his own supplies.

"One," offered Xhommaha, who was the father of Xhabbo.

They were silent for a while, their eyes meeting again briefly, the fear and apprehension naked, finding no reassurance in each other.

"How far is the water?" asked the old grandfather. It was an effort for him to speak. His voice was cracked and dry, and his words were little more than a faint whisper.

Tsonomon looked up at the burning sun, computing distances against its movement in his mind. "Three length of a bow-string," he said eventually.

The old man nodded, and then he lay back on the sand. "You must build me a house," he said, and now his voice was firmer. "I will wait in it, for the thing which all men wait for."

There was a moment of shocked and disbelieving silence, and the stone he had thrown sent the ripple of an old fear through them all.

"No!" Xhabbo cried.

"My daughter," the old man said softly. "It must be."

"No," she said again. "I am strong, I will help you."

"The sun goes down in its own time," he replied. "So it is with the life of a man."

The smile he gave her was gentle and compassionate, and the eyes in the old wrinkled face were serene with an acceptance that came from having in the past built the little houses for those he himself had loved. It was the way of life, of the eternal desert. A man was a small flicker of flame, but there came a time when there was nothing left for the fire to feed on.

"Not while I have the strength," she said.

"Or I," Pxui told him.

The old man stared at them for a few moments, each in turn. He wanted to tell them that it was futile to try and postpone the inevitable, but he was tired and his mouth was too dry, so he closed his eyes and lay back, giving his body to the earth of the desert, drawing comfort from the feel of it as the babe drew comfort from its mother's breast.

They rested for another hour, and then as if some silent communication had passed between them the men glanced from one to the other. They nodded wordlessly, and they touched the women to wakefulness, and then the wife of Exxwa reached out in turn and gently woke her sleeping son.

He sat up, staring about him in dazed bewilderment, and then when he understood that they were going to move again his face crumpled briefly and he reached out to his mother.

They moved off again, into the murderous heat of the sun. The air was broken and shimmering, and the sky reflected partial images of the scorched land so that it was difficult to differentiate between the mirage and the reality, with the gaunt thorn trees growing upside down in the blistering heat-crazed sky.

Pxui and Xhabbo trailed behind the group, each with an arm around the old man, guiding his faltering steps and taking most of the weight of his body on themselves.

Behind them came the lion, limping heavily through the burning sea of sand and sunflame.

It took them almost four hours to reach the dried-out water course. They settled the old man on the bank, where he lay gasping in the shade.

The men ran down into the river bed, and Xhabbo followed them with a skin full of empty shells and a water pipe. They got down on their hands and knees. They dug frantically, the joy of their anticipation giving them strength.

The sands were dry.

Their eyes met, but each pair only mirrored the same fear and consternation and disbelief. When the initial shock released them from its paralysing grip they fanned out quickly, up and down the bed of the water course.

They dug with a new fury and desperation, tearing and clawing at the sand. It was the same wherever they dug.

They went on digging, refusing to believe it, driven by a fresh burst of fear. One by one they gave up, till only Pxui was left, burrowing frantically into the sand.

Tsonomon touched him gently on the shoulder. He looked up, his eyes glazed and unseeing, the perspiration pouring down his face, the tips of his fingers skinned and raw.

"Save your strength," the man said. "It is dry."

The blindness left the boy's eyes. He rose slowly, the sand falling from his knees and arms. He wiped the perspiration from his face and licked it off his hands.

They walked into the shade by the edge of the water course, where the women and the children waited. The women said nothing, because they knew already, and there was nothing to say. The men sank down to the earth, slipping the quivers from their backs.

They sat there gasping, all of them too dazed and stunned to think or speak.

The old man stirred. He groaned and opened his eyes. He tried to sit up, but he did not have the strength.

"Water?" he asked, his voice thin and reedy.

"The sands have drunk it all," Tsonomon replied.

"Xhe-he, Xhe-he!" the old one cried softly.

They were not words with any meaning, but the ancient cry of despair that was as old as his people. He forced himself to sit up, and the effort made his thin arms tremble. His sunken eyes fixed themselves on Xhabbo, steadied on her and then slid to Pxui.

"You used your strength for nothing," he rebuked them both.

"It is my strength," she answered. "While I have it I will use it."

"You are the child of my son," he said. "You must go on alone, so that I may live in you."

She turned to look at the boy. Her eyes were full of love, but there was an ancient sadness in them too, the shadows of an old memory.

"You also could have lived in me," she said softly, the words for him alone. "Now we have nothing."

He held her gaze, and in those timeless moments they were the only two people in all the world. After a while he lowered his eyes. There was nothing that he could think of to say.

She closed her eyes for a few seconds, pressing the lids tightly together. When she opened them they were clear again.

She stared at her grandfather. "When the time comes," she replied grimly. "That time has not yet come."

She glanced round the group, her eyes fierce and glittering with a hard determination.

"If I say that we should make a pit, for the grandfather and the children, who would say that we should not?"

"Let us do it," Exxwa said immediately.

They nodded their agreement, all of them, and then the men rose. After deliberating a moment they selected a piece of deep shade and went to work quickly.

They dug a shallow pit, using their hands and the grubbing sticks of the women. It was about five feet in length, and about two feet wide. When they had finished, they urinated into it in turn, spreading the precious liquid.

They carried the old man to it, and they laid him on the moistened sand. Next went the boy. He began to protest, but one look at the stark face of his mother and the fear he saw there reached deep into him and made him quiet. They laid the infant beside the old man, and then carefully they packed the sand back into place, over their bodies and around them.

They lay there, cooler than they had been before, in their own micro-environment which would reduce the evaporation of their own body juices and the odds against their survival.

"Let us go now," Tsonomon said. "Let us go and see what we can find."

"Stay with them," Exxwa told his wife.

She nodded, and the rest of them moved off, the men slinging their quivers and picking up their bows and spears, the women with their grubbing sticks.

For a moment the lion stared at the woman who remained, and then its gaze went to the group that was moving out. It struck at the flies that were buzzing round its muzzle, and then it got to its feet and plodded heavily after the boy.

They found no fresh spoor, neither did they see any game. They found three of the bitter tubers, and two of another variety. The animals of the desert had passed before them, and they too had been digging.

They dug up a few nuts, and they gathered a few dried-out *xweeke* berries, which was the sound they made when a person bit into them green.

Six lizards and two long-nosed mice fell to their spear butts, and that was all that they returned with after foraging for almost two hours.

When they returned to the bank of the water course they found that Exxwa's wife had gathered wood and lit a fire. They roasted the lizards and mice whole. The food was shared quickly, and they ate the guts and skin.

The two sweet tubers were divided between them, and they bit into them carefully, so as not to spill any of the juice, and then they chewed and swallowed their portions, pith and skin.

All except Pxui.

He had saved half of his meat, and also half of the portion of tuber which had been his share. He got up, conscious of their eyes on him, bleak and condemning. He walked over to where the lion was lying. He halted a few feet from him. The yellow eyes watched him attentively.

He threw the meat, and then the bit of tuber. They landed between the big paws. The lion ate the piece of lizard first, and then it chewed down the tuber.

Pxui watched him chewing for a moment and then turned away. He felt foolish, because it was so little, but the compulsion within him was stronger than his own hunger and thirst. He returned to the group and sat down. They watched him in silence for a while, and then Tsonomon spoke.

"Truly you have lost your senses."

"I must."

For a while no one said anything, and then the old man rubbed the folds of skin on his belly and patted it. He was sitting up, out of the pit now, refreshed by his rest and the meagre nourishment he had taken.

"That was good," he said.

Xhabbo stared at her grandfather. There was love in her eyes, and pain. She remembered sitting between his knees, and listening to his stories. He looked old and frail and weak now, and she wondered how much longer he would last. The thought frightened her, because his death would in some indefinable way be the death of her own childhood.

"A little more," the old man continued, "and once again I might be as strong as a lion."

She started, glancing at the lion, and then the thought which had been hidden at the back of her mind crystallized in a sudden rush.

"The lion," she breathed. "We should kill him and eat him."

A hushed deathly silence greeted her words. She glanced at the others in turn, and in the eyes which met her own she saw the sudden flowering of hope before they shied away uneasily and she knew that she was not the only one who had considered the idea.

It gave her the courage to finally look at Pxui. His face was a mask, but his eyes burned with a cold watchfulness. Her own shame drove her.

"Whose survival is more important?" she shouted. "His or ours?"

"Ours!" cried Exxwa, and he glanced at his son and the babe beside his wife.

"No," the boy said, his voice quiet but harsh. "If I am to be a person, his survival is also important."

"And if you have gone on the long journey, oh my son?" asked his mother. "What will it matter then?"

"We are not walking in the shadows yet, oh my mother."

"And when we are?"

He stared at her for a long while, his eyes wide and full of misery and despair. After that he glanced at them swiftly in turn, but their faces were closed and inscrutable.

"Have you forgotten already?" he shouted. "Have you forgotten the eland that he killed for us?"

"That does not concern us now," Xhabbo pointed out coldly.

"It concerns me," he said, and the pain was deep in him as he searched her face. "Of all the people, it was you. I did not think such a thing would come from you."

"Is my grandfather not more important than a lion?" she asked softly. "The meat and the blood of the beast would give him the strength to go on."

He shook his head in confusion, unable to answer, because truly he did not know. "I should have killed him that day. But I didn't. I licked his tears, and I gave him the chance to live. Because I gave it to him, his life is in my hands. I am his father now."

"We can wait," Exxwa said, and he glanced at the lion, licking his cracked lips unconsciously. "We can wait another day, perhaps two, but if things do not get better——" He broke off, his voice trailing into emptiness, the unspoken implication more chilling than words.

The boy rose. He slung his quiver and his pack, and he picked up his bow and spear. He eyed them in turn, and his heart was pounding, because though their faces were familiar they were as strangers to him now.

"Forgive me, but I will do something," he said quietly, and his right hand lifted and fingered the arrows in his quiver. "I do not know what I will do, but I will have to do something. Therefore you must not think of killing the lion, because I do not know what I will do."

He turned and walked away. They watched him go in silence, and they saw him begin to smooth the sand out a few feet away from the lion. They knew that it was where he would sleep.

"We must leave before the sun is up," Tsonomon said eventually.

"We will walk till the heat of the day drives us into the shade. There we will rest, and then go on again when the sun falls."

He took the harp from his sack and began to tap it. They listened to the hollow notes, soothed by the echoing music. The sun went down, and the sky became red with the fire of its dying.

On the southern horizon the clouds began to collect. They gathered slowly, but then they rose towering into the sky, formidable and black.

Later that night they saw the flashes of lightning and they heard the roll of thunder, but it was still very far away.

6

THEY HAD BEEN walking for four hours, heading south towards where they had seen the lightning the night before. Pxui was some distance to the rear of the straggling group, the lion behind him and almost on his heels.

The animal kept close to him now, closer than ever before, and he wondered if he had somehow sensed their intentions and their animosity.

The old man was failing fast, and they were taking it in turns to help him. The sun climbed higher into the sky. It hung there, and the earth seemed to cower and shrivel under its pitiless onslaught.

His lips were cracked, and his tongue swollen, and his throat was tight and dry, the flesh like cotton. It seemed to the old man that he had been walking all his life, blindly and automatically putting one foot down in front of the other, with no end in sight to the number of times he would have to keep on doing it. He wondered how much longer he would last.

An hour later the group ahead halted and crawled into the shade of a thorn bush. Pxui found his own shade and lay down, and the lion lay down a little way from him.

He watched him for a while, the heaving flanks, the ticks on his hide, heads buried deep and feeding. They were sucking the life from his body, but there was nothing he could do about that.

From his sack he took a piece of the root his mother had given him. He scraped a little of it into the palm of one hand and expressed the juice onto his tongue.

The bitterness made his mouth tighten, but then the spasm passed and he felt his tongue begin to unglue itself from his palate.

He wolfed down the pith that remained, but it only made the ache of hunger deeper and more insistent. It was not the first time he had been hungry, and if he lived, he knew it would not be the last.

A little later Xhabbo limped across the burning sand. She sank painfully to the ground, at the edge of the thin shade.

"It has come," she said. "He cannot go on, and we are too weak to help him. The time has come to build his house."

He stared deep into her eyes. They were hard, but they were also bright with sorrow and pain. He knew what she wanted.

"I am sorry," he said. "I am truly sorry, but I cannot kill the lion."

"I understand," she replied stiffly.

She got up, and her hand rose to the waist of her tassel-fringed loinskin.

"I will help," the boy said, "to make the house."

"No!" she retorted, and her hand moved and the fingers probed within the waistband of her skin covering and brought forth the small arrow she had kept against her body.

She broke it in two, and threw it at his feet, and then she turned quickly, a wildness in her eyes, of pain and other things for which no man had ever made the words. She limped away.

He stared at the broken arrow. He felt as if something was breaking inside him, but then the sharp pain went and left only a black suffocating numbness. It was easier to bear.

He turned and looked at the lion for a while. His lips moved silently, but no words came. He picked up the broken pieces of the arrow, with their delicate decorations. He stared at them blindly for a moment, and then he tossed them away.

A little later he saw them begin to work on the shelter. They made it out of thorn, the roof also. It would keep the wild animals out for a while, but eventually they would become emboldened and break through. The leopard and the hyena, and anything else with an empty belly.

It was the way, when a person survived to grow truly old, and there was nothing that anyone could do about it. The desert made its own laws.

When it was finished, with the old man locked away inside, they rested again. The boy dozed, his mind hovering just below the level of consciousness.

He woke instantly when they began to wail and cry. The sounds of their grief were bitter and full of pain. He began to get up, thinking to join them in saying his farewell, but he sank to the ground again. He was frightened of them, for the lion.

When they had shed the gall of their anguish they moved out. Some of them glanced back, signalling him with a wave.

He pushed himself wearily to his feet and started forward. He halted by the little house of thorn where the old man lay resting.

Within the hut, on the sand beside him, lay one of the precious tubers, and a wooden knife to scrape it. The knife wasn't much, just a stick with one side whittled to an edge.

"Old father?" the boy whispered.

The old man stirred, and he pushed himself up painfully. Pxui squatted, and they peered at each other through the thorn.

"I am here."

"Forgive me, but I could not kill the big beast," the boy explained. "If the flesh of my body would have given you strength, I would give it to you. I would give it to you gladly, so that you might gain strength."

The old man nodded, and then he smiled. It was very gentle, on his old wrinkled face where time had drawn its map. "I do not wait in this house because you did not kill the lion. The sun begins to grow dark for me, that is why I wait."

The boy felt his throat tighten. "I could not do it. I just could not."

"How could you?" the old man replied. "Can a father kill his son when the son has neither harmed him nor disgraced him?"

For a moment the boy wasn't sure precisely what he meant, but then it came to him, and the gratitude that welled in him was so strong it felt like pain.

"You understand?" he asked hesitantly.

"Yes."

The boy reached into the sack on his back. He brought out the four remaining inches of tuber. He cut it in half, and held out one portion to the old man, pushing his arm through the thorn.

The old man took it wordlessly, and before the boy could withdraw his hand he placed in it the root that the others had left him. The boy stared at it, and then he began to shake his head violently.

"Old father, I cannot take it."

"You must," the man replied, his voice strong and firm now. "You have a long way to go, and so does my daughter. She must live, and so must you. Go now, and guide her into the sun for the rest of her days."

"She broke my arrow."

A faint laugh came from beyond the wall of thorn. "Does a hunter brave the sands with only one arrow in his quiver?"

"No."

"Then go, but before you do, reach through the thorn and give me your hand."

The boy felt the brush of ancient fingers against his own, and something was slipped into the palm of his hand. He withdrew it, staring in surprise at the small piece of root which he had given the old man.

"Old father, I——"

"Go!"

There was a bleak and terrible finality in the command. The boy hesitated a moment, and then he rose slowly.

"Thank you, old father," the boy whispered.

The reply came from inside the thorn. "You do not thank a man for acting well. It is his pleasure and his privilege. Go now."

The boy turned away and started out after the others, the lion padding close behind him. He felt a stinging in his eyes, but he had no tears to shed.

It was about two hours later that they heard the faint drone of a distant vehicle. They froze, listening to the sound, trying to pinpoint its direction.

Their first instinctive reaction to it was fear, but that was replaced almost immediately by the knowledge that it might also mean salvation.

"What is it?" Pxui whispered, as he came abreast of the group.

"Listen!"

For a few moments he heard nothing, but then it reached him, the rise and fall of sound that was so faint it might have been the beating of a pulse inside his head.

There was something about the sound that jogged his memory. He struggled with it for a moment, listening intently, knowing that there was a significance to that particular sound. A moment later cold terror swept through him.

"Let us go!" Tsonomon cried. "Let us go and ask for help."

They stared at him in disbelief, and then a moment later hope began to grow in their eyes.

The faint drone of the engine died out. They strained their ears, tense with bated breath, but they heard nothing more.

They stiffened a moment later at the muted crash of a rifle. The rolling echoes dwindled, and then they heard the vehicle start up again.

They started forward, the hope rising in them fresh again. Beneath their hope was the fear that they might be hoping in vain. They lengthened their stride, their small legs pistoning backwards and forwards.

Gradually, imperceptibly, the boy began to lag further and further behind. There came a moment when he could no longer see them, when the straggling line was hidden from his view behind a barrier of bush.

Pxui turned aside swiftly, moving off at right angles to the direction they were taking. He shut his mind to the exhaustion in his body, and he broke into his steady mile-devouring lope. The lion ran behind him.

Within his thicket of thorn, the old man sat, thinking his thoughts. He had no fear, because he knew that wherever the journey led him to, he would just start all over again, as one of the hunters, or as one of those who was hunted.

7

THE CAB of the Land Rover was like a furnace. They had driven all morning without sighting any game. In the early afternoon they had sighted a lone duiker, but it vanished before Jannie could even halt the truck.

"I don't know," Carol commented, taking it all in, "how anyone can live out here."

"They do."

"These Bushmen," she said. "Do you think we'll see any of them?"

"I couldn't say."

She shrugged. "No sense in trying to talk to a man who doesn't want to talk."

He drove on in silence. The thick scrub gave way to open grassland. There was no grass, only burned stubble. The finely powdered earth swirled behind the vehicle in an ochre cloud. It was everywhere, in their hair and nostrils and in their throats.

Jannie saw them at about four in the afternoon, when he was thinking of calling it a day. Motionless they had looked like part of the land, and then bursting into sudden movement they had revealed themselves.

They milled in panic, six gemsbok, galloping erratically in different directions until the bull took charge and they began to run with purpose.

"Look!" she cried. "Do you see them?"

He was swinging the wheel over, beginning to accelerate, when his eye picked up a soft flow of movement in the distance, straight ahead.

He hadn't seen it earlier, because directly beyond it were half a dozen scattered camel thorn trees. The flat terrain had distorted perspective, and it had blended perfectly with the trees until it moved. He swung the wheel back and went on ahead, ignoring the stampeding gemsbok.

"What's the matter?" she cried, excited by the game and the sight of life on the plain. "Aren't you going after them?"

"Straight ahead," he said. "There's a giraffe by those trees."

"Where?" she exclaimed, sitting forward tensely. "I don't see it."

"It's moving past that last thorn tree on the right," he said. "See it now?"

She sat forward, peering through the windscreen, her face almost touching it. "Yes!" she cried abruptly. "Yes, I see it now."

It was about three hundred yards away, moving slowly and unconcernedly past the thorn trees. As Jannie accelerated slightly it halted and turned towards them. It held the regal pose for a few seconds and then began cantering away. Jannie immediately braked and brought the Land Rover to a halt.

The giraffe moved with an effortless grace. The long legs made it seem as if it was moving in slow motion, gliding over the earth, a clipper ship of the desert with the tall column of its neck a proud figurehead that ran before it. It ran for about fifty yards and then halted and turned to stare at them.

"It's beautiful," she said suddenly. "Isn't it?"

Jannie nodded, intent on the animal. He reached behind him and took down the .375 Magnum, lifting it over their heads and settling it across their laps. The barrel lay over his thighs.

"Are you allowed to shoot them?" she asked.

"Not normally, but Spartala wangled a licence from the tribe."

"It seems, well, a shame, to kill something so beautiful."

"It's meat," he replied laconically.

He engaged second and drove forward slowly, his foot light on the accelerator, his eyes fixed unwaveringly on the giraffe. He hadn't driven more than fifty yards when it turned and cantered away casually. Once more he halted the vehicle and watched it, waiting to see how far it would run. It ran a little way and then came to a halt. Once more it turned to watch them.

"Why doesn't it run?" she whispered. "Why doesn't it run away and escape?"

"Curiosity," he replied. "They're very curious, like most animals."

He studied it a moment longer and then drove forward cautiously. He did not approach it directly, but drove towards it at an oblique angle. It made them less suspicious.

The actual distance between them closed slowly. When there was about a hundred and sixty yards separating them he brought the Land Rover to a halt and switched off the engine.

For a moment he sat without moving, his breath coming more quickly. He was reaching for the door handle when he shot a glance at her. He saw the look on her face, the raw excitement, the longing in the eyes that were fixed on his rifle.

"You said you could shoot," he whispered, flicking a glance at the standing animal.

"I can. I used to shoot. Varmints, stuff like that."

"Do you want a shot?"

"You have to be joking?"

"I'm not."

Her breath caught, her eyes wide, and then she breathed out shakily. "I'd love to have a shot."

"Get out," he whispered. "And do it quietly."

He opened his own door and slid out. He crouched and went round the bonnet of the truck, so that the watching giraffe would not see any alteration to the silhouette of the vehicle. He made a quick estimation of the range and altered his sights. He cocked the rifle and handed it to her.

"She kicks a bit, so hold it firm," he whispered. "Take a dead rest on the bonnet, it'll be easiest."

He saw instantly that she had handled a rifle before. She pulled it in snug against her shoulder and then settled her cheek against the stock. Her finger began to curl round the trigger.

He was wondering impatiently how long it was going to take her to shoot when the roar of the explosion took him by surprise. A fraction of a second later, with his ears still ringing from the blast, he heard the wet meaty slap of the striking bullet.

The spinning bullet struck. It rammed its way through hide and flesh. It hit bone and deflected slightly. The nose mushroomed and it plunged on. It smashed on through living tissue, a mindless chunk of copper and lead, furiously intent on achieving nothing more frightening than a state of equilibrium. Vital flesh and sinew exploded and disintegrated as it absorbed the monstrous influx of energy.

The giraffe rocked under the impact of the massive blow. It remained motionless for a few moments and then it whirled and galloped off.

"Oh dammit!" she exploded softly. "I missed."

"Get in!" he cried. "You didn't."

He snatched the rifle from her and ran round the bonnet. He scrambled in, started the engine, and roared after the giraffe, the sand spurting from under the spinning wheels.

He gained rapidly on the animal. He was swinging wide preparatory to cutting in on it when it slowed abruptly and came to a halt. He braked and brought the Land Rover to a stop about fifty yards from it.

"Shoot it!" she breathed tensely. "Finish it off."

"It's had it."

The giraffe turned to stare at them. The short horns on its head, together with its ears, made it look as if it was wearing a four-pointed crown.

It began to quiver. They saw it very clearly from where they were. The movement started in its legs, barely perceptible at first, just a tremor, and then the tremor grew in strength till its vibrations shook the whole body of the animal.

No one had moved or spoken since it began, and no one moved or spoke now. The engine ticked over with the same regular beat. It was the only sound, and it was constant, but none of them were aware of it.

The giraffe took a faltering step forward and then paused. It began to tremble and shake even more violently. It changed the position of its legs, spreading them wide as if it sought to balance itself against the heaving of the earth on which it stood.

The long slender column of its neck began to quiver. Its head began to nod and jerk like a man with palsy. It began to stagger from side to side, as if it were drunk.

It toppled suddenly, legs buckling and giving way beneath it. They heard the thud of its body hitting the ground. She sat unmoving, stunned and silent, and she knew that she had seen the destruction of a temple, the first stone of which had been laid down at the beginning of time.

She drew a sudden stricken breath. Her face crumpled abruptly and she burst into tears. He watched her, his expression gentle. After a while she stopped crying, knuckling the tears from her eyes.

"It's a hell of a thing, and it gets to you," he said softly. "I feel pretty much the same. After a while it doesn't show much, but it's there inside."

He drove forward, halting the Land Rover a few yards from it. The giraffe kicked out feebly and raised its head. She opened the door, began to get out.

"Wait!" he snapped.

"Why?"

"Just wait, unless you want to go up and get your head kicked off."

He watched the giraffe a little longer. It struggled again, its head lifting, but then the long neck crashed back to the ground. He racked the rifle on his lap. The animal was finished.

They left the truck and gathered in a small group round its head. Red foam was bubbling from its nostrils, the froth catching in bubbles on the hairs of its long prehensile lips.

"It's still alive!" she exclaimed, a thread of horror running through her voice.

In that moment the eyes of the giraffe focussed on her. They were the loveliest, most gentle eyes she had ever seen. They were dark brown, almost purple in their depths, and the long curved sweep of the enormous eyelashes made them look disturbingly human.

"Please," she whispered. "Kill it."

Jannie took the knife from Spartala. They stepped in close, taking an ear each. The giraffe tried to twist its head free, but the movement was without strength.

He placed the point of the knife just behind the skull, at the nape of its neck. He thrust it in, grunting with the effort. He twisted the blade from side to side. The giraffe stiffened. A spasm ran through its arched body and then it became still.

The purple eyes became blind and opaque. There was no beauty in them any more, there was nothing. A whole universe died then and was no more, as it did each time death shuttered a pair of living eyes.

He offered her a cigarette, but she shook her head and turned away. She unhooked one of the water bags from the Land Rover and drank thirstily.

She leaned against the wing of the vehicle. She watched them go to work on the carcass, reducing it rapidly with axe and knife to blood-smeared slabs of meat and bone.

She shut her eyes for a few moments, blotting out the sight of carnage. In her mind she saw it again as it had been in life, a stately vessel sailing across the desert sands.

Spartala and Tsexhau threw the last of the meat into the back of the Land Rover. The springs flattened under the thousand-pound load. All that remained of the animal on the desert where it had roamed was a wet smear and a pile of flaccid entrails which would be gone long before the sun rose again.

"Are you all right now?" Jannie asked.

"It was crazy, wasn't it?" she murmured. "To cry."

"No, it wasn't," he replied quietly. "It would perhaps have been crazy if you hadn't."

She gave him a strange searching sort of look. He held her gaze a moment. He began to nod.

"That's one of the things about hunting that people who haven't hunted don't know about," he said. "The good pain."

He turned away abruptly, walked round the bonnet and jerked open the door of the Land Rover. He was about to climb in when Tsexhau let out a startled cry. There was a strange excitement in his voice.

"Look, morena!" he cried. "Wild Bushmen, coming this way."

Jannie followed the direction of his pointing arm. At first he couldn't see them, but then his eyes picked them out. They were quite a way off, but even at that distance he could see them waving their arms frantically, and a moment later he heard their shrill faint cries.

They came on with a dogged deliberateness, people who had reached physical exhaustion and were now forcing themselves to continue by fuelling their bodies with the last reserves of their spirit.

"Who are they?" she cried.

"Bushmen."

She was silent for a moment, digesting the information. "I thought you said they were frightened of people, that they hardly ever showed themselves and were difficult to find?"

"They are."

"They don't look—afraid of us."

"They are, but they're more afraid of dying," he said. "Look at them, use your eyes."

Tsonomon came to a halt. His chest was heaving and he swayed unsteadily on his feet. He held his right hand out, palm up.

"Good day," he croaked. "We saw you from afar and we are dying of hunger."

There was a look in their eyes of people who had come through the shadowlands and could not believe that they were in the sunlight again.

"Tshjamm!" Jannie replied, quickly unhooking both water bags, and then using up most of his vocabulary, he finished the traditional response. "I was dying before you came, but now I live again."

He handed both bags to Tsonomon, who in turn passed one on and then drank swiftly and deeply before handing over the second bag. They drank in turns from the two bags, and Spartala refilled them four times from the twenty-gallon tank in the back of the Land Rover.

They stared in awe and wonder at the life-giving water which flowed from the tap of the tank, the expression on their faces reverent and incredulous.

When they had quenched their terrible thirst they sank to the ground. They unslung their packs and leaned against them, their heads bowed and their arms clasped round their knees, their breath coming in short shallow gasps.

After a while the wife of Exxwa lifted her infant child to her breast. The small hands squeezed at it hungrily, and the sucking lips bruised her nipple. She felt the flow of life from her breast, and on her face was a look of indescribable tenderness made more poignant by the naked relief with which it was mingled.

"They must have drunk about a gallon each," Carol commented. "They look half dead."

"They were."

She took in their dirt- and dust-stained bodies, the hollow gauntness of their sun-seared faces. They were small statured, and the weariness that cloaked them seemed to make them appear even smaller. She felt a movement of something deep inside her. She didn't know what it was, but she knew she had not felt it for a long time.

"What would have happened to them?" she asked. "If they hadn't found us?"

He shrugged. "They'd have made out."

"They don't look like they could have gone much further," she said doubtfully.

"I tell you they'd have made out," he said, his voice rising a little.

She stared at him curiously. "You like them, don't you?"

"I respect them," he said tersely. "You and I wouldn't last out here two days. They live out here."

One or two of them looked up. She saw them glance at her, their eyes shy and curious. And then she noticed, then, that none of them stared at him. They simply saw him, as he was.

Tsonomon stirred. He raised his bowed head. There was a frown on his face, as if he were searching his mind for some elusive image. His glazed eyes cleared slowly, and then abruptly he sprang to his feet, feverishly scanning the burning distances through which they had just come.

"Pxui!" he shouted, in shocked surprise. "My son is not here, and neither is the lion."

Jannie started and then became tense. He had picked out the last word in the staccato outburst. The word he had picked out was ghum, which was their word for lion. He whirled on Tsexhau.

"What lion?" he snapped, the excitement mounting in him. "Find out what they're talking about."

Tsexhau held up his hand, flapping it from the wrist, signalling Jannie to be quiet. He listened intently to their conversation, struggling with the dialect, but he got most of it.

He began to question them. Jannie listened to the rapid exchange, picking out words here and there, his heart beginning to thump painfully. He wanted to believe that the impossible had happened, that the first improbable thought which had flashed through his mind at the mention of a lion was directly related to the enigma of the one which had escaped from his trap.

"What is it, Tsexhau?" he whispered urgently. "What is it, man?"

The tracker listened a little longer, fired one last question at them, and then turned to Jannie. He spoke rapidly in Setswana, and when he had finished Jannie stood there transfixed. He remained motionless for many long moments, and then he started suddenly, like a man waking from a terrible dream. The blindness faded slowly from his eyes.

"I'm going after that lion now," he said abruptly. "Tell them I want one of them to show me the way. The others can wait here, I'll pick them up on the way back and take them into camp."

Tsexhau conversed with them again, and watching them, Jannie saw their eyes become fearful and furtive, and those who had remained seated rose and began to back away.

"They will not go," Tsexhau said. "They say that the boy has done nothing wrong to be punished."

"Dammit!" Jannie exploded. "I don't want the boy, I want the lion. Nothing will happen to him."

Tsexhau spoke to them again, but they shook their heads stubbornly. "They do not want to do it. They ask you to give them some water and some meat, and to allow them to go on their way."

"No water or meat," Jannie replied grimly. "Unless they show me the way."

They spoke together again, and then eventually Tsonomon nodded and stepped forward.

"He says that he will show you the way, if you do not harm the boy."

"He has my word for that, on my father's head," Jannie replied.

"He says also," Tsexhau went on, "that they had to leave behind an old father. He asks that you go to him first and give him water, for he is near to death with thirst."

"No!" Jannie cried. "The lion first."

"He is dying," Tsexhau pointed out quietly.

Jannie clenched his fists, his face twisted in a grimace of fury and exasperation. "All right, dammit, the old father first," he cried. "Now get some of that meat out of the back to lighten the load. Tell them to eat what they want."

They took out the skin of the giraffe and spread it on the ground. With the Bushmen helping, it took them less than a minute to unload half the meat and dump it on the wet hide.

"Right, let's get going," Jannie exclaimed. "Tell him, Tsexhau, to get in front with us."

He waited impatiently, while Tsonomon and the young girl who was Xhabbo went into an urgent conversation.

"What is it now?" he snapped irritably.

"The girl, she wants to come," Tsexhau informed him.

"Why?"

"It is her grandfather, the old father who lies in his house waiting for the hyenas."

"All right," Jannie growled. "Tell her to get in the back with you and Spartala."

"What's happening?" Carol demanded.

"I'll tell you in the truck."

He ran to the door of the Land Rover and jerked it open. He

scrambled in and started the engine. Tsonomon got in warily beside Carol, and her nose wrinkled instantly.

The Bushman stared helplessly at the door, and Jannie leaned across and jerked it shut. He drove forward, glancing from time to time at the terrified Bushman who was pointing out the direction.

"My God!" she exclaimed. "Is that stink coming from him?"

"Yes."

"It isn't possible."

The smell in her nostrils was compounded of sweat, smoke, dung and the dried blood and body juices of long-dead animals, mingled with the smell of the earth itself. It was overpowering, but as she gradually became accustomed to it, she found herself equating it to the terms by which he lived his life, and her distaste was replaced by a half-sensed and atavistic longing. She wondered what it would be like, to live as close as he to the great womb that was the earth.

"You'd smell just as bad if you lived in this waterless waste," he growled.

"Maybe we all need to smell like that now and again," she said pensively, but then she shook her head, as if she were waking from a dream. "Where are we going, mister man? What's it all about?"

"They left one of their party somewhere along the way," he told her. "An old man, and we're going to find him now."

"What did they leave him for?"

"To die."

"What!" she exclaimed incredulously. "They just left him there to die?"

"That's right."

"What are they, savages or something?" she asked, darting a bleak and startled glance at the Bushman beside her. "Couldn't they have helped to carry him or something?"

"They probably did," he replied quietly. "They probably helped him till they no longer had the strength to help him any more. Then they left him, because there was no other way."

"And if they hadn't found you, he'd just die?"

"Either that, or a leopard or a hyena, or something hungry would come along and kill him and eat him."

She thought over what he had said, the stark reality of it frightening and disturbing, but after a moment's consideration she realized that the rest of the world was no different.

"That's the way it goes," she said. "But at least they're going back for him, which is more than a lot of people would do."

He didn't say anything to that. He glanced at the Bushman, and he changed direction to the left, following the signals of his hand.

"What happens after we find him?" she asked.

"We'll take him aboard, and then I'm going after that lion."

"Lion!" she exclaimed. "What lion?"

In the back of the bouncing vehicle, Xhabbo chattered shrilly to Tsexhau. He had fallen in love with her already, not as a woman, but as a symbol of the beauty that was possible in one whose veins carried the unadulterated blood of his maternal ancestors. Once again he felt a great pride that he was half-Bushman: people had not allowed him to feel it for a long time.

It was not long before she had persuaded him to fill six shells for her with water, and after she had packed them into her sack she got him to cut her a large chunk of meat which quickly joined the eggs. With food and water in her possession once again, she felt a comforting sense of security.

"The lion I was telling you about," Jannie replied. "I still can't believe it, but it happened. This Bushman boy, he freed that lion of mine."

"What Bushman boy, for God's sake?" she asked excitedly. "Where is he?"

"He was with the others, and the lion also, right up until the time they heard the shot you fired," he told her. "They started out in our direction, as fast as they could. It was the last time they saw him. They didn't realize he wasn't with them until his father missed him. They seem to think he ran away because he was afraid of being punished for having freed it in the first place, or afraid that the lion would get shot."

"What do you mean?" she asked, her eyes wide with astonishment. "He ran away with the lion?"

"Apparently, they—they're friends," he said. "This boy and the lion."

"My God!" she whispered, awed and delighted, and looking out on the desert, she saw them in her imagination, the pair of them, a small yellow-brown boy and lion running side by side over the burning wasteland. "Isn't that crazy?"

She dallied happily with the vision. She was still in a world of fantasy when she recalled what he had said. She gasped, and she turned to him with a look of shocked astonishment on her face.

"But you're going to shoot that lion," she said.

"That's right."

"Don't," she cried. "Oh please don't shoot it."

"I'm going to shoot it," he said flatly. "I'm going to get it in my sights and take it's head right off."

"Why?" she pleaded. "Why do you have to kill it?"

"It's mine," he replied. "I trapped it and it's mine."

"Do you own them?" she shouted angrily. "Do you own every living thing out here? Who do you think you are? God or something?"

"The skin's worth quite a bit of money," he said, his own voice beginning to tighten with anger.

"It's not the skin you want, mister man," she said harshly. "Why don't you shoot the boy? That would be more in your line, wouldn't it?"

For a moment he was puzzled, but then he stiffened and his face became a mask. "Shut up!" he breathed, his voice a grating whisper. "Just shut your mouth."

The Bushman beside her shouted, and then he began to chatter excitedly. Jannie swung the truck over to the right and brought it to a halt beside the shelter of thorn.

Xhabbo sprang down from the back the instant it came to a halt. She ran to the shelter and began tearing at the thorn, ripping the branches aside. She was joined moments later by the others, and they helped her to tear open the coffin.

The old man was sitting up, staring at them in bewildered anxiety. Jannie squatted beside him, holding out the unstoppered water bag. The old man stared at it uncomprehendingly for a moment, but then the clean sharp crystalline pungency of the water reached his nostrils and he stretched out eagerly and took it.

He drank till it was empty, and even as he drank they saw the life and hope returning to his faded eyes. When he had finished he sighed with satisfaction. It was a deep, deep sigh, and it sounded as if it came from the depths of his parched and thirst-ravaged body.

"You have given me my life," he said gravely, addressing himself to Jannie.

"What's he saying, Tsexhau?"

"He says that you have given him his life."

"I gave him water," Jannie said brusquely, and then to Spartala: "Help him up into the back of the truck. We must move quickly, or the sun will be down before we can find the lion."

Moments later he was wheeling the Land Rover through the scrub again, following his own spoor back. A little while later the Bushman signalled, and when Jannie brought the vehicle to a halt he scrambled out awkwardly and began casting around for tracks.

It didn't take him long to find the place where his son and the lion had broken away. Jannie bent down to study the spoor of the lion. It was fresh, the sand along the ridges of the broad pug marks not yet settled, and when he touched it lightly with the stem of a piece of dried grass it rolled inwards.

But that was not all. The pug marks of the right front foot indicated that it was an animal with an old injury, and further, the right back pug was defaced by a crescent shaped indentation that was deeper than the rest of the print. He knew then, without any doubt, that it was the same lion which he had followed months before.

He spun back to the Land Rover and lifted the .375 down. He ejected the cartridges, catching them as the extractor drew them clear of the breech. He recharged the magazine with soft-nosed cartridges, putting two of the solids into his shirt pocket.

"Spartala!" he barked. "You get in and drive. Tsexhau, you tell the Masarwa to get on that spoor." He threw a quick glance at the sloping sun. "Tell him to run, and I mean run. You ride in front with Spartala, and when he's tired you take over. And don't tell me any more about bloody ngakas ever again."

Jannie scrambled into the back of the Land Rover, trampling over the meat to get forward to the support of the cab roof.

"Can I get up in back with you?" Carol asked.

He started, becoming aware of her again. "If you want."

She climbed in, and a moment later Spartala ground the gears and took off after the Bushman who was loping along on the spoor.

In the back of the truck the old man was seated beside Xhabbo, his lean rump cushioned on a shoulder of meat. He signalled quietly to Xhabbo. She drew a knife from her pack and passed it to him. He cut a hunk of liver for each of them, and they began to eat, biting into it with relish, and wolfing it down half chewed.

Standing beside Jannie, holding tightly to the roof of the cab for support, Carol turned and glanced at the passengers. She stared in disbelief, and then a little flutter of revulsion swept through her.

"They're eating liver!" she exclaimed.

"That's what it's for."

"Raw," she explained. "They're eating it raw."

He threw a quick glance over his shoulder, smiled at them encouragingly and then swung back to resume his sweeping search of the land ahead.

"Nothing wrong with raw liver," he replied. "You'd eat it raw too, if you were as hungry as they are."

"I suppose so," she murmured, but there was doubt in her voice.

Fifteen minutes later Tsonomon came to a halt, his chest heaving. The water he had drunk and the rest earlier had revived him, but even his phenomenal powers of recuperation were not sufficient to cope with the continuing abuse of his weary body.

The Land Rover drew to a halt beside him. He spoke to Tsexhau, in between his laboured gasps for breath.

"He says that his legs are finished," Tsexhau reported.

"Tell him to get in and rest," Jannie snapped. "You take the spoor."

He ground his teeth together in impotent anger as the trackers conversed. He watched them pointing and gesticulating for a few more moments, and then his impatience burst through.

"Come on, hurry it up," he urged. "We haven't got much time left."

Thinking of the spot-light back at camp, he began to curse silently to himself. He glanced at the sun. It was going down fast, and he estimated that he had no more than half an hour of light at the most. After that he wouldn't be able to see his sights, and that would be the end of it, for the time being.

After a final exchange of information the Bushman climbed into the front of the Land Rover. Tsexhau crouched, studying the spoor. He straightened up after a few moments, and there was a look of uneasiness on his face.

"Fresh tracks," he said. "Very fresh."

"Spoor, man!" Jannie cried. "Take up the spoor."

"And the lion?"

"For God's sake, I'm right behind you, aren't I?"

Tsexhau bridled, at the words and the implication in them, but the cold glittering eyes into which he found himself staring were even more frightening than the prospect of the lion.

He turned abruptly and took up the spoor. He broke into a trot, glancing back over his shoulder periodically to reassure himself about the position of the vehicle.

Carol studied Jannie furtively. His eyes were alight with the reflections of some inner fire. They moved ceaselessly as he searched the broken land ahead.

The sun moved rapidly across the remaining quadrant of the sky. It seemed to hover for a moment just above the edge of the distant horizon, and then it began to settle. It sank rapidly, the earth swallowing it.

Jannie threw a swift and murderous look towards the west, as if by its setting the sun had affronted him personally. The light began to change, the shadows deepening slowly, the hard sharp definition fading.

Carol felt the tension draining from her. Muscles which had tightened in fearful expectation began to relax. A blissful limpness began to spread slowly through her body.

"You won't get it now," she said. "I'm glad about that, not for what you might think, but for your sake."

"What do you mean, for my——"

He never finished the sentence. He pounded on the roof of the cab, two swift blows which were so close together they sounded like one. The Land Rover lurched to a violent halt that threw her forward against the back of the cab.

Jannie cocked the rifle and threw it up. She followed the direction of the pointing barrel. For an instant she saw nothing, but then she stiffened.

They were running across a little open pocket of ground, the boy in front, dark copper in the fading light, his straining limbs stretched in speed, the lion a little way behind.

It was a sight she would never forget, that first glimpse of them in the purple light, two creatures fleeing for their lives.

"Don't!" she screamed. "Don't shoot."

She glanced at him. The look on his face horrified her. It was set in a hideous twisted mask, as if he were in the grip of some frightful nightmare.

She saw his finger tighten on the trigger as the rifle tracked its target. She threw herself against him, and even as he staggered and she felt herself falling she heard the shocking explosion of the rifle from right beside her.

She straightened up, her ears still ringing from the blast. She saw him work the bolt of the rifle with a lightning-fast flick of his wrist. He threw it up again, and then a moment later he lowered it slowly.

For a long while he stared blindly at the spot where the lion had vanished. He opened the bolt handle of the rifle, drew it back a little, held the trigger down and then closed it carefully. He laid the rifle across the top of the cab, and then very deliberately, he turned to face her.

He was gasping softly, like a man fighting for his breath and his life. She began to feel afraid, looking into the fine quiet madness that was seething in his eyes.

"Why did you?" he whispered. "Why did you do that?"

"You're killing people," she breathed, her voice a broken croak. "Someone, a woman maybe, I don't really know what happened to your face. You're killing a lion, but you're really killing a person, and you're killing yourself doing it."

She saw him start, his eyes wide and shocked, and then he laughed at her. She felt the palm of his hand smash against the side of her face. There was a stinging flash of pain, and then a merciful numbness blanketed her mind.

The force of the blow flung her back against the pipe rails. She clung to them for support, fighting the dizziness that swept through her in wave after black wave.

She felt the shocking jolt of his open hand against the other side of her face. He continued to hammer at her, first one side and then the other. She clung desperately to the rails, her whole body jerking with the force of each blow.

There was a strange coppery taste in her mouth. It took a while to penetrate her dazed mind that it was blood. She licked at her bruised lips, the taste coming stronger. Through her blurring vision she saw him cock his right hand again.

"Go on," she whispered, the words coming thickly through her smashed lips. "If it'll help you, kill me and think you've killed a lion."

"Morena!" Spartala shouted, vaulting over the side and into the back of the truck. "Enough, morena, enough."

Xhabbo whispered a few words to her grandfather, and then she slipped quietly from the truck. She spoke to Tsonomon, her voice rising in exasperation. When he began to nod reluctantly she touched him lightly on the arm, a gesture of farewell and gratitude, and then she slipped away into the gathering darkness.

Jannie blinked his eyes. The look of blindness in them cleared slowly. He glanced at the woman who was sagging against the rails of the Land Rover, and then he lowered his raised hand, staring at it uncomprehendingly, as if it were something that he had never seen before.

He picked up his rifle and climbed wearily out of the truck. He unhooked one of the water bags and drank deeply.

Spartala helped her from the back of the Land Rover, lifting her up and over the tailboard. He took the water bag from the bonnet and handed it deferentially to her.

In the thickening dusk Xhabbo followed the spoor of the boy and the lion till the light faded out and she could no longer follow it. She unslung her pack quickly and began to collect grass and twigs and dead scrub wood. Using her sticks she lit a fire, and by its light she went on to collect a further supply of kindling.

She made her place by the fire. She drank sparingly from one of the shells, and then took the meat from her pack and began to broil it on the coals. She stared into the fire, wondering how long it would take to catch up with him in the morning.

To the south, great cloud columns began to mass in the sky. A little later, the lightning began to play, and as she watched it strike she felt fresh hope begin to stir in her again.

8

BEFORE THE SUN came up over the horizon, while the land was still clothed in grey, Pxui was up and away, moving southwards toward where he had seen the lightning flash the night before.

The small herd of gemsbok that Jannie had ignored in favour of the giraffe was also moving in a southerly direction: they too had seen the lightning.

The sun edged up over the horizon, a thin sliver that grew rapidly in size till it had cleared the earth. As it began its ascent into the sky, the harmless red ball gradually began to change colour. It went from red to orange, and then the orange faded and gave way to a fiery metallic yellow. The enemy had revealed itself.

He was grateful for the light, but he cringed inwardly. There were no clouds that he could see anywhere, and he knew that it would be another merciless day.

A little later he spotted the two small green leaves peeping from a tangle of grass stubble. He dug the root out with his spear. He brushed the sand and dirt from it and bit into it ravenously.

The cool juices bathed his parched and swollen mouth, and the ecstasy of it made him shut his eyes and in his mind he saw those great stretches of shallow water that sometimes lay like a blue mirror in the desert pans for a few days after it had rained.

He had eaten half the root before he remembered the lion. It was about ten feet away, on its haunches, its eyes like transparent amber in the morning light. They were fixed unwinkingly on him.

He took another bite at the tuber. The mouthful seemed to make his thirst and hunger even more pronounced. He was lifting the tuber to his mouth again when he checked himself with an effort of will that took all his strength.

He looked at the tuber, and then quickly, before he could yield to temptation, he tossed the remains of it to the lion. The animal pounced on it and began to chew.

He started off again, with his shadow to the right and tall on the ground. He glanced at it, and its familiarity comforted him. He began to think of Xhabbo. He found it difficult to conjure up her face. In the eye of his mind he saw only the beads which had hung between her breasts, and the arrow which she had broken. He pushed the thought of her from his mind, because it was too painful to think about.

Two hours later he came across fresh spoor. It was so fresh that it made his heart leap with hope and excitement. There were five cows and one bull, and from the spoor he knew that they had passed only a little while before, moving in the same southerly direction in which he was travelling.

He hitched at the quiver on his back, fingering the notched butt of an arrow, and then he broke into a slow easy lope.

He saw them fifteen minutes later, and he came to a halt beside a bush of white thorn. The thudding of his heart was like a drum beat inside his head. He studied the distant herd for a few moments. They were moving slowly, foraging as they went.

He checked the direction of the wind, and then threw a quick apprehensive glance at the lion. The animal had gone to earth, flat down on his belly, and his eyes were fixed on the moving herd.

Pxui began his stalk. He moved from bush to bush, running crouched and out of sight. Where there was insufficient cover, he wriggled forward over the hot sand with his belly as close to it as the belly of a lizard.

It took him an hour to get into position. The nearest animal was one of the females. It was about forty-five yards away, and still unaware of his presence. Its hide was a sandy grey, and he could see the clear pattern of the black marks on its face and flanks.

He slipped an arrow from his quiver. He notched it to his bow. He knuckled the sweat from his eyes. One at a time he got his knees beneath him, taking the weight of his body on his elbows.

"Now," he told himself.

Twenty yards from where he crouched the lion broke cover, streaking forward, a blur of black and gold.

The boy saw him out of the corner of his eye just as he began to come upright on his knees.

Half-way towards his intended victim the lion stumbled and went down. He rolled over twice, the dust flying, and when he regained his feet the herd had already turned and bolted.

The boy stared at the vanishing animals in stunned disbelief. He became conscious after a few moments of the drawn bow in his hands. Slowly he eased back on the string, and then he unhooked the arrow and returned it to his quiver. He rose to his feet, fixing his eyes on the lion which was limping back towards him.

The animal came to a halt, a little way off. Pxui noticed how thin he was, the ribs showing through the skin, and he wondered why he hadn't observed it before.

He stared into the eyes, and he wondered whether it was only his imagination or whether he had in fact seen a glitter of despair deep in their shining jewelled depths.

He fought it, but the slow-dawning knowledge of what he had to do grew in him inexorably. He remembered long ago where it had all started, and he began to think about the story of the young hunter and the lion. He thought he began to perceive an added dimension within the parable of the legend, but it was too tenuous to grasp completely.

He lifted his bowed head, and now his eyes were stark and unseeing. He glanced about, and he felt a strange numbness creeping into his body.

A little distance off he saw what he had been seeking. He started walking towards it. He reached the tall thorn tree, and he stood there for a while, staring at it, lost in his own thoughts. He began to climb it, and he was crying quietly inside himself, the weariness in him not so much of the body but of the spirit.

He took an arrow from his quiver and notched it to his bow. He made the eland sound, the clicking that its hoofs made on the desert sand.

The lion came obediently towards him, and he remembered how it had been in the beginning when he had first tried to call him. Those days were so far back that it seemed now as if they had only happened in a dream.

The lion halted, just below the tree. He sat back on his haunches, looking up at the boy, the beautiful eyes alight with a puzzled curiosity.

Pxui stared down at him for a moment, and then he began to bend the bow. The golden eyes were hypnotic, and he felt his resolution begin to waver. He bent the bow a little more, trying to swallow the pain in his throat.

"Forgive me, my brother," he whispered thickly. "But I will try to make it quick for you."

There was nowhere that he could do that, except the eye. The thought made him sick, but he forced himself to steady his aim. The glowing golden orb filled his vision.

The bow twanged like a breaking harp string. The arrow flew true, deep into the left eye of the lion. The boy felt as if his heart had broken.

The lion leaped into the air, roaring in pain and shock and surprise. He struck and clawed and bit at the slender thorn tree, and then he span away, mindless with the mortal pain, flattening and devastating the bushes into which he blundered.

He died a few minutes later, and the earth and vegetation looked as if they had been struck by a tornado.

The boy climbed down out of the tree. He walked over to where the lion lay. He stood there, looking down at him. He felt nothing, because inside of him everything was numb.

He heard someone call his name. He did not turn or pay any attention, because he thought the sound had come from somewhere inside his own reeling head. It came again, from closer and almost right beside him. He turned slowly, his eyes blind and unfocussed.

She was standing a few yards away, but he didn't believe it at first. Her figure swayed and shimmered, as if it were made of the sunlight and the air. He blinked his eyes, and she sprang into sudden sharp focus.

"Xhabbo!" he exclaimed softly, and then abruptly he burst into tears, the sounds coming up broken from somewhere deep inside him.

"I heard him roar," she said. "I heard him roar after you killed him with your arrow."

"I also killed something inside myself," he whispered. "But I had to do it, because only I licked the salt of his tears."

He began to feel suddenly light-headed, and the earth seemed to move beneath his small bare feet. He would have fallen then, but somehow, though he hadn't seen her move, he felt her arm around his body and she lowered him slowly to the ground.

He drank deeply from the shell she gave him. He drained it and then drank another one dry. The strength returned slowly to his body.

"The water?" he asked. "Where did you get such sweet water?"

"Later," she said. "Eat first."

He nodded dumbly, taking the meat from her hands. She sat there beside him, their bodies touching. She studied his face, the weariness of it, and as she stared at him she saw the blankness slowly fade and leave his eyes. She reached out, and she wrapped an arm around his scratched and bleeding dust-smeared thigh.

9

AT FIRST LIGHT, people stirred and the camp began to come awake. They stretched and yawned, roused themselves and got up. Some of them walked off a little way into the bush, moving like sleep-walkers, in response to the demands of their bladders and bowels.

Jannie brushed his teeth and then rinsed his face, using the water sparingly. With Spartala assisting him, he filled the water tank in the back of the Land Rover and then topped up with fuel. He checked the water in the radiator, and the engine oil, and then he went over the tyres for cuts.

When he had finished, the aroma of coffee and roasting meat sweetened the morning air. The Bushmen were sprawled round their own fire, the women cooking, speaking softly amongst themselves. Joseph was busy over his own fire, laying rashers of bacon into a blackened frying pan.

Jannie glanced furtively at Carol. She was bent over the basin of water he had filled and left for her, lifting it in her cupped hands and splashing it gingerly over her face.

It was bruised purple, dark shadows beneath the puffed and swollen flesh. She patted her face dry, and then she picked up the small hand-mirror and began to examine her face critically, turning her head from side to side as she made the scrutiny.

He could hardly bear to look, and yet at the same time he couldn't tear his eyes away. She dried her face, using the towel like a blotter, and then she combed her hair out.

She turned towards him. Their eyes met. He looked away uncomfortably, then looked back again, unable to keep his eyes off her swollen face. He felt sick at what he had done, but he hadn't spoken to her since last night, and now he didn't know where to begin, because no matter what he said it wouldn't change what had happened.

Her mouth stretched suddenly, and he was startled and taken aback for a few moments until he realized that she was only trying to smile at him.

"Don't take it hard, mister man," she said. Her voice was blurred and distorted, coming through her swollen lips. "It looks pretty awful, but it isn't all that bad."

"I'm sorry," he mumbled. "I lost my—head."

"I pushed you, mister man," she said. "It's a habit of mine, putting my big foot in my own mouth. I pushed you, but it wasn't to give you the needles." She grinned again, and on her bruised face it looked funny and sad. "That's what it's all about, isn't it, putting the knife in? But—but I wasn't doing it that way."

"How were you doing it?"

She shrugged, and for a moment he thought he saw the flicker of a smile in her eyes, but he wasn't sure.

"You're going after that big pussy cat again, aren't you?" she went on, her voice casual, neither condemning nor approving.

"What if I am?" he said, his hackles beginning to rise.

"Oh nothing. I just wondered whether you'd take me along. After yesterday, you know?"

He stiffened, about to refuse, but then the sight of her bruised face made him feel guilty all over again, and he thought that if he took her it might be some kind of atonement.

"You—you won't do anything like yesterday?" he asked warily.

"Scout's honour."

He nodded. "You can get killed doing things like that, especially if a lion's charging," he said quietly, and his right hand began to lift unconsciously towards his face. "And if—if a woman——" His voice trailed away.

"And a woman what?"

He started, as if he were coming back from far away. He smiled at her wearily. "Tries to knock the rifle out of your hands, it doesn't help matters."

"Oh," she said, and she felt the disappointment rise in her.

"We'd better eat," he went on quickly. "I'm going to get that lion. It was mine, no one had the right to free it."

She felt a strange compassion for him. It was startling and a little frightening, because she hadn't allowed herself to feel anything like that for a long time.

"Do I get to come?" she inquired.

"All right," he agreed. "But don't try to—to stop me."

"It's already too late to do that," she replied cryptically.

He frowned, vaguely sensing the uncharted depths beneath the surface of her words. He turned away, suddenly frightened and disturbed by an awareness that was growing in him.

Twenty minutes later they were rolling through the bush. Spartala was driving, with Tsexhau up in front beside him. Jannie was in the back, his rifle in his hands, with Carol standing to his left. Behind them were two of the Bushmen, Tsonomon and Xhommaha, men who were also fathers.

Spartala wheeled the vehicle in and out through the scrub, following the spoor that they had cut the evening before.

"It's kind of wonderful, isn't it?" she commented, glancing over the burned land. "I mean, it's so empty and desolate, and yet all kinds of things live out here, even people."

"You should see it a few days after the rain."

She was silent for a while, shifting her stance, her feet spread wide against the jolting and bouncing of the vehicle. She glanced at him covertly, studying his expressionless face.

"Who was she?" she asked abruptly. "What happened?"

His head whipped round, anger flaring in his eyes, but the sight of her puffed face and the knowledge that he had been responsible drained it all away.

"I don't know what you're talking about," he said.

"If you say so."

Spartala brought the truck to a halt in exactly the same spot from which Jannie had fired at the lion the day before. Tsexhau jumped out and called to the two Bushmen. They climbed down, still clumsy and unsure about getting in and out. They joined him, and together the three of them went forward on the spoor. The Land Rover followed close behind.

They found the fire that Xhabbo had made, and then they found the place where the boy and the lion had spent the night. The marks of their bodies were there in the sand, close together, and as Jannie studied them he felt a strange awe and incredulity that was close to reverence. He had hunted lions all his life, sometimes out of necessity, as when they killed his cattle, but mostly for the pleasure it gave him. He knew their savagery and their ferocity, and yet it was there now in front of his eyes, evidence which pointed to the impossible.

The trackers moved on. They halted again a little later, and Tsexhau beckoned to him. He jumped down off the back of the Land Rover and strode forward.

"What is it?" he asked eagerly.

"Fresh spoor again," Tsexhau replied, pointing. "Very fresh."

Jannie nodded, knowing what he was getting at. "Can you follow it?"

"Easy."

"Tell these two to get back in the truck," Jannie ordered. "I'll come with you."

Tsexhau turned and spoke quickly to them. They needed no prompting. It was a *lion* that they were tracking, and yesterday it had been fired on by the red man. It would know now that it was being hunted, and it would give no quarter. They climbed into the back of the vehicle with alacrity.

"What's happening, mister man?" Carol called out.

"Stay in the truck," he warned her.

He cocked the rifle, and with Tsexhau moving beside him, they went forward together. He paid no attention to the spoor. That was the tracker's job. His work was to search for the lion, to find and destroy it before it got to him.

A little further on Tsexhau paused, puzzled by the information that came to him from the writing on the sands. He went forward slowly, and then he came to where the lion had broken cover, the pug marks deep and elongated by the speed at which it had moved.

He went on cautiously, and then when he saw the fresh spoor of the gemsbok he thought he began to understand. He started off again uneasily, and now the tracks of the boy and those of the lion were once again running close together.

The Land Rover crept along behind them, the sound of its engine a steady and ever-present rumble.

"Tsexhau!" Jannie cried abruptly.

He reached out, grabbing the tracker by the arm and halting him. They stared in astonishment at the smashed and flattened brush. A moment later Jannie saw the lion.

Instinctively the rifle leaped to his shoulder. He had the lion in his sights instantly, his finger beginning to tighten on the trigger. He checked the movement abruptly, and then slowly, incredulously, he lowered the rifle.

He studied the lion a moment longer, and then he went forward cautiously. He halted ten yards from it, his rifle up and ready to fire. He studied it intently, and then an instant later he noticed the shaft of the arrow head which protruded from its eye socket. He uncocked the rifle and slung it from his shoulder.

He heard the Land Rover come to a halt directly behind them. A moment later the sound of the engine died. In the sudden silence which followed he heard the tick and pop of cooling metal.

"So," he breathed quietly, and there was a grim satisfaction in his voice. "He killed it himself."

He started forward, oblivious to the others who had joined him and were following close behind. Four feet from the dead animal he came to a shocked and incredulous halt.

In the sand beside the dead lion was a stoppered ostrich egg shell and a single arrow. His breast began to fill with a strange and over-powering tumult.

His vision blurred, and on the retina of his mind he saw it again, like a flash of lightning that briefly illuminates the dark night sky, the prints that their bodies had made as they lay close together in the sand.

He bent down and picked up the big white shell. From its weight he knew that it was full of water. He shook it, listening, and then he put it back carefully in exactly the same place it had been before. He knew what water meant, to the children of the desert. He felt small, and very humble.

This had been no simple killing, as he had thought it was in the beginning when he first saw the protruding arrow shaft. There was a deep love here, and no man killed the things he loved recklessly or with impunity. There was always a price that had to be paid.

"He killed it," Carol whispered, shocked and incredulous. "He did, didn't he?"

"Yes."

"Why did he do that? They were running through the evening together only yesterday."

"I don't know."

She stared silently at the body of the dead lion. It was thin, the fur patchy in places, and it didn't look like anything that you could either love or be afraid of any more. It just looked dead.

"The shell," she said. "What's it doing there? And the arrow beside it?"

"They bury their own people like that," he said heavily. "Water for the journey, and a bow and arrow to hunt along the way. He didn't leave his bow, because he still has to hunt. He didn't light a fire either. They usually light a fire, at the foot of the grave, because it's dark where they're going, and they need the light to take them into the day beyond the darkness. Maybe he didn't have his fire sticks, or he didn't have the time."

"He must have loved that lion very much," she said.

"Why did he kill it then?" he asked, shouting almost. "Tell me that, why did he kill it?"

"I don't know, maybe he loved it too much," she replied, and then she turned away suddenly, her eyes brimming. "I don't bloody know, mister man. All I know is that if you hadn't trapped it he probably wouldn't have been forced to kill it."

There was a corollary to that, but he couldn't put his finger on it, and then Spartala cleared his throat loudly two or three times and the interruption broke the fragile thread of his thoughts. He turned to him, the blindness slowly leaving his eyes.

"What?"

"Shall we start?" asked Spartala, fingering the knife at his waist.

Jannie regarded him in blank surprise, and then he began to shake his head violently. "Get the shovel."

"Morena?"

"I said get the bloody shovel."

Spartala hesitated a moment, then he walked back to the Land Rover and came back swinging the spade.

"Dig a hole," Jannie ordered. "A big deep hole to put the lion in the ground."

Spartala's eyes widened in disbelief, but he turned away quickly from the sudden anger which leapt into his master's eyes. He began to dig.

Jannie looked up, into the deep blue vault of the sky. The vultures were beginning to circle already. A shiver ran through his body, and he looked away quickly.

His glance fell on the ground, a little way beyond the dead lion. He saw the two sets of small footprints which marched forward through the sand side by side. He followed them with his eye, till they became too distant to discern with any certainty. He felt a sudden burst of pain deep inside his chest.

It took them twenty minutes to dig the hole to his satisfaction. The four of them took it in turns, and when it was finished they dragged the lion to the hole and rolled it in.

Jannie walked to the edge of the grave, and he bent down and placed the shell of water and the arrow on top of the body of the dead lion. They buried the king.

When all trace of his existence had vanished below the desert sands, and only his footprints remained on the earth, Tsonomon and Xhommaha approached Tsexhau nervously and began to whisper urgently. He listened, nodding from time to time, and then he turned to Jannie.

"They tell you that they go now, and they ask you to wait," he translated. "They go to find their children."

"I'll take them."

"They do not want it. They ask you to wait. The children will hear the noise of the engine, and they will run because they are afraid."

"I understand," Jannie replied. "Tell them I will wait."

The last of the circling vultures dropped its left wing and peeled away. It picked up an updraft, and levelling off it began to soar, a living sculpture black against the brilliance of the sky.

"Remind me," he told her quietly, "to pick my traps up on the way in."

"You going to quit hunting?" she asked, eyeing him curiously, even a little contemptuously.

"No—just the traps."

She stared at him for a few moments longer, and then suddenly she began to grin. "For a second there I thought you were getting soft," she remarked. "Or trying to con yourself or pull a snow job on me."

"I'm afraid I don't understand."

"It doesn't matter," she replied. "As long as you understand yourself."

10

THROUGHOUT THE AFTERNOON it got steadily and frighteningly hotter. There was a charged stillness in the air, as if earth and sky were waiting for some portentous happening.

To the south, great black clouds rolled billowing into the sky. The earth darkened as they moved northward, filling the sky and blotting out the sun. Lightning began to flash on the blackened ominous horizon, and the stentorian roll of thunder was like music in their ears.

Watching the clouds, studying them anxiously, Jannie felt a quickening of his spirit. There was hope in him, but no certainty, because he had seen it too often, the rain beginning to fall, evaporating before it reached the earth and the subsequent wind that it generated ripping the clouds apart and driving them away over distant horizons.

Against the superstitious promptings of his mind he supervised the rigging of a tarpaulin overhead, hoping that the Gods in whose charge the desert lay would not take his presumption as an affront and deny the parched earth.

He glanced at the group of Bushmen at the far side of the clearing. His eye fell on the boy, the one who had been with the lion. There was a blank vacancy to his expression, as if he were in the grip of some deep and terrible depression. He had tried earlier to question him, to find out why he had killed the lion, but the boy had turned away, shy and sullen and remote.

It was dark by the time the tarpaulin had been rigged to his satisfaction. The odour of grilling meat began to fill the air, and here and there the firelight picked out a shining yellow-brown face, the light reflecting from high cheekbones and black slanted eyes.

The lightning struck intermittently, closer now, the flash and crackle followed almost immediately by the reverberating roar of thunder.

"Will you eat now, morena?" Joseph asked him, coming through the shadows and materializing at his side.

"Later, I want to drink a little first."

Joseph nodded, and he was beginning to turn away when Jannie called him back.

"Here, give this packet of cigarettes to the Masarwas," he said. "And don't lose any of them on the way."

He drained his glass and poured himself another drink. He sat back heavily, his legs stretched out and the weight of his body on his arms.

There was, he thought, a certain magic about a hunting camp. He didn't know quite what it was, but he thought it had something to do with people being together, drawn close by the vastness of the desert which surrounded them.

"How's your glass?" he asked.

Seated a little way from him, Carol stirred reluctantly. She tore her gaze from the mesmeric flames of the fire and looked at her glass.

"I could use another," she said.

He poured a solid measure for her, and then topped it up with water from the bag.

"Listen to the thunder," she said softly. "You know, it always kind of makes me feel safe and snug."

She went back to staring at the flames. He studied her shadowed swollen face in silence, and then glanced across at the group of Bushmen. Most of them had finished eating, and he saw them begin to hand round the cigarettes he had given them.

Pxui lit his cigarette with a burning ember. He drew the smoke into his mouth, his cheeks hollowing as he sucked. He closed his eyes, and in an ecstasy of fulfilment he drew the smoke deep into his being. He held it within him, savouring the full warm feeling that it gave him, and then he raised the cigarette to his lips again.

He reduced it rapidly in four drags to an unmanageable stub, and then he lit another. By the time he had finished the second one, he was feeling beautifully light headed.

He began to think about the lion. He felt a sudden eviscerating burst of loneliness and shame. He tried to push the memories from his mind, but they persisted.

The story of the lion and the young hunter came again unbidden to his mind, and he began to examine its subtleties once more in the light of what he himself had done.

In the story, the lion had killed the man because he had fallen asleep on his journey through life, and that was the price he had to pay. But he had also licked the tears of the hunter, showing his compassion. Why then had he killed him, and immediately after lain down beside him and died?

He thought about it, but he could find no answer, and he was about to terminate his nebulous groping when the first glimmer of light penetrated the blackness of his heart.

He wondered if it was shame and remorse, which had made the lion lie down and die after killing the young man, especially after having licked the salt of his tears?

But that did not help him, because he was a man and not a lion. He wondered whether a man was weaker than a lion, or whether it was the other way around. He decided after a while that they were not different, both of them weak and strong at the same time, each in his own way. But that did not help him much either, because he had killed the thing he had taken pity on and grown to love.

He was sinking into a deeper depression when it came to him, flashing through his mind like a bolt of lightning and illuminating what had been hidden before.

He had killed the lion out of compassion, because he had known he could not survive without him, and if he had not killed him, both of them would eventually have perished. He had killed the thing he loved, and in the process he had died a little, but he had not done it selfishly and for himself. He knew also that everything started to die the first moment after it was born.

He was beginning to feel a little bit better, more righteous and more noble, when the lightning struck again, and in the flash of clean and austere light he felt a horror growing within him.

Unlike the lion in the story, he had not acted out of love. He had killed him simply to survive. He had given himself, from the beginning, the pleasure of exercising a compassion he should have been wise enough not to indulge in, because in order to extract any meaning from it, he should have been prepared to back it with his own life, just as the lion in the story had done.

He was starting to despise himself when the lightning struck once again. He had not given him the chance of life because he cared for him. He had gambled on the act of setting him free, and having won he had used the lion for his own ends.

And then just as he was beginning to feel more miserable than he had felt before, he realized that all of the things he had thought were true in their own way, and that legend, like life itself, was only a means of making a man think for himself, without self-deception, and in a final burst of revelation he knew there was no truth to the story of the lion and the young hunter.

He glanced across the clearing at the red man who sat there with his glass in his hand and his own woman beside him. In a way, he knew that it was he who had given him his knowledge.

He got up, and he crossed the clearing with a lightness in his feet. He came to a halt in front of Jannie. For a moment he was as still as a statue, and then he lifted his arms and rolled his eyes downward so that the pupils vanished and only the whites were visible beneath the slitted lids.

He began to sway rhythmically, his whole body moving to the motion. The muscles in his stomach contracted abruptly, bunching into a compact ball. The ball began to move, slowly at first, and then faster and faster. It moved in and out, up and down and from side to side, as if it were some separate and mysterious entity. And as he watched the gyrating ball from within, it seemed to expand and change in shape and colour till it was looking back at him like the eye of the lion. He spoke silently, out of his own pain, and he heard another voice answer him, from out of the depths of his belly and the eye of the lion.

> "I am ashamed and in disgrace.
> But I came to you for help and you licked my tears.
> Not for you did I do it, but for myself.
> Whom did your act of compassion benefit?
> Myself of course. I have Xhabbo, I have my legend.
> I had my life, for a little longer."

The great golden eye inside his belly winked shut and then appeared again.

> "But I killed you in the end, did I not?
> You helped me while you could, you killed me when you had to.
> I am a hyena, I am unclean.
> It was I who fell asleep on my way through life and walked into
>   the trap. Was that your fault?
> No, but I gave you life and then took it away.
> Life took it away, not you. Who can you depend on for your own
>   survival if not yourself?
> My people.
> Only if they can depend on you."

The eye blinked out again. The sweat ran down his face as he danced on, but he was not aware of it. He waited in fear for the eye to open once more.

> "If only you had learned to obey me and stay by my side while I
>   was hunting.
> I must obey myself. To stay alive I had to obey my own nature.
> But it caused your death.
> And death has many forms.
> If you had obeyed me I could have hunted for both of us.
> And made me a slave? I would rather be dead."

The eye grew in size till it seemed to him that the eye and he were one. And now it spoke to him.

"Why did Xhabbo break your arrow?

She wanted me to kill you.

Why didn't she kill me herself?

You belonged to me.

Have I not already explained that such a thing is impossible?

Why then did she break my arrow?

She was setting a trap.

I don't understand, I killed you in the end.

You knew why you were killing me, and you took the responsibility for your act.

She wanted to kill you for her grandfather.

Did she?

She loved him, did she not?

She did, but she also loved the love *she* had for him.

Is that wrong?

It is natural.

What then do you speak of?

Those who kill and blame the necessity of death on others.

Again I do not understand.

You broke faith with what was your own nature in setting me free. You are beginning to learn the price of freedom.

There is a darkness in my mind.

This is only your first dance.

There is too much, I will never understand.

Now listen. Why did you shoot your arrow into Xhabbo's rump?

To let her know I loved her, and find out whether she loved me.

Did you cause her pain, by shooting your little arrow into her body?

I——

But you also gave her pleasure, did you not?"

The eye suddenly grew even huger, and then slowly it began to contract till it was only a pin-point. It glowed with a violent unearthly light, and then extinguished itself abruptly and there was only darkness inside him.

He remembered only snatches of the dialogue which had swept through his mind, but then the essence of it struck at him.

For an instant he was terrified, with his Gods dying before his eyes, and then he understood that only the living could continue to search for meaning in the vast arena of the desert.

And then he realized that what the old gods had said was no

different from what he was beginning to think about now, but that in between there was so much incidental and organized chaos that the truth was obscured. To be immortal, he did not need a legend. To live his life with what he knew and learned, that in itself would make one.

He felt a sudden terror at his new freedom, and also a shattering excitement.

His eyes opened slowly, as if he were coming back to reality from a place within his body that was very far away. He stood there for a moment, glistening with sweat, and then suddenly he smiled at Jannie. He turned and went back to his people as silently as he had come.

There was a moment of stunned silence, and then Tsexhau leaped to his feet, his eyes on fire with admiration and excitement and a luminous pride that went as deep as his own manhood.

"Oh you Bushman!" he cried in ecstasy. "You child of a Bushman, you!"

The wife of Exxwa took a lyre from her sack. She began to play it, her calloused fingers stroking the strings like a woman bringing pleasure to her lover. Tsonomon joined in with his harp, and a moment later they were all singing quietly in the night.

"What was that all about?" asked Carol.

"He was thanking me," Jannie said. "In the biggest way he knows."

"For what?"

"I'm damned if I know," he said, deeply puzzled.

"Ask him," she urged.

"It couldn't have been the cigarettes," he mused reflectively. "I've given them three or four packs already."

"Ask him," she said again. "Go on and ask."

He hesitated, uncertain, wondering if the boy would again refuse to speak, but then his own curiosity got the better of him.

"Tsexhau!" he called. "Ask him, why he did that dance for me?"

He held his breath while the tracker made his swift interrogation, and then abruptly Tsexhau swung back to face him.

"He thanks you," he said, "for giving him the lion, even if it was only for a little while."

For a moment Jannie was bewildered, but then he thought he understood. As the glimmer of understanding grew, he felt glad that he had not taken the life of the king himself.

"What did he say?" she asked eagerly.

"He thanked me for giving him the lion, even if it was only for a little while."

Her eyes widened slowly, and then her bruised face grew suddenly gentle. "Oh mister man," she breathed. "Do you know what he's telling you?"

The answer to the corollary he had been thinking about when Spartala had coughed that morning and disturbed his thoughts became clear. If he hadn't trapped the lion, the boy would never have had to kill it. He would not have known it either.

"I'm not sure," he said hesitantly, lost in the labyrinth again. "I'll have to think about it."

He drained his glass and filled it again. There was that good warm feeling inside him from the brandy, and he felt his mind begin to detach itself, floating free, beginning to soar, like a black bird against a white sky.

The lightning flickered and struck with ever-increasing frequency, the flashes momentarily ripping the darkness apart and turning night to day.

"You know," she said softly, "I still kind of find it hard to believe."

"What?"

"About what happened," she said. "You know what I mean."

He stiffened almost imperceptibly and then relaxed. "Why do you keep asking me about it?"

"So that you can face it, without guilt and shame, as a fact."

His mouth curved, a dry ironic grin. "I already have."

But the eyes that held her own were steady and grave and full of an old pain that mocked her, and in that instant, with a sudden mind-crunching twist of perception she saw both the truth and the nature and significance of his distortion, and all she could think of was the brutal waste of time and life that it represented and the ruin and the pointless anguish it must have caused.

"It was her, it was your friend!" she gasped. "She was the one who had the rifle that day."

He jerked as if she had struck him, and then he exploded. "Shut your fucking mouth," he screamed at her, his scarred face hideous in its naked agony. He drew a great sobbing breath, and then said tiredly, without much conviction: "I told you, it happened in the forge."

He turned away from her and picked up the bottle, but his hands were shaking so badly that he couldn't hold it steady enough to pour himself a drink, with the bottle mouth rattling against the rim of the glass.

She took them gently from him and poured him a hefty shot and then topped the glass up from the water bag. She handed it to him, watching silently as he lifted it in both hands in an effort to keep it steady. He drank half of it at one swallow, and after a while he began to feel the turmoil within him begin to subside.

Lightning struck again, very close, and the thunder that followed made it feel as if the earth had leaped in shock and surprise.

"I hope it rains," he murmured. "Otherwise we'll have to leave tomorrow."

"I thought you were staying five or six days."

"We've just about used up our water," he informed her. "I wasn't counting on guests."

"Well," she said, after a long silence, "I really have enjoyed it."

"What are you going to do?" he asked.

"Go on, of course."

"Where to?"

"Don't know, just on."

He stared at her, his heart suddenly beginning to beat fast, and the thought of the vacuum she would leave behind filled him with a frightening loneliness more intense than he had ever felt before.

"Why don't you stay on a while with me?" he asked, bringing it out hesitantly. "I mean at Ramabana."

She faced him, her eyes disturbingly steady, an ironic gleam in their depths. "Is that a proposition, mister man?"

"I don't know what it is. It might be a—beginning."

She sighed deeply, as if something vital within her had been pierced and she was breathing out her life, or an old death. She began to shake her head slowly.

"Thanks, mister man, but I have to go on."

He had been hoping, but now the hope was gone and he was back to where he had been before.

"Suit yourself," he said lightly.

"I intend to."

"Would you mind," he said irrelevantly, "not calling me mister man? My name's Jannie."

"Sure thing, mister man."

Her eyes widened, and she clapped her hand to her mouth. She stared at him aghast, and then the moment passed, and then suddenly both of them were laughing.

Lightning struck again, blindingly bright. The earth seemed to leap and quiver. The thunder deafened them, and a moment later the rain roared down. It drummed against the tarpaulin, and the sound of it filled their ears, drowning out the chatter of the Bushmen who ran for its protection.

As the water streamed from the tarpaulin they began to fill their shells. Spartala and Tsexhau busied themselves with the splashing stream that cascaded from the opposite side, channelling it into the first of the 44-gallon drums.

11

THE SKIES WERE black and overcast when Carol stirred and woke in the morning, and it was still raining lightly. She sniffed deeply, the clean, pungent smell of raw earth quickened by the rain.

It was strangely quiet, except for the patter of the rain. She was puzzled by the enveloping silence. It was as if something was missing.

She washed at the basin, using the water lavishly. She was combing out her hair when she realized with a sudden start what it was that had been puzzling her. She spun around, alarm and a strange inexplicable feeling of loss in her heart.

"The Bushmen!" she cried. "Where are they?"

He gestured silently to her, telling her to come. She walked over to where he was standing, at the edge of the clearing. He pointed.

She stared uncomprehendingly at the half-washed-out footprints for a moment. They went straight out, into the desert.

"They've gone?" she inquired, her voice small and hesitant.

"Yes," he replied. "They've gone home."

Her sense of loss mounted, but then she felt a kind of indignation rising in her.

"They left," she exclaimed. "Just like that, without even thanking you for saving their lives?"

The bruises had darkened on her face, and she looked somehow very vulnerable despite her resentment. He smiled at her in quiet amusement.

"How can you thank a man for that?"

"If you can't thank him for that, you can't thank him for one damn thing."

"You can't thank him," he said, and there was a quiet certainty in his voice. "All you can do is maybe help another person one day, someone who's also in the same kind of trouble."

She stared at him, her eyes wild, and then she looked away abruptly and stared blindly at the footprints in the sand that the rain was slowly washing away. The loneliness inside her grew till she thought that she would choke.

"I'm going to stay on a few days," he remarked. "Would you mind?"

"I'd like it."

He cleared his throat, hesitant again. "Won't you change your mind? About staying a while at Ramabana?"

"Oh God!" she cried softly. "You don't know anything about me, you don't even know how I think."

"That's what time is for," he said softly. "To find out."

"And if you don't like the way I think, the things I've been?"

"I don't want you to think the same way as I do," he said. "That would be almost like killing you."

Her mouth worked slowly, the crushed lips writhing as if she were in pain. For a moment longer she stared unseeingly at the vanishing footprints. Unlike her own, they were leading somewhere. She turned suddenly to him.

"You better make me think what you think, mister man," she whispered fiercely. "Otherwise I'm going to kill you, and I don't want that."

He stared at her incredulously, and then slowly he began to smile. A sudden flurry of wind beat against them, and then the rain began to fall harder.

They turned together. He took her hand, and they ran for the shelter of the tarpaulin. Beyond its inimical protection, the thirsty earth continued to drink. It drank deeply, and the rain, like love, quickened the seeds that had been waiting patiently for so long. To grow and endure, and then to die.

"I hope it works," she whispered, still holding his hand.

"It will."

She turned to stare at him. His face seemed to shimmer like deep reflections in a wind-ruffled pool, and then it dissolved and slowly reformed again. For a moment there were no scars on his face, and she saw it as it might have been.

She looked away, and then . . .

She turned back again, and the fleeting vision had vanished, and his face was as it was. She wondered what it would have been like to know him without the scars, and then she knew that she would never know unless he could first see himself.

She wondered whether she might be able to illuminate both faces for him, so that in the process she might begin to understand them herself.

. . . And then . . .

She realized that when he had learned those two faces of his, more would be born for her to learn about. The cataracts fell from her eyes, and suddenly she saw her own mask.

Jannie turned to her in surprise and consternation as she burst into tears. The rain continued to fall gently, searching the sands for latent life.

The use of symbols and euphemisms by man is a desperate attempt to keep intact his crumbling illusions about his own nature and the reality of his true significance in the scheme of things.

SPAEDES